MAYBE TOMORROW

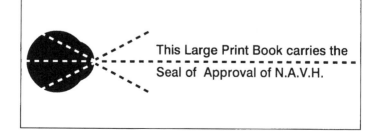

This Large Print Book carries the
Seal of Approval of N.A.V.H.

MAYBE TOMORROW

Joan Hohl

Thorndike Press • **Thorndike, Maine**

Published in 1999 by arrangement with Zebra Books, an imprint of Kensington Publishing Corporation.

Thorndike Large Print® Americana Series.

The tree indicium is a trademark of Thorndike Press.

The text of this Large Print edition is unabridged. Other aspects of the book may vary from the original edition.

Set in 16 pt. Plantin by Al Chase.

Printed in the United States on permanent paper.

Library of Congress Cataloging in Publication Data

Hohl, Joan.
    Maybe tomorrow / Joan Hohl.
       p. (lg. print)   cm.
    ISBN 0-7862-1860-6 (lg. print : hc : alk. paper)
    1. Large type books.   I. Title.
[PS3558.O34759M39 1998]
    813′.54—dc21   98-56291

MAYBE
TOMORROW

Prologue

The two teenaged girls sat side by side on the sofa, a tray with the remains of a pizza set on the low coffee table in front of them.

A flickering, shadowy, grayish-white light from the TV illuminated the darkened family room. The sweeping theme music from a video of an old movie poured from the stereo speakers as the credits scrolled across the screen.

"Oooh . . . wasn't that wonderful?"

Leigh Evans slanted a wry look at Sheila Porter, her neighbor and best friend since the second grade. She rolled her eyes as Sheila swiped a hand over the tears unabashedly streaming down her cheeks.

"It was a movie," Leigh reminded the seventeen-year-old. "And unrelated to real life."

Sniffling, Sheila tossed her a superior look. "But it could happen — people do fall in love, you know."

"Oh, sure." Leigh's voice held a note of ridicule only teenagers were capable of striking. "It happens all the time; rich man meets poor girl. Instant attraction. Love conquers every problem. Spare me!"

Bristling, her pale blond hair shimmering in the living-room light, her delicate features quivering, Sheila drew her small frame taut and glared at Leigh.

"Leigh Evans, you are the most cynical person I have ever known," Sheila accused.

"Well, I may be cynical," Leigh shot back, "but I'm not stupid. I know that some Mr. Handsome, Rich and Wonderful, like the hero — gag — in that dumb movie, is never going to walk into the burger joint where you work, take one look at you, fall madly in love and take you away from all this!" She indicated their surroundings with a broad sweep of an arm.

"I know that." Sheila's well-endowed chest heaved in a mighty huff. "But that doesn't mean someday, somewhere, I won't meet a really terrific guy and fall in love."

Leigh gave her friend a pitying look. "Boy, you're in for trouble, girl, if you really believe all that sticky stuff about love and the happily-ever-after crap."

"Oh . . . you . . ." Sheila bounced off the sofa. "You make me crazy. I'm going home."

"You're sleeping over." Leigh showed her perfect white teeth in a grin. "Remember?"

Sheila deflated. "Right." She stared at her

grinning friend for a moment; then her naturally sweet nature reasserted itself and she smiled. "How many times have we had this argument?"

"Four thousand, two hundred and twenty-two," Leigh answered at once. Leaning forward, she picked up a limp piece of pizza, tore off the tip and popped it into her mouth.

"You made that up." Making a face at her friend's obvious enjoyment of the now stone-cold snack, Sheila plopped back down onto the sofa.

"Of course." Leigh shrugged and favored her with a smug look. "But it's got to be close to that."

Sheila's expression turned from sour to pensive. "You know, it's about the only thing we ever argue about — falling in love, I mean."

"Ummm." Leigh murmured around the second bite of pizza in her mouth. She chewed, swallowed and arched auburn eyebrows. "So?"

"Why don't you believe in love, Leigh?" Sheila asked, not for the first time.

Convinced she had more than ample reason for her beliefs, Leigh always gave her the same answer.

"It's an illusion created by men to enslave women."

One

It was a near perfect morning. A hint of blossoming fragrance wafted on the breeze. Sunlight sparkled off the multi-windowed high-rise office complexes lining the streets of Center City, Philadelphia.

After an extended, snow-snarled winter, spring had finally arrived in Pennsylvania.

Green was the color of the day: the deep lush green of new grass and unfurling tree leaves and the jewel-toned green of the smart suit Leigh had chosen for her working day. It was also the color of the pure emerald green of her eyes and the green of the traffic light at the corner.

In a whimsical departure from her usual workday style, Leigh had let her auburn hair flow loose and free instead of smoothing it back into a neat pleat. The long tresses bounced and swished against her shoulders as she paced along with the crowd crossing the street. Intent individuals like her, they were hurrying to their jobs in offices and shops.

Her own place of business was located in the third building beyond the intersection.

As she did every workday morning, Leigh paused on the sidewalk to run a critical but satisfied glance over the showcase window.

The showcase was quite small in comparison to other huge floor-to-ceiling showroom windows. Leigh didn't mind. In her admittedly biased opinion, her window, while spare, had a definite touch of elegance the more elaborate and cluttered showroom windows lacked.

She had re-dressed the window the week before Easter, when the weather had actually turned springlike with butter yellow sunlight and a mild breeze.

Understated, almost stark, the display caught the eye of passersby, Leigh noted from her position at the edge of the sidewalk near the curb.

As her welcome to the gentle season, Leigh had chosen a tall, slender glass vase in bottle green, fashioned in the shape of an unfurling plant. From a narrow base, the vase branched off into two long pointed leaves, one lower, curving backward, the other higher, its arch less pronounced. A length of misty sea green silk swirled around the slightly bulbous base. Inside the vase, she had placed one white lily, standing tall, regal, the traditional representative of the season of resurrection, renewal, life.

That single magnificent lily had aroused the interest and inquiries of several prospective customers over the previous four days.

Very effective, Leigh decided, a tingle shivering through her as she raised her eyes to the letters scrolled in gold across the upper section of the window: INTERIORS by LEIGH.

Her spirits high, her step jaunty, Leigh mounted the three steps up to the door and swept into her domain.

"Morning, Sheila," she said to her friend and receptionist/assistant. "Is there coffee?"

"Yes, of course," Sheila fairly bubbled. "But there's something even better than that."

Making a beeline for the automatic coffeemaker set on a credenza behind and to the side of the reception desk, Leigh smiled and shook her head. "There is nothing better than coffee at nine o'clock in the morning."

"Yes, there is," Sheila said, her sparkling blue eyes alight with excitement.

"Really?" Filling a mug with the dark brew, Leigh dumped in a measure of powdered creamer, stirred, then, cradling the mug, turned to examine the young woman's face, intrigued by the glow of expectation shining from her eyes.

"And are you planning to tell me . . . or are you just going to sit there, squirming?" she asked, dry-voiced.

"You have an appointment in exactly . . ." — Sheila paused for a quick glance at the digital clock on the corner of her desk — "twenty-five minutes."

"An appointment at nine-thirty?" Leigh arched auburn brows, her curiosity aroused by Sheila's bright-eyed ebullience. "Since when . . . and with whom?"

"Since about two minutes before you walked in," Sheila said, a tremor of exuberance in her voice. "And with none other than Mr. Michael St. Claire, no less."

Leigh stared at her friend in mute astonishment for a full thirty seconds. "*The* Michael St. Claire?" she finally asked in awed tones of disbelief.

"The one and only." Sheila sprang out of her chair as if unable to sit still another moment.

"Michael St. Claire of the St. Claire Development Corporation?" she persisted.

"The very same." Sheila laughed, dancing in place next to her chair.

"And he made an appointment . . . to see me . . . here . . . at nine-thirty this morning?" Leigh pressed, wanting, *needing* absolute clarification.

"Yes. Isn't that what I've been telling you?" Plucking the forgotten mug from Leigh's hands, Sheila grabbed her arms and proceeded to waltz her around the reception area.

Leigh automatically kept in step, too stunned to assimilate the information.

"Blows you away, huh?" Sheila was laughing between gasps for breath.

To put it mildly, Leigh thought, common sense reasserting itself as the sensation of soaring euphoria took a reality tumble. Coming to an abrupt halt, she frowned down at her diminutive friend.

"Why?"

"Why what?" Sheila frowned back at her.

"Why me? Why Interiors by Leigh?"

Sheila continued to frown. "Why not?"

"Oh, come on," Leigh said impatiently. Retracing her steps, she returned to the desk, picked up her mug, took several steadying sips of the now cooling liquid, then stared narrow-eyed into the baffled expression on her friend's face.

"What?" Sheila demanded.

"St. Claire is a powerhouse, a mover and shaker in the world of real-estate development," Leigh answered.

"So?" The blonde frowned.

"He can well afford to be very selective,

make a choice from any one of the big, upscale and expensive firms of interior designers. Why would he choose me?"

"Now wait just a minute," Sheila protested, her small slender body quivering with indignation. "You've worked damn hard ever since opening your first showroom six years ago in Lancaster, and you've done nothing but beautiful work." She defended her best friend . . . to her best friend.

"Thank you, but —" Leigh began.

"Don't interrupt me." Sheila slammed her hands onto her narrow hips. "I'm on a roll."

Grabbing a quick breath, she paced to the desk, her stance militant. "You've had a few upscale clients yourself, ever since you relocated to this place three years ago — very vocally appreciative clients, I might add." Her delicate nose twitched. "Darn it, Leigh, you've made a ripple on the surface of interior design in the area, and you know it as well as I do."

"A small ripple," Leigh conceded, her tone gentled with affection for her loyal friend. "But in a very large pool of established talent," she hastened to point out. "I just can't imagine why someone like Michael St. Clair would decide to engage a relative unknown when —"

"He said you were highly recommended to him," Sheila interjected.

"By whom?"

Sheila moved her shoulders in a helpless shrug. "A business associate, he said. He didn't give a name." She glanced at the clock. "If he's as punctual as he's reputed to be, he'll be here in less than fifteen minutes. If you think it's so important, ask him then."

"I intend to do precisely that," Leigh said, turning to refill her mug before heading for her connecting office/workroom. She paused in the doorway to glance back at Sheila. "Would you mind making a fresh pot of coffee? Please?"

" 'I intend to do precisely that,' " Sheila mimicked, grinning at her friend and employer.

Sheila's obvious attempt to blunt the claws of nervous tension digging into Leigh had had the desired effect.

She knows me too well, Leigh mused, smiling at her small friend before entering her office and closing the door.

Out of sight of the other woman, she slumped back against the door, her breathing erratic, her body trembling, her carefully constructed shield of cool composure exposed for the fragile facade it was,

16

had always been.

Michael St. Claire.

Jesus.

Leigh shivered.

This meeting with St. Claire could prove to be the chance of a lifetime, she thought, an excited tremor roiling in her stomach, her one-in-a-million chance to break into the arena of large accounts.

Her suddenly cold fingers gripped the warm cup. Her gaze skipped around the room, searching for any overlooked sign of dust, any disarray that would reflect negatively upon her professional attitude and approach to business.

She felt queasy and half-sick, but fortunately not from the scene that met her eyes. As usual, and not by accident, both separate and distinct work areas were spotless.

Leigh let her gaze rest for a moment on the section fronting the street that contained her desk, client chairs and a classic credenza on which were set two spring plants, one with a burst of yellow daffodils, the other a clay pot of fragrant purple hyacinths.

Satisfied with her minute perusal, and having noted the neatness of the tastefully decorated area, she switched her gaze to the other half of the spacious room. The entire

17

far wall was taken up with deep shelves loaded down with catalogues and sample books, large and small, thick and thin, from furniture makers, fabric manufacturers, wallpaper and paint companies, *objets d'art* and a myriad of manuals and reference books. Her slanted work table and stool were set in front of, and within an easy arm's reach of, the shelves.

The remaining walls were painted a warm, earthy sage, the woodwork a natural honey shade. Wall-to-wall plush carpeting in rich nutmeg covered the floor. Clean-line, loose-woven draperies in a ripe wheat shade framed the windows. On the wall facing her desk a counterpoint of deep apricot brightened a long swag of dried flowers and greens.

Leigh nodded her head in silent approval of the invitingly comfortable yet business-like tone of the room. Hoping St. Claire saw it in the same light, she crossed to her desk, careful not to splash liquid over the side of her coffee mug and onto her suit or the carpet.

St. Claire.

Merely thinking the man's name increased the tremor in her hands, her entire being. For while it was true that being associated with him professionally could be of enormous benefit to her career, his reputation instilled a strong sense of caution.

Leigh tightened her grip on the coffee mug, causing an ache in her fingers, and raised it to her excitement-parched lips. Questions swirled inside her head as she glanced at the small elegant desk clock.

How did he hear of me?

What could he want of me?

What is he really like?

That last was the question that intrigued.

From all accounts, Michael St. Claire was on the fast track to legendary status, seemingly overnight. Springing from nowhere, he had emerged on the Philadelphia scene, a sudden power in the field of real-estate development. Speculation about him — and his past — was rife.

Leigh had heard and read all sorts of wild and implausible stories and rumors about him.

At various times, it was said, even in the papers, that he originated from Los Angeles, Chicago, St. Louis, Houston, New York City, London, Amsterdam.

At other times, it was rumored, even reported, that his beginnings were as a carpenter's apprentice, a numbers runner, a building inspector's assistant, a street-gang leader, a spy for a free-wheeling pimp.

At exclusive gatherings, it was murmured, then later it appeared in print, that his private life had included a blazing affair with a married Hollywood super star, a secret marriage to the daughter of a reputed gangland boss, a suspect and almost slavish devotion to an influential businesswoman, a hush-hush liaison with a famous homosexual.

It was whispered, then eagerly reported, that he was observed in elegant, dimly lit restaurants and exclusive clubs, escorting various, stunning female companions . . . whom he changed with the same regularity as he did his hand-tailored shirts.

It was also said, and duly reported, that he was a bastard, in the legal sense of the term.

His birth status was the one and only speculation Michael St. Claire had ever responded to: he confirmed it.

He was the mystery man of the moment. The darling of the gossips and the seamier members of the fourth estate. The spin was in full whirl — the interest voracious.

The few known facts about him — his business acumen, his apparent wealth, his avoidance of publicity, his refusal to dance attendance to the tune of media, his rigidly guarded personal life — all combined to enhance his titillation value.

The man exuded attitude.

From the bits and pieces Leigh had read and heard via the active gossip grapevine, his attitude blended supreme self-assurance with an undeclared the-hell-with-what-anybody-says-or-thinks stance.

That he was supposedly handsome as sin added spice to the spin mixture.

Leigh had never set eyes on the man, her only reference being grainy and blurry newspaper photos of him, caught on the fly, so to speak.

Being neither naive nor fool, Leigh knew better than to swallow whole and without doubt everything said or printed about the man. In a society seemingly avaricious for the smallest titillating tidbit, every person with so much as a hint of celebrity was fair game for the gossips.

And Michael St. Claire was the current specimen on the slide under the microscope.

Sitting at her desk sipping coffee, staring at the slim third hand on the clock marking each passing second, Leigh couldn't quite decide if she felt sympathetic, fascinated, frightened or repelled by the prospect of her quickly approaching interview with the much discussed, but seldom seen or heard from, Michael St. Claire.

Two

The rumors, the spin on him regarding appearance, had been way off base, Leigh reflected, covertly studying the man Sheila had ushered into her office.

He stood an impressive six feet, four inches or so of lean, muscled perfection. The perfection of his body was mirrored in his face. He was a golden blond all over — from his gleaming spun-gold hair, styled longer than fashionable, to areas below, judging by the meager patches of his sun-bronzed skin that were visible.

His elegant figure was shown to advantage by the expertly tailored suit enhancing his blatant maleness.

His polite smile revealed even white teeth.

Michael St. Claire was not handsome as sin, Leigh assessed, quashing an instinctive shiver.

Quite the contrary in fact. The man possessed an almost unreal masculine attraction. His countenance, his entire form, projected a breathtaking, golden angelic beauty, the terrible golden beauty reminiscent of a picture she recalled from her childhood, an artist's depiction of a glowing and glorious avenging warrior angel. An angel who also happened to bear the name Michael.

There was one major difference, however. In addition to his glowing and gloriously angelic appearance, this Michael possessed a devilish and terrible sexual magnetism.

The conflicting attractions were formidable.

Leigh felt the pull, resisted — and quickly reinforced her armored facade.

The image of cool reserve, she rose and circled the desk, her right hand extended in greeting.

"Mr. St. Claire," she murmured, suppressing a gasp of shock as his long slender fingers closed around her hand. His skin was warm, dry, creating a friction against her palm that shot shards of electric sparks tingling up her arm. She had never before experienced anything remotely similar to the sensation. It unnerved her, which in turn, only deepened her reserve.

"Ms. Evans." His response was soft, formal, his voice low, smooth, every bit as attractive as the rest of him.

The tingling sensation intensified, fracturing to invade her entire being. An instinctive sense of self-preservation urged her to show him to the door, rather than to the chair positioned in front of her desk. Pride wouldn't allow it. Suppressing the impulse, she smiled, unobtrusively disengaged her hand from his and motioned to the chair.

"Won't you sit down?" she invited, retreating to the relative safety behind her desk.

"Thank you." He returned her smile and moved with innate grace to the chair.

Good heavens, she mused, affected against her will. His smile was of and by itself utterly devastating — pleasant, charming and demoralizingly sensuous all at the same time. The fluidity of his movements was a blatant sexual assault on the senses.

Calculated? Leigh asked herself, instantly alert to the danger this man and that smile posed for anyone, most especially any woman.

Not this woman, she vowed in silent determination, closing herself within — and keeping him outside — of her carefully constructed protective armor.

Deciding to forgo the conventional offer of coffee and get right to the point, thus expediting their business, she offered him another, cooler, more remote smile.

"What can I do for you, Mr. St. Claire?"

Michael went blank for an instant, a mental state he was not accustomed to or patient with.

But, Lord, he mused, the immediate effect of this woman on him, on his senses, his libido, was beyond comprehension.

He had been apprised of her talent . . . but not a word had been spoken about her beauty.

And this highly praised interior designer was beautiful. He had utilized the few seconds to his advantage, taking her measure when the perky little receptionist ushered him into the office. Her immediate impact on him had frozen the polite, impersonal smile on his lips.

Leigh Evans's facial bone structure was classic Celtic; high cheekbones, slim nose, well-defined jawline. Her eyes were a fantastic, exciting, challenging turbulent green. Her mouth — oh glory, her mouth — was wide, its lips full, luscious, and when she smiled just now . . . He suppressed a shudder.

Her smile contained the seeming contradictions of cool reserve and hot sexual promise.

The texture of her skin was smooth, fine;

her complexion creamy. Framing this delightful picture was a mass of long and thick auburn hair he suddenly ached to touch, test, curl his fingers into.

She was tall, somewhere around five ten or eleven, he'd noted when she circled the desk to greet him. And every inch of her was slender, curvaceous. Her incredibly long legs were shapely, the sight of them recalling secret fantasies he'd harbored since his teens.

What the hell, he thought in momentary confusion. He was turned on — rock hard — for God's sake, and thankful he was sitting down, his uncomfortable physical condition concealed from her eyes by the desk.

On the spot, he could think of many things she could do for him, all of them exciting — and not one of them appropriate to a business meeting.

But this was beyond weird, Michael mused.

Sure, he had experienced quick interest and physical attraction to a woman before, with many women, in fact. What straight man hadn't? But he had never before felt quite this intensity, this immediacy.

Ludicrous, maybe, but there it was, like it or not. The strange part of it was, Michael couldn't decide whether or not he did like it.

Strange barely defined it.

Fortunately, during the mere moments he had pondered his unusual response to her, he had not dropped the thread of her opening question.

"I want my office redecorated," he said, in the candid, up-front manner natural to him.

"By me?"

The slight flicker in her green eyes revealing surprise impressed Michael. He quashed an urge to smile. Though it was clear she was anxious, it was equally obvious to him she was working hard at concealment.

"Yes." He inclined his head, making it easier to hide the unruly twitch of amusement on his lips. "That is . . . if you want the commission."

She drew in a slow, deep breath.

He wished she hadn't, for the action drew his gaze to the uplift of breasts pressing against the crisp linen of her suit jacket.

"Why me?"

The underlying shakiness in her tone snagged his wandering attention. He reluctantly released his visual lock on her bosom and raised his eyes to hers.

"Your work was highly recommended to me." Beneath his bland tones, Michael was wondering why Leigh Evans's stunning looks had not been mentioned along with the high quality of her work.

"By whom?"

A tiny quirk of a smile escaped his control. Amused, he awarded her excellent marks for composure under duress. The woman possessed class in abundance.

He gave a negligent shrug. "A business associate . . . and close friend."

"I see."

Michael found himself once again fighting the urge to smile. For while she appeared contained, he could detect signs of her frustration; Ms. Leigh Evans was near to exploding with the need to challenge him, bombard him with questions. The very fact that she held her curiosity at bay elevated his estimation of the strength of her character.

An errant thought about the strength of her legs, most particularly her thighs, while wrapped around a man's hips, tested his own character.

"Are you interested?" he said in mild inquiry, while mutely urging: *Say yes, say yes*. The mere idea of having no reason to see her again was not to be considered.

"Of course I'm interested."

Silently applauding her calm demeanor,

Michael slowly released the breath he hadn't realized he was holding. He rewarded her with a brilliant smile. Satisfaction warmed him at the tiny flash of response she quickly banked in her fantastic emerald eyes.

Those eyes would glow for him, Michael promised himself on the spot. Sooner or later, hopefully sooner, her entire being would glow, shimmering with sensual pleasure, in response to him, only for him.

"Then shall we set up an appointment for you to see my office?" Holding her steady gaze — and again applauding her fortitude — he slid a slim appointment book from his inside breast pocket.

Breaking the visual contact, she lowered her eyes to the larger, leather-bound book on her desk. The crackle of turning pages disturbed the quiet in the room. "I'm free next Tuesday afternoon." She arched delicate dark auburn brows. "Will that be convenient for you?"

Flipping the slim volume to the appropriate page, he scanned the date; he was booked solid from one-fifteen till six. "I'm cleared from four-thirty on," he said, determining to make the lie truth and to extend the meeting to dinner for two. "Will that work for you?"

"Yes." Picking up a gold-toned pen, she noted the appointment in her book.

Removing the pen attached to his slim pocket book, he followed suit. Then replacing the book in his jacket, he retrieved an embossed business card.

"We can discuss financial matters after you've had a look at the place," he said, prepared to agree to any price, however exorbitant, she might quote. "If that is satisfactory to you?"

"Quite satisfactory," she murmured in response.

Thrilled as a teenager in the throes of a hormonal explosion, he nodded. Then, standing, he offered his card to her. "Until Tuesday, then?"

She accepted the card, careful not to touch his fingers, he noted with some amusement.

"Until Tuesday," she repeated, rising and again circling the desk in a gliding, arousing-as-hell stroll to extend her hand to him. "A pleasure, Mr. St. Claire."

"Mine," he gently insisted, "Ms. Evans."

Sitting still and upright at her desk, her hands folded atop her appointment book, Leigh stared at the door through which Michael St. Claire had exited moments before.

She could still hear murmurs of his parting conversation with Sheila. A shiver coiled its way up her spine, making the short hairs at her nape quiver.

She had misjudged him, she acknowledged, inhaling a deep breath in the hope of calming the emotional flutter feathering her nerve endings.

The man was not dangerous; he was positively lethal. His male beauty alone was a shock to the system. His eyes — those orbs of crystal blue clarity and keen incisiveness — glittered with potent sexuality.

Reluctant as she was to admit it, Leigh had felt the impact of his piercing stare; her nipples were still tight and achy in reaction to the casual and brief glance he had rested on her breasts. Fortunately, the layered materials of lacy bra, silk blouse and linen jacket had concealed her startling, involuntary response to that visual touch.

And yet, though she might wish it, in truth Leigh could not fault his manner. St. Claire had conducted himself with scrupulous politeness, displaying an almost old-fashioned gallantry that was beyond reproach.

So, then, under the circumstances, why was she suffering the familiar aftereffects of having been visually undressed, her feminine attributes thoroughly assessed by his dissecting crystal blue gaze?

The experience had been unnerving, to say the least. Tiny aftershocks continued to tremble through her. On reflection, Leigh could hardly believe she had actually agreed to meet with him again in four days' time, when every instinct she possessed screamed a silent inner warning to distance herself from him.

Lowering her eyes, Leigh stared at her open appointment book, at the name she had written in the space . . . the solitary mark on the otherwise blank page.

"So . . . what happened?" Sheila cried, bursting into the office.

Calmly, calmly, Leigh told herself, managing a faint smile as she raised her eyes to her hyper friend.

"He offered me a commission to redecorate his office," she answered, somewhat amazed at the steadiness of her voice. "I have an appointment to see it next Tuesday."

"*Yes!*" Sheila exclaimed, leaping into the air like a demented ballerina. "Oh, Leigh," she gushed, whipping around the desk to hug her. "This is the opportunity you've been waiting for. Michael St. Claire . . ." she broke off, her tone tinged with awe, her blue

eyes, so different from his in their innocence, bright with expectation. "He can
make you."

Or break me, Leigh fearfully acknowledged, in more ways than one.

"I know," she agreed aloud in somber
tones.

"Scared?" Sheila asked, her eyes suddenly
serious, probing into Leigh's.

Leigh gave a strangled little laugh. "Yes
. . . no." She shook her head. "I'm terrified."

"But why?" Sheila's laugh was sponta-
neous, lighthearted. "You're talented —
really talented." Her laughter dwindled to a
dreamy smile. "And Mr. St. Claire is so very
handsome, and so utterly charming."

And so coolly calculating. "It's terrifying in
its importance to my career," Leigh
answered, choosing to keep her personal
opinion of the man to herself.

"Oh, Leigh, I know." Sheila's smile
turned soft with affection. "But I also know
you'll do a superior job for him." She pulled
a mock-stern expression. "When are you
going to allow yourself to accept the reality
of your worth, of your own exceptional
talent?" she demanded, scowling.

She definitely knows me too well, Leigh
amended her earlier assessment, smiling
despite her mounting trepidation. It was an

33

old familiar scold, one Leigh had heard Sheila level repeatedly since coming to work for her soon after Leigh had opened her first showroom. Her response was automatic.

"Maybe tomorrow."

Sheila made a rude, snorting noise, and a sardonic reply. "Yeah, yeah. I've heard that before."

"Then again, maybe not," Leigh dryly added the codicil, which also had become automatic.

"You're too cool, Evans," the bubbly blonde retorted, her grin robbing the charge of its sting. "You always were." She rolled her eyes. "You get these minor attacks of inadequacy before every new commission, regardless of how large or small. I don't know why I even thought of being concerned about you for a minute there, when I know — and so do you — that Mr. Michael St. Claire will be very impressed and satisfied with the end results of your work."

"Opening-night stage fright, perhaps," Leigh suggested, dry-voiced, her sense of humor, and equilibrium, back on an even keel. "I understand even some of the most acclaimed actors and actresses suffer the symptoms."

"I'm so glad I have no outstanding talent," Sheila said, heaving a dramatic sigh of relief. "Because, from where I stand, talented people appear to be rather strange."

Her deliberate shot hit the intended target; Leigh's burst of appreciative laughter rang in the room, shimmered on the air, releasing her inner tension.

When her laughter subsided, she gazed fondly at her best friend. "What would I do without you?" she asked, enjoying her first easy breath since Michael St. Claire had stepped into her office.

"Oh, you'd think of something." Sheila tossed her a grin as she headed for the connecting door to the reception room, dismissing her own importance with a flick of her hand. "Extraordinarily talented people always do."

"Perhaps," Leigh tossed back, "but I'd probably be bored out of my mind in no time, if you weren't around anymore to keep me company."

Sheila stuck her head back inside, a big grin on her pretty face. "I love you too, friend." She hesitated, a dreamy look darkening her eyes. "And talking about love . . ." She sighed. "Just imagine what it would be like to be loved by Michael St. Claire."

"Romantically?" Leigh asked.

Sheila's eyes narrowed.

"Or physically?" she continued, her cool

tone reflecting a sudden chill inside.

"Oh, brother," Sheila groused, making a sour face. "Both, of course."

"It's all physical," Leigh quoted her mother.

"Not again. Honestly, I —" The blonde began her familiar protest.

"And it's all phony," Leigh interrupted, finishing the oft-repeated saying of her deceased parent.

Sheila lifted her hands, palms up, and raised her eyes, as if imploring strength from above.

"Romantic love is an illusion," Leigh instructed.

"This is where I came in," Sheila groaned. "I feel like I'm in a time warp."

The telephone on Sheila's desk rang.

"Well, right now, you'd better warp yourself back to work," Leigh advised, her tone more of a request than an order. "Business as usual . . . Michael St. Claire notwithstanding."

The phone shrilled another ring.

Leigh arched a brow.

Giggling, Sheila retreated, but was back, sticking her head around the door moments later.

"That furniture you special-ordered for Mrs. Standfield's formal dining room has arrived at last. The man on the phone wants to know if they can deliver Monday morning."

"Yes, please," Leigh said, obviously relieved to get it after weeks of delays and excuses. "I'll finally be able to finish that project. He's still on the line?"

"Yes."

"Get an approximate time, Sheila. I don't want to spend the entire day waiting for them."

"Will do." Sheila disappeared again, only to return within seconds. "He promised the delivery truck will be there sometime between nine and eleven."

Leigh heaved a sigh. "Good. Mrs. Standfield will be delighted."

"Mrs. Standfield's already delighted," Sheila reminded Leigh. "She adores the transformation you've made of her home, and you know it."

"Yes," Leigh admitted. "She has been a dear, very enthusiastic and supportive."

"Not to mention very impressed by your refusing to accept payment until the work is complete," Sheila drawled.

Leigh shrugged. "I couldn't."

"You couldn't have paid all of your expenses next month either if this stuff hadn't arrived," Sheila retorted. "Then what would you have done?"

"I don't know." Leigh shrugged again, went on facetiously, "Ask St. Claire for an advance?"

"He certainly can afford it," Sheila said, taking her boss seriously.

"Oh, really, Sheila," Leigh said in exasperation. "I was only joking."

"Well, I'm not. I mean, the man's supposedly loaded." Her expression grew dreamy, and she sighed. "Gee . . . imagine what it would be like to be married to a man not only that handsome, charming and sexy, but that rich."

" 'Handsome is . . .' " Leigh taunted with the partial quote. "And there's not enough money in the world worth trading your independence for."

Rolling her eyes, Sheila pulled her head back, but chided, "One of these days, Leigh, you're going to fall like a lightning-struck tree. And I'm gonna laugh all the way to the wedding."

"Don't hold your breath," Leigh retorted, laughing as the slamming door punctuated her taunt.

To be loved by a man like Michael St. Claire.

The errant, aberrant thought dried the laughter in Leigh's suddenly tight throat.

The concept wasn't worth consideration, she told herself, her step brisk as she returned to her desk. She didn't have time to waste speculating on the opposite sex. To her thinking, it didn't warrant the effort.

Men didn't love; they owned, possessed, enslaved.

Her slender body shook with induced memory. The echo of her mother's bitter advice from sixteen years before tolled inside her mind.

Men will tell you they love you, just to get you to have sex with them, Dottie Evans had said to her friend, unaware of her young daughter in the next room, overhearing this denouncement of the male species. *And then they'll marry to have a ready supply of sex. You know how that old saying goes; a wife is something you screw on the bed — and does the housework? Well, the saying is true. When a man says he's in love, he lies. What he is, is in rut.*

She had been so young at the time, Leigh recalled, too vividly. She had just turned twelve, a very impressionable emotional age, made more so by the onset of her menstrual period a few months before.

Dottie had gone on and on to her unmarried, unattached friend, expounding on her theme of the traditional, atavistic and ingrained faults of all men.

Naturally, her mother's words had had a profound effect on Leigh, making her wonder, question and, sadly, view her father in an altogether different, sullied light.

Leigh might have forgotten her mother's denigrating charge against men, outgrown it as she made the transitions from young girl to teenager to young woman, if she hadn't then started to notice her mother's unhappiness, bordering on depression . . . and if she hadn't been such a bright, inquisitive kid.

Instead, as she grew, matured, Leigh stood apart, observing the interaction between her mother and father — and the opposing sexes in general, removed from the play, while remaining one of the group.

She was popular and well liked by both girls and boys during her middle-school and high-school years, and later, with the young women and men in college.

Yet, Leigh had continued to observe, even though she had reached the conclusion before graduating from high school that her mother's accusations were correct.

Though it was unpalatable to her, for she genuinely enjoyed the company of males, there was no other conclusion Leigh felt she could reach, since every man she knew, however casually, appeared to be constantly in a state of sexual arousal — and they weren't too discriminating or selective in their choices of bed partners, either. Sadly, it soon became evident to Leigh that it had always been so.

In the cause of research, she had made an extracurricular study of history, not of dates of events and discoveries, nor of the war games men had ever played. No, Leigh had concentrated her search on the oldest of wars, the one seemingly declared the day man first appeared on the earth — the ongoing, neverending war between the sexes.

Her research had been rewarding, in so far as, to her satisfaction, history not only confirmed her beliefs, but added another, that being the female of the species had a justifiable right to be enraged against the opposite sex. In Leigh's interpretation, men had been treating women badly from day one.

By the time Leigh donned cap and gown for her college graduation services, she had further concluded that the masculine tendency seemed to be to do the majority of their thinking with a part of the anatomy located quite some distance below their skulls.

Nothing had occurred in the intervening

years to change or alter Leigh's conclusions. None of the men she had met, dated or spent any amount of time with, regardless of how interesting, charming or amusing, had proved the exception to her mother's rule. To a man, they all appeared little more than predators on the prowl, out for the next sexual kill.

Too bad, for many of them were fun to be with.

Not once did she entertain the idea that her thinking process, her judgment, might have been skewed, tainted early on by bitterness.

And not once did she think to examine the female species under the same harsh and revealing light.

However disappointing the results of her unknowingly biased observations, in the end, Leigh accepted her mother's scathing opinion of men.

While many men might be entertaining, fun to be with, they all were, at heart, little more than clothed animals, always on the scent for a female in heat.

In the intervening years, Leigh had met not one man who had managed to change her perspective but many who, by their actions, had confirmed it.

Pity.

Shrugging off her reflective mood, Leigh resumed her seat behind her desk.

Sufficient to the day, she told herself. There was work to be done today, in preparation for Monday, when she and her business would once again be solvent. She'd handle Tuesday on Tuesday.

A small, confident smile curved her lips.

She'd handle Michael St. Claire on Tuesday as well.

Three

Michael was humming at full throttle. Charged, revved up, he had managed to accomplish a prodigious amount of telephone and paperwork after returning to his office from his meeting with Leigh Evans.

At the end of the day, when everyone, including the receptionist and his personal assistant had left the executive floor of St. Claire Development in the tall Center City office building, Michael relaxed in his plush desk chair, waiting. He didn't have time to get bored.

A smile touched his lips at the *burring* summons of his direct phone line. He lifted the receiver before the *burr* sounded again.

"Hello, Barbara." His voice was soft with affection, heavy with amusement.

"You've always been an impudent scamp," the low, cigarette-roughened voice drawled.

"And you wouldn't want me any other way," he returned, chiding, chuckling.

"Well?" she demanded.

"Well, what?" He played obtuse.

"Your angelic appearance is deceptive,

Michael." With her broken-glass textured voice, she chastised him. "Actually, you're really a devil."

Giving his amusement free rein, he laughed aloud. "And you love me, despite my devilish ways," he said when the laughter subsided, then qualified, "Or because of them."

"There's that," she admitted, her throaty laughter echoing his own. "Now, cut to the chase, St. Claire."

Delighted with her, Michael grinned. "I love you like mad, Ms. Saunders. You're so refreshingly direct."

"If I were there, I'd direct my palm to your grinning face," she returned, in tones not stern but tender. "And I love you back like mad . . . but . . ."

Her pause was his cue; he took it. "I made an appointment with the lady to see my office next Tuesday afternoon."

"That's fine . . . But what did you think of her?" Impatience crept into her voice.

A teasing light flared to dancing life in his eyes. "Cool. Reserved. Very professional."

"Michael." A note of warning.

He laughed again, but to himself, not aloud. "Okay. Leigh Evans is gorgeous, stunning, a visual assault on the libido of any healthy, normal male." His tone was both indulgent and teasing. "That what you wanted to hear, Babsy?"

"I'll kill you."

"Only you could," he conceded, knowing it was unnecessary to add if anyone could. "But I'm afraid the repetitiveness of the threat has diminished its impact."

"I detest that nickname."

"I know."

She made a rude noise in his ear.

He laughed into hers.

"You're in rare form, aren't you?" she observed with a growl-like purr. "Spirit soaring."

"Yeah, I'm feeling pretty good," he admitted without hesitation.

"Got plans, do you?"

"Elaborate plans." An image of Leigh Evans filled his mind, swamped his senses, tantalized his body. He moved restlessly in the butter-soft leather chair.

"Seduction plans, perhaps?"

"Mind your own business, darling," he said in a pleasant-sounding drawl, the mental image telescoping to Leigh's legs — her long, long legs. A shiver of anticipation skittered from his nape to the base of his spine, then curled around to tingle the root of his masculinity.

The familiar voice at the other end of the

line abruptly banished the image, though the tingle remained.

Barbara laughed. "I do beg your pardon, but . . ." She broke off, and he could hear the distinctive click of a lighter, hear her indrawn breath, and he imagined he caught a whiff of the acrid scent of her exhaled cigarette smoke in the air.

"But?" he prompted, shaking his head in despair of her absolute refusal to relinquish her long-standing habit, despite the health warnings against smoking.

"But it's so novel, my darling, so titillating," she wryly responded. "What was that last young lovely's name? It's been so long — over a year, isn't it? — I've forgotten."

"Of course you have," he murmured, his voice dry as dust, loaded with disbelief. "Her name was Emma."

"Oh, yes, the veddy upper-class British heiress. Whatever happened to dear Emma, anyway?"

Michael had to laugh. Barbara could be such a bitch, if she set her mind to it. Idly, he wondered how Leigh Evans might fare in a go-round with Barbara, and decided it would be interesting to watch. But back to Emma . . .

"She married a sheikh drowning in oil

money," he said, smiling at the memory of the elaborate nuptials.

"And is now very likely ensconced in purdah," Barbara opined with a raw-voiced laugh. "Really, Michael, your refusal to consider matrimony with your assorted, however infrequent, paramours drives them to extreme measures."

"I never promised any of them forever, never deceived them on that or any other count," he needlessly reminded her. "As you well know."

"Yes, I do," she agreed. "I taught you well . . . You are honest to a fault, in all respects."

"I thank you most humbly for the tutelage, and for the blessing of your guidance." His soft tone was strengthened by sincerity. "They — you — have served me well."

"You've been an apt pupil — one might even say eager." Her raspy voice was smoothed by indulgence. "I assure you, the pleasure was mine."

He was quiet a moment, memories swirling, bringing a reminiscent smile to his lips.

He and Barbara went back a long way together, to the days of his untrained, impetuous youth. She had taught him much about business — and life. And, as she had reminded him, he had been an eager — no, greedy — pupil.

"But enough of the mushy stuff," Barbara said, her no-nonsense tone sweeping through his reverie. "I want to hear exactly what you have in mind — professionally, of course," she was quick to clarify, before he could again tell her to mind her own business. "What are your plans for this evening? Do you have an engagement?"

"No, I'm free," Michael said, eyeing the folders of estimation reports stacked on his desk. "I was going to crunch some numbers."

"Is that stiff-necked houseboy of yours expecting you home for dinner?"

Michael grinned and produced a sigh born of long suffering. "You know damn well Clancy is forty-seven years old, Barbara, and hardly a boy."

"Man or boy, he is overbearing, arrogant and full of himself," she retorted. "Actually, what he is, is a major pain in the ass."

It was an old complaint of hers, and one Michael wasn't in the mood to pursue at the moment. "The pain in the ass is not expecting me home for dinner," he said with emphasized patience. "What did you have in mind?"

"Come have dinner with me, at my

place," she invited. "If you're good, I'll help you crunch numbers."

Not a small offering, Michael knew, as Barbara Saunders had built a formidable business of her own with her uncanny talent with numbers.

"I'll be very good," he promised, his amusement coated with mock solemnity. "What time?"

"Now. Later. Whenever. I'll be leaving the office right after we hang up."

"Then I'll see you in an hour or so," he said, aware it would take at least thirty-five to forty minutes in rush-hour traffic for him to get to her river-view condo, whereas it would take her about twenty-five from her office. "Have the martinis chilled."

"But of course, darling," she returned in her rough-voiced purr.

"And potent."

"Is there any other way?"

Michael was still smiling at her rejoinder minutes after cradling the receiver. Barbara never failed to amuse him — except when she was giving him royal hell for some personal or business error she believed he'd committed.

Accepting that she was most often correct in her estimation of his rare blunders, whether with a woman or a business client,

Michael took her tongue-lashings in the manner they were administered — for his own benefit.

He respected and admired this forceful businesswoman, and he loved her without question or doubt, content in the sure knowledge that Barbara returned his feelings, despite her irascible manner.

Looking forward to a mutually entertaining and satisfying evening, Michael pushed back his desk chair, stood and scooped up the pile of folders as he circled the desk.

He had much to accomplish before Tuesday.

Anticipation lending a spring to his stride, he left the office . . . which really didn't need redecorating, since he seldom gave it more than a passing glance anyway.

After the spirit-lifting balminess of Friday, the weather went downhill. A front swept through Pennsylvania during the night, bringing intermittent showers and cooler temperatures. The rain fell on and off throughout the weekend and into midday Monday.

Leigh spent the weekend fending off intermittent bouts of nervousness about her quickly approaching appointment with Michael St. Claire and worry over the possibility of the special-ordered, extremely expensive furniture being damaged by inept handling in the inclement weather.

Monday morning she called a halt to the jitters; she didn't have time for all this angst, she upbraided herself. She had a project to finish.

Fortunately for Leigh's peace of mind, the delivery men knew their business. Not only had the elegant, beautifully crafted pieces suffered no damage in transport from the West Coast, they were covered and handled with care by the two-man crew.

Standing to one side in the dining room, her anxious and excited client quivering beside her, Leigh directed the placement of each exquisite piece in the large room.

When the men had finished and departed, Leigh, a gentle smile curving her lips, allowed the fluttering older woman to assist her in completing the final touches by adding small decorative pieces.

While Leigh centered a tall candelabrum, twined with live vines and bearing slender citrus-scented tapers, Mrs. Standfield arranged delicate pieces of gold-rimmed crystal inside the imposing, multiwindowed breakfront.

Leigh experienced a feeling almost of letdown with the work at last finished, but her mood changed to one of elation when Mrs. Standfield, effusively heaping praise on her head, handed Leigh a hefty check, along with her heartfelt gratitude and thanks.

Leaving the old stately Mainline house — the lack-luster and outdated interior of which she had transformed into a showcase — for what she thought was the last time, Leigh drove directly to the bank, deriving immense satisfaction from depositing the large remuneration into her dwindling business account, thereby protecting her personal account.

From the bank, Leigh proceeded to a small shop she frequented often, for herself and clients. The shop dealt exclusively in collectibles and *objets d'art*. However, this visit to the shop was not for herself or a client; she was in search of a suitable fifth–wedding anniversary gift for her brother and sister-in-law.

Leigh knew her sister-in-law's tastes were expensive and ran to the ostentatious. Since she was once again if not flush at least solvent, Leigh decided to indulge the spoiled woman, for her brother's sake, though she did not like his wife.

The refined, elderly shop owner did not disappoint. Within five minutes, and without so much as a wince at the price tag, Leigh handed over her gold card in payment for an exquisite hand-carved wood, smooth-as-silk Oriental figurine.

Consoling herself with the fact that the gift card the shop owner handed to her was gratis, she signed it with a flourish, then handed it back to the man to be packaged with the figurine for United Parcel shipment to her brother's home in one of the more upscale suburbs of Lancaster.

That particular chore taken care of, Leigh headed back to Center City. Certain she'd never find a parking space close to her showroom, she returned to the garage located a block and a half from her apartment, where she paid a minor fortune every month to park her car.

Leigh didn't mind having to walk, as the sun was playing peekaboo with the dispersing cloud cover and the air was mild, with a rain-washed fragrance. Since it was by then already long past noon, she stopped at a nearby coffee shop for a soup and half-sandwich lunch before strolling the few remaining blocks to her showroom.

"Well?" Sheila said the minute Leigh walked into the office. "Did she love it or did she love it?"

Leigh laughed. "She loved it."

"Of course." The blonde's shrug was nonchalant. "And so will Mr. St. Claire."

The mention of his name recalled the pending appointment, reactivating Leigh's earlier nervousness. Her stomach lurched, threatening to reject her lunch.

"We'll see," she murmured, bringing all her willpower to bear on calming her anxieties.

Whether in response to the return of the bright sunshine and milder temperatures or to her own impatience with herself for succumbing to the rampant uncertainties of her secret and deeply buried insecurity was moot. But she had had enough of the inner fidgets, and that was that.

From that moment on, Leigh diligently worked at shoring up her flagging confidence in herself, her ability.

The problem was, she didn't have the unqualified success she would have preferred.

Sheila, the only person aware of Leigh's carefully guarded vulnerability, and only because she had been on the scene before Leigh had learned the art of concealment, was a staunch ally in support of her friend's battle.

"Darn it," Sheila finally exploded later that afternoon, her normally laughing blue eyes flashing with concern, her small fists planted on her narrow hips.

"What?" Leigh asked, sounding ingenuous.

"You know what," her friend retorted. "You've been prowling like a caged lioness, for heaven's sake. Will you put it together?" She shook her head in despair, setting her riot of short pale blond curls into a swirling dance. "I mean, honestly, I know he's got a formidable business reputation, in addition to being the most delicious-looking man ever, but at the end of the day, Michael St. Claire is only a mere mortal, just a man."

Sheila may have appeared the metaphoric representation of the brainless and ditzy blonde. In fact, she was not. She knew what she was about, and her reference to St. Claire as "just a man" did the trick.

Just a man. Just another man. Very likely, most probably, out for an ego-stroking score, in one form or another, Leigh reflected with ingrained cynicism.

From that point forward, she was back on track, her insecurities shoved into submission, the breach in her facade of confidence and composure sealed with the cement of determination and purpose.

Telling herself that with her finances replenished, she could refuse the commission if she chose to do so, by Tuesday afternoon Leigh felt prepared for anything . . . even the near legendary St. Claire.

Attired in a tailored, pinstriped, charcoal gray suit over a crisp white cotton shirt, low-heeled black leather pumps, the narrow strap of a matching leather bag slung over her shoulder, her unruly hair tamed and smoothed into a figure eight twist at the back of her head, she strode into the lobby of the office complex, a picture of cool conservative confidence.

The outer surface of the recently constructed, tall edifice was impressive, the interior even more so. A sea of gold-veined black marble flowed over the floor and splashed midway up the enclosing walls, causing Leigh to wonder with cynical detachment if the quarry in Italy now lay exhausted.

The gold-toned hands on a large, prominently positioned wall clock stood at twenty-five after four.

A quick perusal of the directory led her to one side, where there was an older man seated on a high stool behind a podiumlike desk. After locating her name in an appointment book, he directed her to the bank of elevators for the stratospheric floors, two of which were occupied by the St. Claire Corporate Offices, the highest being the exclusive executive level.

Naturally.

The express lift delivered her to her destination, while her stomach felt it was still at ground level.

Determined not to be overwhelmed by the sensation of having been shot from a cannon, she paused to draw a deep breath before alighting, her professional eye scanning the area.

Instead of marble, Leigh sank into plush, mourning dove gray carpeting when she stepped from the lift. A large reception desk was set to the right of a wide corridor. A window of glass made up the wall behind it. The spacious section between contained the waiting area, which had more the appearance of an elegant private living or sitting room.

The scattering of pale gray and teal patterned chairs were deeply padded, comfortable looking; and the occasional tables were of expensive and gleaming solid wood. The added decorative touches of white, ceramic-based table lamps and artful arrangements of live spring blooms in bulbous teal vases lent a definite note of cachet.

Impressive . . . Which, Leigh acknowledged, was the whole point of the scheme.

Refusing to feel in any way daunted by the classy, intimidating reception area, she approached the receptionist with her head high and a smile in place.

"Ms. Evans?" asked the sleek, attractive brunette before Leigh had come to a stop at the desk.

"Yes," she answered with deceptive calm, damning the twinge of tension attacking her stomach muscles.

"Mr. St. Claire is expecting you." Rising, the woman smiled and motioned Leigh to follow her.

Head up, spine straight, shoulders squared, Leigh trailed behind her along the broad thickly carpeted corridor, past several doors to an unmarked one at the very end. Swinging that door open, the receptionist ushered Leigh inside and to another desk, behind which sat another sleek, attractive woman.

"Ms. Evans to see Mr. St. Claire," the receptionist said, formally . . . and unnecessarily in Leigh's opinion, since she had already said St. Claire was expecting her.

"Oh, yes." Smiling, the woman behind the desk stood and extended a hand to Leigh. "I'm Rosalie Farrella, Michael's assistant. Pleased to meet you, Ms. Evans."

"Leigh . . . please," Leigh responded, accepting the woman's hand and returning her smile while trying to quash her curiosity as to the possible role this woman might play in Michael St. Claire's life other than as his assistant.

Not that it matters, of course, she thought, assuring herself she didn't care in the least.

The thirty-something woman was lovely, small, slim, with a creamy complexion, a mass of long dark hair and deep, soulful black eyes. Her voice was pleasing, her manner businesslike, brisk but friendly.

Preoccupied with her thoughts, Leigh didn't hear the receptionist silently exit the room.

"And I'm Rosalie," she said, her smile widening to reveal small white teeth. Stepping away from the desk, she moved to yet another door in the wall to her right. "Michael asked me to show you right in," she said, turning the knob and pushing the door open.

Drawing yet another silent, steadying breath, Leigh stepped forward when Rosalie moved aside, gesturing for her to enter before returning to her desk.

Leigh was on her own. Okay, go for it, she told herself, striding with contrived, bold confidence into St. Claire's well-guarded sanctum.

"Ah . . . Ms. Evans, right on the minute." He smiled. "I do appreciate punctuality."

He was not seated behind his desk — his huge solid oak desk — as she had expected, but standing before a wall of windows overlooking the city.

The view beyond the windows was spectacular, the sight of the golden smiling man breathtaking.

His expertly tailored — and obviously outrageously expensive — navy blue business suit enhanced the slender muscularity of his long form, a dark and striking counterpoint to his allover golden appearance. His crisp white shirt looked even whiter in contrast to the dark suit and red-striped navy tie.

Damn, he was gorgeous.

The thought undermined Leigh's hard-won confidence, forcing her to regroup her defenses. Railing in silent frustration against her involuntary response to his undeniable attraction, she quickly mended the frayed edges of her cloak of cool reserve by reminding herself that most blonds looked great in navy blue. Sheila immediately sprang to mind as an example.

"I also appreciate punctuality," she replied, pleased with the note of remoteness she'd managed to attain. "Time is money," she quoted. "Trite, perhaps, but true."

"Ummm." His smile developed a crooked slant.

Was he laughing at her? Leigh wondered, studying the sheen in his eyes — reflected sunlight from the windows or . . .

"Will you have a seat . . . a cup of coffee?"

Leigh shook her head, ceasing her speculation while refusing his offer. "No, thank you. I think I'd just like to have a look around . . . if you don't mind?"

"Not at all." A flick of one hand indicated his invitation to explore. "That is what you're here for."

Leigh managed a faint smile and a brief nod before turning away, only then taking note of the spaciousness of his office, which in fact was one of a suite of rooms she quickly judged to be much larger than her apartment.

An open doorway to the left led to what was obviously a meeting room, furnished with a long rectangular conference table surrounded by a dozen well-padded leather armchairs. Beyond the meeting room, she could glimpse a small, compact kitchen. She could only presume that if there was a kitchen, there was also a bath en suite.

Her gaze encompassing the area, she glanced around, not really surprised to discover that his office had been professionally decorated with style and taste, in muted, variegated shades of gray and cream, soothing to the eye, thus conducive to concentration for both solitary work and business meetings.

Yet, something struck Leigh as not quite right about the look, the feel of it.

A frown knit her smooth brow.

What was it that jarred? In truth, it was beautiful, the handiwork of a talented decorator. So what —

"It doesn't fit, does it?"

The sudden sound of his voice was startling; the very closeness of him unnerving. Exerting control, Leigh kept herself from a reflexive response, and drawing a breath, slowly she turned to face him.

Michael St. Claire wasn't merely close, he was practically on top of her.

"I beg your pardon?" Leigh took a half-step back, covering her automatic retreat with a sweeping glance around the room. "What doesn't fit?"

"The decor." His voice was smooth as glass, his tone coolly polite. But the gleam in his eyes let her know he hadn't missed her deliberate move away from him. "It's expertly done, both masculine and appealing, but cold and generic." His glance followed the path of hers. "There's nothing reflective of me, of my personality in here."

Of course. She should have seen it, and yet . . .

"One needs to be familiar with a person before his — or her — personality can be incorporated into a decorative scheme," she said, giving substance to her thoughts.

"I know, and the decorator who put this all together did not know me, couldn't know me, as I never met the man, never had so much as a cursory chat with him." His smile, though bland, held a suspicious hint of satisfaction.

"I see," she murmured, thinking come to that, she didn't know him either.

"I sincerely hope so."

Leigh was at once wary, uncertain as to what he meant by the remark. "I'm afraid I don't understand what you're getting at," she reluctantly admitted, for some obscure reason not even sure she wanted to understand. And, dammit, he was still too close for her peace of mind.

She took another half-step back.

And then another.

A knowing, annoying smile twitched his lips; then he abruptly turned and strolled to the far corner where a plush sofa and three chairs were grouped around a glass-topped coffee table positioned to advantage before the window.

With what she felt was a deliberate display of fluid, almost boneless-looking grace, he settled his considerable length into one of the creamy-toned chairs.

"Come, Leigh, have a seat," he invited with a negligent wave of his elegant, long-fingered hand at the sofa and chairs in the grouping. "I've asked Rosalie to bring us coffee."

She hesitated, too aware of his use of her given name, aware also of undercurrents she didn't understand — didn't want to understand, because, as unimaginable as it seemed, and as innocuous as his comments had been, they had struck her as somehow sensual in nature.

"Then I'll explain 'what I'm getting at,' " he went on after the brief pause.

Leigh had almost decided she no longer wished to hear his explanation. She was out of her element here, and she knew it. She had dealt easily with other men, all types of other men. And yet, Michael St. Claire was leagues ahead of her in experience and sophistication. The metaphorical distance separating them was great, but not nearly great enough in her estimation.

She felt crowded, and she didn't appreciate the feeling.

She didn't want to sit down or have coffee.

Yes, I do, she decided in the next instant, hating the sudden shakiness in her legs, swallowing against the sudden dryness in her mouth and lips.

She hesitated a moment longer, her gaze caught, held captive by his steady regard.

He arched one impossibly gold brow.

Damn him. She could not, would not allow him to get away with subtle intimidation.

Her eyes glaring defiance, she strode to the nearest chair, silently daring him to laugh at her trepidation.

He didn't. Maintaining eye contact, he pressed a button on the intercom set on the low, glass tabletop. He didn't even have to speak.

"Ready for coffee, Michael?" Rosalie asked, obviously responding to some form of alert, a buzz or light on the unit on her desk.

"Yes, please," he said, his crystal gaze never wavering from Leigh's guarded eyes.

Locked into the strangest visual duel Leigh had ever engaged in, they waited in silence for Rosalie. To her heartfelt relief, the interval was brief.

Within minutes, Rosalie breezed into the office, carrying a large tray. Crossing to them, she flashed a friendly smile for Leigh as she settled the tray on one end of the table. Then, her movements brisk, efficient — which Leigh judged earned her an exorbitant salary — she proceeded to set out a tall, gleaming silver coffee server, a small silver creamer, an oval silver salver containing packets of sugar and sugar substitutes, a pair of delicate Limoges cups and saucers and a matching plate of assorted petits fours and lacy cookies.

Oh, to be in Paris, now that spring is there, Leigh paraphrased to herself in silent disparagement, impressed against her will and not happy about it.

"Will there be anything else, Michael?" Rosalie asked, her tone relaying an eagerness to serve.

Leigh wondered if Rosalie had ever heard of the woman's movement or equal rights. On the other hand, she felt grateful, for the question at last drew his gaze from her.

"No, this is fine." He favored his assistant with a warm smile. "Thank you, Rosalie." However politely stated, it was a dismissal.

"You're welcome." Her smile serene, Rosalie nodded to Leigh and departed to the outer office.

The door closed with a faint click.

The soft sound reverberated through

Leigh's nervous system. For a moment, panic unfurled inside her at the idea of being trapped, alone with him, at his mercy; and she had to fight to control an urgent instinct to run.

The absurd notion brought Leigh up sharp.

Run?

At his mercy?

Indeed not, she chided herself. She never ran from a challenge, she had never been at any man's mercy and she certainly had no intention of initiating the experience with this particular man.

Gathering her senses, her composure, and the remnants of her resolve, Leigh steeled herself for St. Claire and his promised explanation, whatever form it might assume.

Four

"Cream and sugar?" His voice was soft, polite, his words common, almost prosaic, and yet they succeeded in drawing her gaze back to his.

Even prepared as she was for the impact, his eyes, clear and direct, had a profound effect.

"Just cream, thank you," Leigh murmured, fighting the unfamiliar enemy of involuntary response to the sensual power glittering in those fantastic blue depths.

Another ridiculous notion, she upbraided herself, leaning forward to accept the fragile cup he held out to her. Still, ridiculous or not, Leigh was careful not to make physical contact with his hand or fingers.

He smiled.

She fumed.

Irritated, yet fascinated, she watched him raise the cup to his lips for a test taste. The sight of the fragile china cradled in his broad, long, slim-fingered hands should have appeared ludicrous. Instead, the impression was one of casual elegance, the delicate pieces cherished and protected by his inherent strength.

She suppressed a shiver, and chided herself for indulging in such unusual and immature imaginings.

"Sweet?"

She started. "What?"

He gave a negligent wave. "Would you care for a sweet . . . a cake, a cookie?"

"Ahhh . . . no." Leigh shook her head, experiencing a sudden breathlessness caused by her fanciful idea that he had addressed her with an endearment.

"They're very good," he said, choosing a chocolate-iced petit four and severing it in two with his white teeth. "I love sweets, have since I was a kid," he confessed, popping the remaining half of the cake into his mouth. "Most especially chocolate."

"Hmmm . . ." she murmured noncommittally, her early-warning senses quivering at the devilish gleam in his eyes.

"It's the next best thing to sex."

Leigh went stiff — on the surface. Inside, well, she wouldn't think about the spreading warmth inside. Her inner body heat sapped every drop of moisture from her throat and lips. Raking her mind for a scathing, slapdown response, she took a quick sip of coffee; the hot liquid seared her tongue, which in turn fired her temper.

"I beg your pardon?" Her voice was as stiff as her body, stiff and cold with censure.

Michael grinned, ruining his previous impression of the politely mannered host. "Have I offended you?"

Resenting the skin-prickling effect of his disarming grin, her temper running hot and her control running out, Leigh blasted him with a green-eyed glare and an imprudent charge. "You do realize, don't you, that in the current politically correct thinking, your remark could be construed as harassment?" She then cringed inside at the hectoring sound of her own voice.

She had overreacted. She knew it, but having talked herself into a corner by taking the high ground, she could see no dignified way out.

Leigh didn't know what kind of reaction to expect from him — a freeze-out, an apology, an angry countercharge. But she certainly didn't expect what she got.

Tilting back his gold-kissed head, Michael let rip with a burst of deep, rich laughter. The sounds of his amusement ricocheted off the walls, and Leigh's eardrums . . . and her senses . . . and her emotions.

Unwilling to acknowledge, never mind examine, the shiver-inducing effect of his enchanting laughter, Leigh chose instead to compound her initial overreaction by feeling insulted.

Enough.

The word exploded in her frazzled mind, sending an order to her brain to move. The command was instantly obeyed. Her shaking hands betraying her agitation, Leigh set the cup on the low table before rising to loom over him.

"I'm so glad you're enjoying yourself, Mr. St. Claire," she said, intermingling wryness and sarcasm. "But, at the risk of sounding stuffy, I can't say I appreciate being the brunt of your humor." She hooked the thin purse strap over her shoulder. "So, if you'll excuse me, I'll —"

"I won't," he declared, gently but firmly, bringing her up short and frowning.

"What?" Disbelief colored her voice.

"I won't excuse you," he said, rising to tower over her. "I'm sorry if I was out of line — I assure you it was not my intention."

Unconvinced, despite his seeming sincerity, Leigh remained skeptical.

"Please, sit back down, finish your coffee. We have a lot to discuss."

Michael St. Claire had reverted to the impeccably mannered businessman, his expression somber and solicitous, the gleam in his eyes banked by concern.

Leigh didn't buy it for a minute, but he was offering her a way out. And, though she might have been too quick to climb onto her high horse, wouldn't it be an act of professional suicide to stand on the shaky ground of principle simply to appease her sensibilities?

"That is, if you still want the commission," he said into the lengthy silence.

Crunch time.

Her recent financial reversal aside, Leigh knew she would be utterly stupid to now squander this chance of a lifetime.

Swallowing her pride, she capitulated. "Yes, I still want the commission."

There, she had done it — but she didn't like it. God, how she hated game-playing control freaks.

Resentment simmering inside her, and hating the idea of being so easily manipulated, most especially by a master of the art, however charming, Leigh nevertheless resumed her seat and picked up her cup and saucer.

"Good." His voice, his nod and his movements were brisk as he mirrored her actions. He took a sip of the liquid, made a face. "It's gone cold — would you like a refill of hot?"

With a quick shake of her head, Leigh gulped down the tepid brew in her cup and even managed to contain a shudder of distaste. "No, thank you."

"Okay, then let's get down to business."

There was a soft double click when, as if synchronized, they placed their delicate cups and saucers onto the table.

Sitting back, Michael pierced her with his crystal blue gaze. "How about dinner?"

Dinner? Leigh went blank for a moment. Dinner? What did dinner have to do with . . . ? Her eyes narrowed. Was he at it again, insinuating, making it personal? Would he actually dare to once more step over the line of accepted, proper professional behavior?

But of course he would. Leigh mocked herself, her unfortunate naiveté. Michael St. Claire had a reputation for daring just about anything. Why should she believe she'd prove the exception to his rule?

Renewed anger burned her throat, adding acid to her tone. "What about" — she paused to let the acid drip off the end of her voice — "dinner?"

Something — surely not admiration? — flashed across his expression, darkening his eyes.

Leigh experienced a tremor, deep inside, that didn't bear thinking about. She employed a cool, arch look, prompting him to respond.

"This evening . . . you and I," he said, his voice smooth as fine old bourbon.

Like hell. Leigh clamped her lips to contain the thought. Wouldn't be politic, or very smart. Instead, she fell back on one of the oldest excuses going.

"Sorry." Her voice outsmoothed his. "But I'm afraid I have a previous engagement."

"Ummm." His expression said he didn't believe her, but he didn't voice his skepticism.

She waited, holding her breath.

He smiled.

Leigh suppressed a shiver.

Michael glanced around, taking in the beautiful, yet inappropriate decor. His perusal brief but thorough, he returned his gaze to her.

"As stated, I never met or spoke with the decorator. He didn't know me." Once again, he raised that one damned gold-kissed eyebrow. "I just thought we could spend some time together, get to know each other, our likes and dislikes, our personalities . . . quirks and foibles," he explained in tones too reasonable, too casual.

He paused.

Sensing a zinger, she waited again, a sensation akin to tiny insects crawling beneath her skin coming over her.

"That is, if," he coolly continued, "we are going to work together."

As intended, Leigh didn't miss the slight emphasis he had placed on the word "if." It was blackmail, pure and simple. No, there was nothing pure or simple about it. It was blatant. Chauvinistic. Enraging. It was effective.

"Another time perhaps?" she suggested, gritting her teeth and swallowing the surge of bile in her throat.

"The weekend? Friday . . . Saturday evening?"

Well, at least he had the grace — or sense — not to smirk, Leigh mused, her palm itching in anticipation of wiping a victorious expression off his handsome face.

"I'm free Friday," she said, initiating the end of the meeting by rising. She had to get out of there, away from him, before she said or did something rash, like telling him to go to hell — and take his commission with him.

Michael stood as well, circling the low table to escort her to the door. He came to a stop next to her, too close to her. From this vantage point, she noticed that his "perfect" looks weren't all that perfect.

Pacing beside him to the door, she surreptitiously examined his features.

Fine lines, masked by his burnished tan, radiated from the corners of his eyes, and the grooves bracketing his mouth were deeper than they appeared from a distance.

For some inexplicable reason, the betraying signs of his age — somewhere between thirty-five and forty, she judged — made him seem more human.

Even so, he was gorgeous.

He said something.

She blinked. "What?"

"I asked what time — six-thirty, seven?" He leveled a puzzled look at her.

"Six-thirty," she said too quickly, hanging on to her composure for dear life. They were almost to the door, just a few more steps to freedom.

His arm shot past her, hand curling around the doorknob. "If you'll give me your home address . . ."

No way. The silent denial stiffened Leigh's spine. "Name a place. I'll meet you there."

He shook his head, smiled; and again Leigh had the fanciful idea she detected a flicker of admiration in his eyes.

Yeah. Right. Take a reality check, Leigh, she advised herself, stifling a demand for him to open the door. The brief flicker she'd caught flaring in his eyes most likely had

had more to do with satisfaction than admiration.

She expected an argument. That expectation was swiftly confirmed.

"I had a particular quiet country inn in mind, where we could relax, chat in comfort," he said, a dash of chiding in his tone. "It would be pointless to go in separate vehicles, don't you think?"

What Leigh was thinking — like advising him to get lost or getting lost herself — didn't bear thinking about. She couldn't; she had a career to consider.

"Very well," she agreed, reluctance warring with a confusing, frightening surge of anticipation. "But" — she continued, her firm tones drawing a wary frown from him — "I would prefer we change the time to six . . . and that you pick me up at my office."

He stood silent a moment, his blue gaze delving into hers, and once again she caught that flicker of *something* in his eyes. Then he shrugged. "Whatever. The time isn't the important factor; getting to know each other is."

He waited a moment, letting his comment sink in, then hit her with the clincher. "And by the way, you can name your fee." He shrugged. "Whatever it is, I'll accept it."

Name her fee. Stunned, Leigh stared at

him in speechless wonder. Name her fee! Just like that? Without preliminary discussions? It was unheard of.

Maintaining visual contact, his hand moved, turning the doorknob.

Reminding herself to breathe, Leigh returned his steady regard with an equanimity she wasn't close to feeling.

"Until Friday, then, Leigh?" He smiled and nudged open the door.

"Yes . . ." Controlling an urge to bolt from the room, she stepped forward, then paused at the doorway to give him a cool glance over her shoulder.

He had caught her with the fee bit; pride wouldn't allow her to leave without a zinger of her own.

"But, Mr. St. Claire," she finally continued, her pulses leaping in anticipation of her daring. "I already have an idea for the decorative theme for your office."

"Really?" She had caught him off guard, and it showed. "What theme?"

Tamping down trepidation, she favored him with a serene smile and took the plunge that possibly might cost her the commission after all. She let the barb fly.

"Why, early caveman. What else?"

Michael was still smiling when the *burr* of

his direct line sounded thirty minutes later.

"So, how did it go?" Barbara asked before he'd even had a chance to say hello.

His smile grew into a self-deprecating grin. "I struck out," he admitted.

"That's one for her. I think I like this woman already." Her raspy laugh rang in his ear. "If I'm not mistaken, this is the first woman to hand you a setdown. No . . ." She rushed on before he could respond. "There was that one, that sweet thing, who was much too young for you — in experience if not actual years."

"Barbara." Michael's voice was soft, controlled, a warning in itself.

She went blithely on. "If I recall correctly — and I do — your strength, your very personality terrified her. Poor dear." She clearly relished her theme. "But that isn't the case with this particular woman. Is it, darling?"

He sighed, tempted to verbally slap her down, yet fully aware she'd merely laugh and slap back. "No, that isn't the case with this woman," he admitted, envisioning the fire in Leigh's green eyes as she'd delivered her parting shot. "She as much as called me a caveman."

"Oh, it's too precious," she hooted, her throaty laughter abrading his ears. "I changed my mind. I don't already like this woman — I love her."

"Uh-huh," he grunted. "But it's only the first inning, don't forget," he drawled. "I have plenty of time to improve my batting average."

"Yes," she agreed, too sweetly. "But darling, will you get the opportunity?"

Michael chuckled in appreciation; Barbara did enjoy needling him. "Of course, my dear," he returned, as sweetly. "Dinner . . ."

"When?"

"Friday."

"Rogue."

He laughed. "I do my best. And you, sweetheart, read too many romance novels."

She gave a very unladylike snort. "But at least I don't see myself in the role of heroine," she retorted, defending her reading matter. "Whereas your best might prove to be your undoing one of these days."

"Indeed?" Michael grinned, delighted with her form of chastisement. "In what way?"

"Sooner or later, one of your women is going to bring you to your knees," she said in eager anticipation. "My only hope is that I'm around to witness the event."

Though Michael loosed a purely masculine chortle of ridicule, the vision of Leigh Evans filled his mind, took command of his senses, hardened his body.

"Don't make book on it, Babsy," he advised, confident his body's reaction was nothing more than carnal lust. "You could lose a bundle."

"While you could lose your so well-guarded heart," she prophesied. "Of which, you only have one." Her voice lowered to a rough purr. "I, on the other hand, would only lose money, of which I have plenty."

A fact Michael knew full well; Barbara was loaded. But the subject was beginning to really annoy him, and he was feeling too good to be annoyed.

"Yeah," he shot back. "But do you have a date this evening for dinner?"

"Yes, but I'd reschedule in a second for a better offer. Are you making one?"

"I am," Michael said, pondering the identity of the about-to-be dumped dinner companion; Barbara never hesitated in being ruthless to her advantage. "Who would be the unlucky recipient of your change of plans? Male or female?"

"Male. A recent, casual acquaintance," she said, her tone dismissive. "No one you need concern yourself about."

"Who's concerned?" His tone matched

hers. "Your casual . . . er, dare I say, dalliances, are your business," he drawled. "And could be the better offer."

"Let's hear yours, darling," she commanded.

"Dinner at my place," he said. "I owe you one."

She groaned loudly. "Prepared by the pain in the ass, I suppose."

"No," he said, laughing. "Expecting to have dinner with Ms. Evans, I gave Clancy the night off. I will be preparing our dinner."

"Interesting," she murmured, a smile making her smoke-roughened voice shimmer. "Tell me more."

"Your favorite," he murmured back, in tones of sheer, decadent enticement.

"California cheeseburgers?" She moaned, as if in the throes of sexual ecstasy.

"And Texas fries."

"Oh, Michael."

"And creamy cole slaw."

Barbara moaned again.

"And chocolate petits fours for dessert," he added as further inducement. Why waste them?

"I can't bear it," she cried, muffling laughter. "It all sounds so sinful — so nutritionally unacceptable."

"Yeah," he agreed, his voice conspiratorial. "But what the hell, let's live dangerously."

"Oh, Michael, you're so deliciously naughty."

"Only naughty? I'm crushed." He chuckled. "So, what'll it be? You wanna be naughty with me?"

"You're on," Barbara cried, erupting in a delightful burst of girlish-sounding giggles.

God, I love that woman, Michael thought a moment later, his smile tender as he replaced the receiver.

Five

Rampant adrenaline propelled Leigh from the heights of Michael St. Claire's lofty aerie to the sidewalk in front of the tall building.

By giving in to her desire to leave him with a stinging exit line, Leigh acknowledged that she also had probably left him with second thoughts about rescinding his offer.

But damn, she simply could not walk away allowing him to believe he could have everything his way.

Could she?

Churned up inside, her feelings a conflicting mix of anxiety and elation, Leigh opted to walk the less than a mile route between the office complex housing the St. Claire Corporation and her apartment building, hoping to relieve the tension tying her nerves into knots.

Besides, getting a cab at that time on a weekday was a near impossibility.

The brisk walk did help, and she had calmed down considerably by the time she turned onto the quiet street of old, mostly well-kept, three-story row houses located some five or so blocks south of City Hall.

The age of the buildings and the neighborhood was attested to by the few remaining iron-ringed hitching posts set at intervals along the curbsides and by the occasional boot scraper mounted to the side of a front door on the landing of a four-step entrance to a building.

Leigh's building still boasted both hitching post and boot scraper, markers that lent a sense of history, continuity and permanence that appealed to her.

After collecting her mail from the box in the small foyer, Leigh mounted the narrow staircase to her apartment, which took up the entire second floor. Unlocking the door, she stepped inside and released a sigh of relief.

She was home — safe from the machinations of the movers and shakers of her corner of the world. The sensation of sanctuary she experienced every time she shut her door behind her was one she never explored or questioned.

She felt it, and she accepted it.

With the delighted permission of her landlord, Leigh had slowly redecorated the flat, room by room. Her efforts had turned a dull and ordinary living area into a vibrant and cozy oasis.

It was her own personal space. Leigh

loved it, and on this particular afternoon, she needed its soothing influence even more than usual.

Still quivering with aftershocks from her disturbing meeting with St. Claire, she went straight to her bedroom. The prevailing colors of the Williamsburg green carpet and walls, contrasted by white woodwork, curtains and bed coverings, with highlighting decorative touches in deepest mulberry, always induced a calming effect she now sorely needed.

Dropping her purse onto the luxurious lacy white down comforter draped on the bed, she stepped out of her shoes and began unbuttoning her jacket.

Ten minutes later, her suit hung neatly in the closet, her blouse and hose deposited in the mulberry hued, lidded storage urn she used for a clothes hamper, her face cleansed of makeup, her business attire replaced by soft leggings and a loose cotton pullover, Leigh left the bedroom, padding barefooted through the living room to the kitchen.

The long rays of the lowering sun shafting through the kitchen windows bounced spangles of gold off the ecru walls, sheened the dark chocolate finish of the walnut cabinets and gilded the deep emerald green veins streaking the antique white countertop.

The remnants of tension eased from her at sight of her pristine kitchen. There was something so homey and reassuring about kitchens.

Coffee? Or tea?

Decisions, decisions, Leigh mused, smiling as she crossed to the cabinet above the stove next to the sink.

Green tea, she decided, lifting the metal container with its Oriental motif from the shelf. Hadn't she read somewhere that green tea was beneficial to one's blood pressure?

And her blood pressure certainly had been aggravated during her interview with Michael St. Claire.

Recalling that baffling, infuriating interview provoked an uncomfortable sensation at the base of Leigh's skull.

Dammit, she railed in silent frustration, banging the tea tin onto the countertop. With his chameleonlike changes from charming businessman to sexual predator — to coercive son-of-a-something-or-other — Michael St. Claire had coolly, skillfully manipulated her into accepting his invitation for dinner on Friday evening.

She didn't want to have dinner with him. Most especially, she didn't want to have dinner alone with him — didn't want to be anywhere near him, didn't trust him.

St. Claire gave every appearance of a man on the prowl, and she didn't appreciate being his prey.

A twinge of pain in her knuckles drew Leigh's attention to her right hand, her fingers gripping the tea tin.

Damn all men, and their lecherous natures, she thought savagely, straightening her fingers to ease the gripping tension.

Grabbing the gleaming emerald green tea kettle from its permanent resting place on the stove, she filled it with cold water, then set it on to boil.

Minutes later, sitting at her glass-topped kitchen table, Leigh cradled a steaming cup in her hands and inhaled the fragrant aroma of the tea.

What to do? she mused, taking a tentative sip of the hot liquid. St. Claire struck her as a man who would not appreciate being thwarted. Quite the contrary, in fact. He had made it as crystal clear as his eyes that he was a man not only used to, but hellbent on having his way.

And — Leigh shuddered — at present, he appeared hellbent on having his way with her.

What was it with domineering men, anyway? How many times during the previous fourteen years had she asked herself that same question? Was it part of their collective psyche, this inner drive to be king of every physical and emotional hill, to reign supreme over every female?

Of course some women had, through blatant or devious methods, reigned — Cleopatra, Eleanor of the Aquitaine, Elizabeth I, militant feminists down through the ages, her sister-in-law, to name a few. But, in Leigh's personal opinion, by and large the effect of their efforts on the average male had been minimal.

At an early age, Leigh had chosen not to venture onto the battlefield in the war between the sexes. Convinced the spoils would not be worth the certain-to-be-inflicted scars, she had opted to observe the action from the sidelines.

There had been a brief moment of deviation from purpose when she was a junior in college, tempted by curiosity to know what all the twittering was about. About nothing it turned out . . . at least so far as she was concerned.

And Leigh had liked the guy, a good-looking senior with a kind of off-the-wall sense of humor, fun to be with. She had dated him several times and, as he hadn't made any demands on her, had enjoyed herself.

But human nature being what it was, temptation and curiosity flared to life inside her the first time he kissed her, really kissed her.

Deciding it was time she gained the reference of experience for herself, rather than drawing conclusions from the tales of ecstatic pleasure relayed by her friends, Leigh determined to "go all the way" if the guy made a move on her, which she was positive he would.

And of course he did, two dates later. They had been out in a group, for pizza and beer. Her guy had drunk only two beers; Leigh had no way of knowing he was extremely susceptible to alcohol.

They made it to the bed — her dormitory bed. Foggy and overeager, he groped at her in between sloppy kisses, murmuring nonsense about how beautiful and sexy she was.

Turned off, but set on her course of enlightenment, she had tolerated his clumsiness until, on the threshold of penetration, he'd muttered the fatal words, "I love you." Thoroughly disgusted with herself as well as him, Leigh had reared up and shoved him off her seminude body and onto the floor, where he promptly fell asleep. She had left him there and spent the night with a friend in the next dorm.

But her experiment hadn't been a total failure, for the fiasco had reaffirmed her belief. In reaction, she had ruthlessly suppressed whatever natural sensuality she may have possessed.

Not having been tempted since then, at twenty-eight, she was a modern anomaly — an adult virgin. And she didn't care. In fact, she liked it that way.

She had gone her own route, content, safe, secure and unassailable behind the wall of reserve she had so carefully and painstakingly constructed, leaving the field of battle to the majority of women who apparently not only enjoyed but relished the sexual clash.

So, she mused, barely tasting the tea she swallowed, why should she now so much as entertain the idea of joining that messy fight by even crossing intellectual swords with Michael St. Claire?

The answer to that one was easy, summed up in three words. Economics. Career advancement.

Leigh certainly wasn't desperate, in regard to the economic angle. She now had money in the bank, and she had clients, a definite and a promising. The definite was a two-bedroom condo located near City Line, on which she had already done some preliminary work. The promising was a larger vintage Cape Cod in Haverford.

Not shabby by a long stretch, she assured herself. But, in all honesty, not the clout and prestige of a St. Claire commission, either.

Sighing, she refilled her empty cup from the brightly colored, flower-strewn, squat fat teapot she had purchased in a discount store.

Anything but a snob, Leigh didn't hesitate in scooping up treasures wherever she found them.

And, of course, the biggest treasure of all would be the St. Claire commission. The only drawback being that Michael St. Claire was the central element of the deal, and from all indications, he appeared to have an agenda other than the redecoration of his office — a personal agenda.

Leigh sipped the tea, grateful for the warmth permeating her suddenly cold interior.

She had not been imagining things; St. Claire had designs on her. There had been undercurrents, unstated but blatant sexual intentions throughout both of their interviews.

Leigh felt it, knew it, she just didn't know the why of it. Why her, when he had been seen squiring the accepted beauties and sophisticates, not only of Philadelphia but of all the major cities in the U.S. and Europe?

While Leigh was aware that her professional endeavors were beginning to be noticed, in the realm of interior design, she was still a very small fish in a shark-infested sea.

So then, why had St. Claire singled her out, for either personal or professional reasons?

He claimed she had been recommended to him by a friend and business associate.

A former client?

Leigh frowned into her teacup as she did a quick mental search of her files. The exercise really wasn't necessary; there hadn't been that many of them. And she couldn't picture any one former client as either a friend or associate of Michael St. Claire.

Not that it mattered in the long run.

Her dilemma remained the same. She had two choices. Have dinner with him, or lose the commission — if it was still on offer after her denigrating exit line.

Leigh sighed. Though personally satisfying, having as much as called him a caveman had not been exactly brilliant, and definitely it was not professional. Come to that, it hadn't even been true. Granted, the man had made a thinly veiled sexist remark, but that hardly made him a caveman.

It merely made him a man, like other men.

Well, not quite like other men, Leigh conceded, feeling a fine, hair-stirring quiver at her nape.

To tell the truth, she had never met a man quite like Michael St. Claire before in her life.

By all rights, it should be against natural law for any one man to have been so endowed with all of nature's bounty, blessed with near perfect beauty of face and form, grace of movement, intelligence and charm.

Who dared quibble with the tiny flaw of self-perceived male superiority?

Leigh dared.

But then, she had made a dedicated study of the predatory sexual instincts of the male of the species.

She had believed herself immune to the allure of the beasts, and to their varied approaches. Her involuntary response to Michael St. Claire cast doubt on her immunity, her own self-perceived superiority.

Was she equal to the challenge he presented?

Pride straightened her spine and sparked a glitter of defiance in Leigh's eyes.

Her career, her entire future was at stake.

Damned if she'd quit the field without a fight. She'd accept his challenge and his command cloaked in an invitation to dine.

The decision made, Leigh took a swallow from her cup and grimaced. The tea was cold. But that was all right, she was now warm, her blood fired by purpose.

Feeling better, less wary and unsure, Leigh got up from the table, rinsed her teacup, then set about the business of getting a meal together for herself.

She was stirring pasta into boiling water when the phone rang. Lowering the heat under the pot, she gave the noodles a final swirl with the long-handled fork before crossing to the wall-mounted lipstick red phone.

St. Claire? Leigh weighed the possibility, eyeing the instrument suspiciously, then snatched up the receiver as it shrilled a sixth ring.

"Hello?"

"I was about ready to hang up."

Leigh's grip on the cool plastic eased at the sound of her father's voice.

"Did I catch you at an inconvenient time?" Apology and anxiety were mingled in Andrew's voice. "I can call you back later if —"

"No, Dad, it's all right," Leigh assured

him. "I'm cooking and had to turn down the burner first," she explained.

"Oh. Good. I'm glad I'm not disturbing you." The relief in his voice was unmistakable.

Leigh suppressed a sigh born of despair and regret. Her father always seemed wary and uncertain with her. She had given him reason to feel trepidation. In her judgment, *he* was directly responsible for her mother's unhappiness and bitter disappointment with life.

"You're not disturbing me at all, Dad," she said, giving silent thanks for diverting her thoughts from another, seriously disturbing man. "What can I do for you?"

He hesitated a moment, then swiftly said, "Could you drive home this coming weekend?"

Alarm streaked through Leigh. Her father rarely asked anything of her, least of all that she come home — to the house her mother had considered little more than a prison.

"Is something wrong?"

"No. No." He was quick to deny. "But Saturday is your brother's wedding anniversary and —"

"I remembered," she cut in, impatient with him for his apparent need to remind her. But then, her brother was a male, the firstborn and favorite child, thus not to be overlooked on any occasion. "Don't worry, Dad. I've already sent a gift I think they'll like."

"Yes, I know. Brett called me, said it was delivered early this afternoon." His tone took on an odd inflection. "He also said Evelyn was absolutely thrilled with the piece — said it looks like it cost a bundle."

A hint of censure there? she wondered. She dismissed the speculation at once. No. Censure of his daughter-in-law might reflect on his son. Can't have that.

A cynical smile twisted Leigh's lips; Evelyn had just about everyone fooled with her sweetness-and-light act. "It did." She wryly confirmed her sister-in-law's estimate. "And I'm glad they like it."

"But that isn't why I called you."

"No?" Leigh managed to keep exasperation from creeping into her tone. "Then why did you call? And why did you ask if I can drive home this weekend?"

There was a hesitant silence for a second, almost as if Andrew were dreading her reaction. Then he rushed into an explanation. "I'm giving a small anniversary dinner party for Brett and Evelyn Saturday evening. Naturally we all want you to be here for it."

Sure. Leigh smothered a snort of disbelief. In her admittedly jaundiced opinion, her family wanted her company like they wanted a month of rotten weather. Other than when they needed something — like a quick infusion of ready cash — not one of them displayed a desire to have her close by. She was too independent, too quick to judgment, and much too often proven correct.

There was one exception: her nephew, four-year-old Andy, named — with calculated forethought, Leigh felt certain — for his grandfather. Andy, still young, still innocent, gave every indication of enthusiastic affection for his aunt. And she was crazy about him.

"Leigh, are you still there?"

Andrew's anxious-sounding question drew her from her unpleasant reverie. Releasing a silent sigh, she replied. "Yes, Dad. I'm sorry, but I, er, was reviewing my schedule, trying to recall if I'm free this weekend."

"You work weekends?" His obvious surprise was predictable to Leigh; Andrew had always held a nine-to-five, five-day-a-week position.

"When necessary, yes," she said.

"Well, do you?"

"Do I what?"

He heaved a very put-upon sigh. "Do you

have anything scheduled for this weekend?"

"I do have an engagement Friday evening," she answered, thinking with chagrin that had he called over the last weekend, or even yesterday, she would have had a legitimate excuse for declining St. Claire's invitation. "But —"

"A date? With a man?" He interrupted her, his eager interest evident.

"With a man, yes. But not a date. It's merely a meeting over dinner with a business associate, Dad," she said, quick to quell speculation and dampen his apparent hope, though why he would think a display of parental concern about her continued single state was called for, she hadn't a clue, when he had never shown the slightest interest before in her activities, either personal or professional.

"Oh."

Though his disappointment rang with genuine regret, Leigh remained skeptical. He had been distant and withdrawn for too many years to convince her of any sudden interest now.

"Why the heartfelt 'Oh,' Dad?" she asked, testing the depth of his newfound and unexpected fatherly concern.

"Well, I . . . just thought . . . ummm." He began in fits and starts, only to go on in a galloping rush. "I thought if he's someone special to you, you might want to invite the gentleman along as your escort."

Leigh rolled her eyes, tempted to tell him that she didn't know any *gentlemen* — only men. But, appalled by the very idea of having Michael St. Claire escort her home for a family celebration, she hastened to make her position as crystal clear as that man's blasted eyes.

"He is not special to me, Dad," she said, her tones hard and repressive. "There is no special man in my life." And not likely to be anytime soon, either, she added to herself with cool assurance. "I'm much too busy building a business to bother with any romantic involvement."

"Too bad," he murmured. Then, in a soft, confusing and somehow unsettlingly sad voice, he went on, "You're very much like your mother, Leigh."

Too bad? His comment haunted Leigh long after, having told him that other than Friday evening she was free for the weekend, she had agreed to driving to Lancaster Saturday morning and they had said their goodbyes.

She brooded over the possible meaning behind her father's remark while preparing a light dressing for the overcooked, mushy pasta.

Why the somber tone? Leigh wondered, eating the food without actually tasting it. As if her being like her mother was a cause for remorse.

Resentment began to simmer while she cleared away the supper things. Although she didn't know the particulars of their private life, from what she had overheard when her mother had enlightened a friend as to the nature of men, and later had learned from her own observations, Leigh firmly believed that Andrew Evans had made her mother's life miserable.

Granted, she had never been witness to her father raising a hand or even his voice to his wife, but in some manner, he must have abused Dottie Evans, if not physically, then psychologically and emotionally.

Leigh had been devastated by the effects of her father's remoteness and unconcern for her mother. She had stood by in helpless fury as her mother's despair deepened into scathing bitterness.

Leigh had suffered shame at the sheer relief she had felt on escaping the darkening atmosphere in her home when she'd gone off to college. And her shame had been compounded by searing guilt when her mother had succumbed to a massive heart attack the year following Leigh's graduation.

Remnants of that shame and guilt remained, burdening her conscience on occasion . . . like now, after hearing her father bemoan her similarity to her mother. And that on top of his belated pretense concerning her lack of male companionship and a romantic love life.

Love . . . Indeed!

Feeling vulnerable and vaguely hurt for some ridiculous reason, Leigh left the tidy kitchen and went straight to her bedroom. Swinging open the closet door, she stood on tiptoe, stretching to reach the far corner of the high shelf. Her fingers groped around an assortment of handbags and the two felt hats she possessed, then closed around the familiar feel of a small cardboard box.

Cradling the container in her hands, she crossed to the bed, sat down on the edge, lifted the lid, brushed back the surrounding tissue and carefully removed the only keepsake that was her mother's.

It was an inexpensive music box, but beautiful all the same, and precious to Leigh.

It was made of stained mahogany, its gleaming finish very close to the color of Leigh's hair. Set into the lid of the box was a small gold-plated filigree heart, with a crack running diagonally through it.

Leigh's mother had purchased the box for herself seven or eight years before her death, and had treasured it — for the same reason Leigh herself now treasured it. When the lid was lifted, the mechanism in the box played a tinny, tinkling rendition of the song "Tomorrow," a tuneful reminder for Leigh of the painful pitfalls of love.

Because, for Dottie Evans, the sunshine of love never shone, and tomorrow never came.

Listening to the hollow-sounding musical notes bolstered Leigh's spirits, and drawing a deep calming breath, she reinforced her determination to fashion her own tomorrows, independent of the desires and machinations of any man — Michael St. Claire and her father included.

Six

Friday dawned sun-bright and warm, lifting the spirits of most of the end-of-the-work-week citizens.

Despite her reluctance for the pending dinner engagement with Michael St. Claire at six that evening, Leigh felt her own spirits rise as she wove a path through the crowd on the way to her showroom. Her spirits took a hit the minute she stepped into the reception room. Her employee and best friend fired off the deflating shot.

"Are you going out to dinner with Michael St. Claire dressed like that?" Sheila demanded, sweeping a shocked look over Leigh's stilled form.

Wanting to make a definite statement, and with cool determination, Leigh had decided to send a silent but pointed message to St. Claire by deliberately not dressing up for the occasion which she considered a command performance, thus not in the least auspicious.

"What's wrong with the way I'm dressed?" Leigh responded irritably, put on the defensive and hating it.

"Well, nothing — for the office," Sheila said, casting another encompassing look over Leigh's now taut body. "I mean, that's a terrific business suit, but —"

"But?" Leigh prompted, narrowing her eyes.

"Oh, Leigh, you know," Sheila said. "It's a tailored, gray business suit."

"So?" Leigh scowled. "This is a place of business."

Sheila threw up her hands. "But you're going out to dinner from here. *And you're wearing low-heeled shoes.*"

The squeak in Sheila's voice triggered Leigh's sense of humor and she burst out laughing.

"What's so funny?" the blonde demanded, slamming her small hands onto her narrow hips.

"You are," Leigh answered despite another bout of laughter brought on by her friend's aggressive stance. Shaking her head, she crossed to the desk. "Is there coffee?"

"Of course." Sniffing, Sheila motioned to the full glass pot on the warming plate of the coffeemaker, in full view of her employer. "As you can see for yourself."

The smaller woman, bringing to mind a tiny fluffy dog acting tough, had Leigh quashing another urge to laugh. "What are you getting so worked up about, anyway? I told you this was merely a business meeting over a meal." She grimaced. "One, I might add, that I could do without."

Sheila rolled her eyes. "Oh, Leigh, what am I going to do with you?"

"About what?" she asked innocently, knowing precisely what Sheila meant.

"About men," Sheila retorted. "Darn it, Leigh, men like Michael St. Claire conduct business in their offices, or on the golf course, or in lounges over drinks and cigars — at least with male associates. They invite women they are interested in to dinner."

Having her own suspicions concerning St. Claire's intent confirmed caused a hollow sensation in Leigh's midsection, a sensation she also could do without.

"I think you're wrong," she said, praying she was right. "I've heard about St. Claire's taste in women." Her voice went bone dry. "I don't fit the description."

"Gossip. Rumors." Sheila dismissed them with an airy wave of her hand. "I say he's attracted to you."

Leigh experienced an odd inner tingle, a fluttering . . . too close to excitement to be considered. "Then I say, too bad for him, because the attraction is not mutual." She hoped she spoke the truth, feared she didn't.

She didn't need or want Michael St. Claire to be attracted to her; she didn't want any man attracted to her. A physical attraction could only cause unnecessary tension in their working relationship — if there was to be a working relationship.

And yet . . . and yet Leigh had unusual difficulty quashing the expectant shimmer inside her.

The inner conflict nagged, as did her friend at Leigh throughout that seemingly endless day. Shortly before five, Sheila even went so far as to suggest that she remain in the office past her quitting time, while Leigh made a quick trip home to change into something more appropriate — and more feminine.

Leigh met Sheila's suggestion with the scorn she deemed it deserved and a firm refusal.

The hour between Sheila's reluctant departure and Michael St. Claire's arrival dragged, each endless minute fraught with uncertainty.

Though he was early, she was standing on the stoop outside her showroom, enjoying the warmth of the dying afternoon sunshine when Michael St. Claire drew his car to a halt parallel to the vehicle parked along the curb.

Feeling a jolt too close to anticipation to be examined, Leigh directed her concentration elsewhere, examining his vehicle instead.

His car was a top-of-the-line, custom-fitted, glossy black Cadillac. What else?

Even when double-parked on a traffic-congested Friday evening, St. Claire played the gentleman, stepping out and circling the car to open the door for her.

Quickly descending the steps and across the sidewalk, Leigh was there to meet him. "It wasn't necessary for you to get out," she said, motioning to the lengthening line of cars behind the Cadillac.

Horns blared. Several drivers lowered their windows to voice their irritation in words unsuitable for young children, some underlining their obscenities with hand gestures.

St. Claire was impervious to the racket. "I thought it was," he said, his smile serene.

With enviable aplomb, he ignored the noise and ushered her into the purring vehicle. The clamor grew in volume as he retraced his steps around the car then, blessedly, was silenced by the door shutting with a solid-sounding thunk.

Luxury cars have their uses, Leigh wryly reflected as St. Claire set the vehicle into smooth motion.

And the car certainly was luxurious. The interior was in dove gray, the seats of soft cushioned leather. The dash appeared to have more gadgets than the average jet plane, one of which gave the air temperature and humidity both outside and inside of the vehicle. The carpet on the flooring beneath Leigh's feet was a deep pile like the one in the living room of her apartment.

The fact that, in her gray suit, she blended to the point of disappearing into the seat was not lost on her.

Or him.

"If it weren't for the beacon of your red hair, I'd have trouble locating you," he drawled, taking advantage of a snarl in traffic to skim a crystal-bright glance over her.

A slur perhaps against her choice of attire? Leigh mused, resentment stirring at the man's audacity.

"One might say the same of you," she drawled back, returning his skimming perusal. And it was almost true. Like Leigh, he was dressed in a gray business suit — silk, of course — its expert tailoring molding the material to his broad shoulders. But to her dismay, unlike her, he didn't disappear into the seat. His tall, burnished gold form *owned* the seat, figuratively as well as literally.

Life simply is not fair, Leigh acknowledged, directing her frustrated gaze to the windshield.

"One might," he agreed, amusement the strongest thread woven through his response.

In other words, one might also be fooling one's self, Leigh fumed, positive she'd correctly read his unspoken jibe. The man certainly didn't lack a sense of the visual effect of his innate power and attractiveness.

Without due consideration or so much as a thought, Leigh retaliated. "One might also wonder what in the hell one is doing here — getting lost in the upholstery."

He laughed.

Leigh sighed, wishing his laughter wasn't quite so appealing.

"One is going to dinner," he said, flashing an utterly demoralizing grin at her. "In case one has forgotten."

Up until then, Leigh had paid scant attention to either their location or direction. "Where are we going?" she asked, just as he zipped the powerful car into the stream of traffic heading west on the expressway.

"Valley Forge," he answered, and without sparing a glance for her, smoothly steered the car around a slow-moving van with an out-of-state license plate. "Actually, a little beyond that. Would you like some music?"

"Music?" The sudden switch threw her for an instant, but only for an instant. "No. But I would like to know *precisely* where we are going."

He chuckled, but again didn't spare a glance for her from the predictable madness of the early evening Friday traffic. "I'm not abducting you if that's what you're afraid of," he said, his white teeth a brief gleam in the dimming light. "Although, I admit, the idea has merit."

His voice, deep and bemused, sparked a flashing image in her imagination. A brief vision of being swept away like the quivering heroine of a historical novel, to be ravished by an arrogant, handsome golden knight who acknowledged no rule of conduct but his own.

The image was gone almost as quickly as it had appeared, leaving her with a feeling of defenselessness against the strength of his magnetism.

Defenseless?

Like hell.

Leigh's hackles rose — along with every

insecurity she had believed she'd success-
fully subdued, buried. Tiny goose bumps
rose on the surface of her skin in reaction to
an inner chill.

"Abducting me would be pointless," she
countered, slanting a cool look of amusement at him. "Since my family has no
money to speak of for ransom, you would
see no profit from the ill-conceived venture."

"Ahhh . . . But what if the point of the
venture was not financial profit?" Michael
spared her a sparkling, devilish glance.
"What if the purpose were adventure — in
the form of an illicit weekend with a desir-
able woman?"

So he offered proof that she had not imagined the simmering tension emanating from
him on their very first meeting. That the
tension had been — and still was — simmering inside her was not only intolerable
but unthinkable.

Leigh took refuge in anger.

Damn him — damn all men and their
penchant to cast every dealing, however
mundane, with members of the opposite sex
in the light of sensuality.

No, Leigh immediately corrected herself,
her eyes narrowing on his strong profile. In
this case, sensuality was much too euphe-

mistic a term for what St. Claire had made clear was blatant, basic sexual intent.

"Adventure?" She arched her brows. "I don't think so," she added in a bored drawl. "Besides, I'm already booked for the weekend."

"With a man?" His voice, while soft and smooth, held the distinct cutting edge of demand.

"Of course," she lightly responded, in retaliation to his imperial tone, unexpectedly grateful for the telephone call from her father summoning her home for the weekend.

"Anyone I might know?" Again that edge flicked softly out at her.

And once again she played it light. "I doubt it," she said. "He doesn't move in your circles — nor do I, come to that," she was quick to point out.

"Circles . . . Brings to mind a dog chasing its tails," he murmured, slicing a glittering look at her. "I don't move in circles, Leigh," he instructed, falling silent as he steered the car onto the sharply curved 26B exit off the expressway and then onto Route 202. "I blaze my own path."

Leaving a wide swath in your wake, no doubt, Leigh mused, recalling rumors and gossip about him, his business acumen, his reputed *affaires d'amour.*

"I'm delighted for you," she said, her voice crisp in denial of a sudden unsettled sensation in her stomach. "I'm also hungry," she went on, blaming the odd feeling on a need for food. "Is it much farther?"

"No." Even as he spoke, he shot off 202 onto another highway, and moments later onto a narrower, black-topped side road. "Almost there."

Almost where? Leigh wondered, glancing out the window, completely clueless as to their whereabouts. Mere minutes had elapsed since he had left the expressway, so it stood to reason that they were still somewhere within the environs of King of Prussia, she reasoned.

Leigh was surprised a few moments later, when Michael steered the car off the road and onto a parking lot adjacent to a well-lighted, medium-sized old country inn. She was surprised because, although it appeared well kept, there wasn't a thing prepossessing about the place.

"Not what you were expecting?" Michael asked, swinging open his door, stepping out, and starting around to her side.

Following his example, she slipped out and met him at the front of the car.

Leigh ignored his arch expression and

turned to examine the building. In truth, the inn was the exact opposite of the upscale, lavishly appointed and expensive restaurant she had been expecting.

"Actually no, this is not what I was expecting," she admitted, moving her shoulders in a faint shrug. "I was imagining a more, well, elaborate setting, a lot of glamour and glitz, if you will."

"You wanted glitz?" he asked, taking her arm to lead her to the entrance to the inn.

"No." Leigh gave a quick shake of her head. "But I had thought you might prefer —"

"Ubiquitous waiters fawning over me?" he interrupted, finishing for her.

A wry smile tugged at her lips. "Something like that," she said, slanting a sidelong look at him.

Anticipating a scowl from him, Leigh was startled to find him grinning at her.

"I detest all that unnecessary fuss," he said, opening the entrance door and ushering her inside. "I much prefer a quiet, relaxing atmosphere." He flicked a hand to indicate the inn's interior, which mirrored his description.

Pleased with what she saw — soft lights set on white-clothed tables, a casual ambience — Leigh offered him a smile, and an agreement. "So do I."

"Aaahh," he murmured, his tone a soft caress. "We already have something in common."

Leigh felt a thrill — and was quick to squash the sensation. She opened her mouth to voice a crushing reply, to the effect that a preference in dining facilities hardly constituted a common bond, but the words died on her lips as, since he had turned away from her to approach the host, she would only have been speaking to herself.

With quiet dignity, the host escorted them to a table by the window, dark now, reflecting their own images.

"Kendall will be your server," he informed them, handing over menus. "Enjoy your dinner."

"What do you think?" Michael probed, his eyes gleaming from the reflected light.

Leigh gave him a wry look. "He's not ubiquitous at all," she said with cool nonchalance.

He laughed.

I wish he wouldn't do that, Leigh thought, forced to squash another tiny thrill.

"Good evening." The young man who came to a stop at the table looked like the all-American college boy, clean-cut, attractive. "My name's Kendall, and I'll be your server. Can I get you a drink?"

Michael looked at her questioningly.

She nodded, then turned her attention, and a smile, to the waiter. "Hello, Kendall. And, yes, I'll have a glass of chardonnay, chilled, please."

"Very good." Kendall smiled back at her before attending to Michael. "And you, sir?"

"A martini, dry, two olives. Bombay gin."

Leigh waited until Kendall walked away before observing, "I heard martinis are making a comeback."

"For me, they never went away," Michael said, grinning with devastating effect.

Repressing yet another thrill, Leigh put on a smug expression. "So it would appear there is something we don't have in common."

"A minor thing, and only half-right, at that," he retorted, his eyes mocking her smugness. "For, you see, on occasion I also enjoy a glass of chilled chardonnay."

Smartass. Leigh didn't give life to the thought, of course. It wouldn't be polite in a public place, but she did convey her opinion with a sardonic look.

His soft chuckle told her he got the intended message, and was amused by it.

Leigh stifled a sigh. It simply was not fair

that the sound of a man's chuckle could wreak such havoc with a woman's nervous system. In self-defense, she snatched up the menu, using it as a shield to block his handsome face from view.

The devil had the gall to compound his chuckle with a rumbling laugh of delight.

Leigh figured this did not bode well for a comfortable evening. But only time would tell.

"I see young Kendall bearing down on us with our drinks," Michael said, lingering strands of laughter woven through his words. "Were you planning on coming out of hiding any time soon?"

"Hiding?" Leigh lowered the menu to present a coolly composed expression to him. "From you?" Deciding it had to be her turn to laugh, she did so, and was rather pleased by the droll tone of it. "You should live so long." She despaired at resorting to the old, overused retort, but it was the only thing she could come up with on the spot.

He didn't respond, for the waiter came to a halt at the table to serve their drinks. "Are you ready to order now, or would you like a little more time?"

"Leigh?"

She turned her head, glancing up with a smile for the waiter. "I'm ready. I'll have the lemon chicken breast with the roasted new potatoes and a Caesar salad."

"Excellent choice," their server said, returning her smile before shifting his attention to Michael. "Sir?"

"Since you feel it's an excellent choice," St. Claire drawled, "I'll have the same."

Silence.

Leigh sipped her wine, eyeing him warily over the rim of her glass.

He sipped his martini, returning her regard with bright-eyed amusement. Then he raised his glass to her in salutation. "It seems we have something else in common."

"Lemon chicken and Caesar salad?" she asked derisively. "I think that's reaching . . . just a bit."

"Not at all." He was unperturbed by her mocking tones. "In the spectrum of things in common, likes and dislikes, lemon chicken and Caesar salad, or any other foods, count as much as . . . say, tastes in music, entertainment — movies, theater, sports events" — he lowered his gaze to her torso — "even colors, like the navy I favor — and you admired — the gray you were wearing on Tuesday and we both favor today."

Caught wanting for an immediate response, Leigh stared at him in consternation for a moment. But she couldn't let it rest there, couldn't allow him to believe he had convinced her with such ridiculous presumptions.

"Come to think of it," he went on, while she was gathering her defenses, "I'd submit that even our professions complement each other, in so far as I'm in the business of constructing buildings and you decorate them."

Now that was just a bit too much. Leigh nearly choked on a sip of wine. "I'd submit that you're really stretching it," she retorted when she got her breath back. "One type of wine, two foods and two colors hardly constitute a spectrum of things in common."

He gave a slight nod of his head. "Granted," he surprised her by admitting. "But then, getting to know each other, about each other, our likes and dislikes, was the purpose of this dinner engagement, wasn't it?"

Well, he had her there, Leigh conceded, murmuring a grudging, "I suppose so."

"Suppose?" Michael challenged, the smile twitching at his lips telling her he knew he had won that round.

The arrival of their waiter, bearing a tray held aloft, the weight supported by his fingertips, spared Leigh the ignominy of backing down.

The food was served without fuss or flourish. The waiter withdrew with a murmured, "Enjoy your dinner."

The salad was premixed, saving them from the ceremony of having the host perform the ritual at the table. Everything looked and smelled delicious.

Leigh glanced at Michael, who was watching her with keen expectation, then down at her plate. The tantalizing scent of lemon teased her taste buds. Surrendering to hunger, she consigned Michael to the devil, and proceeded to follow the waiter's advice.

To his credit, St. Claire had the sense to remain silent while following her example.

The meal progressed in surprising harmony — at least the absence of tension surprised Leigh. Perhaps the expertly prepared chicken, the clear, delicate lemon sauce, the lightly herb-flavored potatoes and crisp salad were conducive to a mellow mood, she mused, savoring a morsel of the oven-browned potato. Even more surprising, and unusual for her, she ate every bite of her meal.

"That was wonderful." Sighing in repletion, she set the fork on her plate. "Thank you." The smile she offered him was genuine and easy.

"Yes, it was, and you're welcome." Michael returned her smile in kind. "But it's the chef we should thank."

"I'll relay your compliments to him," Kendall said, appearing as if out of thin air. "Now, dessert and coffee . . ."

"Oh, no dessert for me," Leigh interjected.

Michael gave a negative shake of his head.

"A liqueur then, or cappuccino?" he persisted, glancing from Leigh to Michael.

They answered in unison.

"Cappuccino."

Kendall raised his eyebrows a notch. "With the works? Flavoring and —"

"What flavoring?" Leigh interrupted him with undisguised interest.

"Kahlua, raspberry, chocolate, cin—"

"Chocolate." They again spoke simultaneously.

"Whipped cream, sprinkles — the works?"

"Oh, yes." Leigh heaved a dramatic sigh.

Nodding agreement, Michael commented, "It sounds even better than dessert."

"Very good." Kendall flashed a grin. "And, trust me, the cappuccino here is *very* good."

They laughed in unison.

Laughing with them, the waiter departed for the kitchen.

"Yet another thing we have in common?"

Michael's soft question brought an abrupt halt to Leigh's laughter. "So it seems," she agreed, unwilling to relinquish the unexpected easing of tension between them.

Yet even so, there remained this awareness, of her as a woman, of him as pure male. The sensuality had diminished from a sizzle to a low hum, but it was there, constant. Leigh could no more deny it than she could ignore it.

That didn't mean she had to like it; she didn't. The awareness made her feel too vulnerable. Still, it wasn't a complete negative, for it put her on her mettle, alerted her senses, sharpened her wit.

She stayed quiet, allowing him to savor his tiny victory, until after Kendall served the whipped-cream-mounded drinks. Then she fired a soft inquiry.

"Now what?"

"Now what . . . what?" Michael shot back, his voice even softer than hers.

"Do we play twenty questions, in between sips of this decadent concoction?"

Arching one burnished brow, he dipped his long-handled spoon into the whipped cream, then raised it to his parted lips. A shiver skipped over the surface of Leigh's skin, penetrating to the bone, as his lips curled into the bowl of the spoon to scoop the sweet into his mouth.

"Such as?"

She shrugged. "Oh, you know. The usual inanities of interest. I think it begins with: what's your sign? Then goes on to deeper, heavier stuff, such as: favorite colors, preferred foods . . . more veggies or lots of meat. Perhaps a confession of a secret passion for fast food — cheese steaks, soft pretzels and the like."

He shook his head, laughing.

She sallied on. "Of course, from there it naturally leads to entertainment preferences: movies — comedy, horror, action adventure, six-guns and saddle sores? The theater — plays or musicals? Vacation spots — blazing beaches or frozen mountains? Do you like to dance, slow or fast? Music — ballads, rock and roll, heavy metal, show tunes. We won't even mention rap." She paused for breath.

Laughing harder, Michael gasped for breath.

Since she appeared to be amusing him, she went with the flow. "Then, after the preliminaries, it proceeds to serious, more personal stuff." She gave him a suggestive look.

"Please, don't stop now," he choked out between chuckles.

"Underwear — boxers or briefs? Sheets — cotton percale or satin? Pajamas to sleep in or nothing but —"

"My skin," he inserted, his laughter replaced by the sexiest drawl she had ever heard.

"I'd have bet my showroom on it," she drawled back, determined that he not hear the tingling effect of his sensuous tone in her voice.

A slow smile worked its way across his mouth.

Leigh's throat went desert dry. Lifting her cup, she sought relief with a gulp of cappuccino. Though still quite hot, the chocolate-flavored coffee soothed parched edges — at least until he spoke.

"You have a whipped-cream lip liner," he murmured, his gaze fixed to the spot. "I'd love to lick it off."

Dead stop. For everything. Heart. Breath. Thought. At least, that's how it felt for an instant. Of course, her heart didn't stop. She continued to breathe, if rather shallowly. Thoughts whirled through her head like dervishes, careening off the walls of her skull. But she did retain the presence of mind to dab her napkin over her lips.

"Do you want to play?"

Leigh's thoughts came to a screeching

halt. Play? Play what? As if she didn't know.

"What?" she asked, as if she hadn't heard — or understood — his question.

"Do you want to play the twenty questions game?" Michael articulated.

Leigh caught herself in time to prevent a betraying sigh. "No, thank you. I've been subjected to it a time or two, and found the answers uninteresting."

"I agree. Too cut and dried." His nod was sage, his expression somber.

She didn't trust either for a moment.

"Much better to learn as we go." His smile so challenging it cancelled sage somberness.

"Go." Leigh latched onto the word. "I'm ready to go now . . . home that is," she said, finishing off the last of her drink. "Are you?"

With open reluctance, Michael drained his cup before answering. "Yes."

Seven

He escorted her from the restaurant with a guiding hand at the small of her back. Unnerved by the warm sensations radiating from the spot, Leigh strode through the dining room and across the lot at a near trot.

"I think I'd like some music now," she told him, while she was still fastening her seat belt. "Something smooth, easy listening, if you have it."

"Sure." Lifting the lid of the compartment between the seats, he rifled through a stack of CDs. "Sinatra, Diamond, Billy Joel, Nat King Cole, Bing . . ."

Bing? She only listened to Bing Crosby's recordings at Christmas time. Yet the very fact that Michael kept some along with the others gave Leigh a bit of insight into his music preferences.

"Cole," she said, feeling a need for the soothing effects of the late singer's mellow voice . . . and an even stronger desire to avoid conversation as much as possible with this disturbing man seated too close to her.

To underline her desire, when the strains of "Dance, Ballerina, Dance" swirled through the interior of the car, Leigh rested back against the head support and closed her eyes.

Fortunately, Michael took the hint. He concentrated on driving, while she concentrated on the music. Barely a dozen words passed between them from the restaurant to her apartment. She was half-asleep by the time they arrived. The cessation of movement jolted her out of a light doze.

Fully expecting Michael to double-park until she had exited the car and entered her building, Leigh reached for the seat belt, preparing to offer him a polite thank you and a swift good night. But the car was moving again before her finger touched the release, not forward, but back . . . *into a parking space?*

Leigh was jolted again. No, it wasn't possible. She could never find a parking space on the street. No one she knew could.

Michael St. Claire had done so — as if he had phoned ahead and reserved it.

Did the man lead a charmed life? Leigh railed to herself. More to the point, did the man actually think — hope — she might invite him in?

Fat chance.

"You needn't have parked," she said, depressing the seat-belt release before the car came to a complete stop. "It's only a few steps to my building — I'll be perfectly safe."

He applied the hand brake before slanting a dry glance at her. "I'll see you to your door, anyway."

Leigh might have argued the point, but Michael was already exiting the car. Sighing, she pushed open her door and thrust one foot onto the sidewalk, just as he finished circling the car to her side. She stepped out and straightened as he bent to offer his assistance.

It was a near-miss collision. The top of Leigh's head brushed against Michael's jaw.

She felt clumsy, and she was never clumsy. *Damn.* She stammered an apology. "I . . . I'm sorry . . . I should have looked."

"I'm not," he interrupted her, so close to her she felt the flutter of his warm breath, caught a whiff of the combined scents of the cappuccino and the martini he'd drunk. "You . . . your hair smells good."

"Th-thank you." *Damn, I never stammer either.*

Flustered, she extracted the keys from her bag, then swung away from him to stride across the sidewalk and up the steps to the door of her building. Michael was right behind her. She nearly collided with him again when she turned.

"Thank you," she repeated, this time without the stammer. "It was a lovely dinner. I —"

He again interrupted her. "I'll see you to your apartment door. Second floor, isn't it?"

"Yes, but. . . ." She caught herself before asking him how he knew. Men like Michael St. Claire had ways of garnering any information they desired.

"I insist," he said, obviously misinterpreting her hesitation.

"I'm not going to invite you in, Michael," she said, deciding the time had come to make her position clear.

"I know." He smiled. The implacable look of him convinced her that he would not budge.

He was standing so close, he was making her nervous . . . Everything about him made her nervous. Giving up, she opened the outer door, bolted across the small foyer, and rushed up the stairs to her own door.

Michael followed at a more leisurely pace. Leigh was turning the key in the lock when he halted beside her. She turned to give him a bright smile and a hasty good night. Her smile faded and the words got stuck in her throat as he curled a hand around her neck and slowly drew her to him.

Leigh stifled a gasp in response to the tingling sensations aroused by the warmth of his palm against the sensitive skin of her nape.

His lips feathered over hers.

"Mi-Mi—" She was stammering again, but it didn't matter, as his mouth captured her parted lips, silencing her feeble attempt at protest.

His lips were cool, his breath warm, his kiss hot. The heat of it zinged from her mouth to the most sensitive and vulnerable feminine part of her.

Shocked by the allure of his probing kiss, Leigh went stiff in rejection.

His tongue invaded, searing the interior of her mouth, scorching her senses, laying waste her resistance. She began to tremble, felt her body soften and, in desperation, fought a clamoring urge to surrender her taut lips, herself, to the enticing fire of his mouth.

It was a battle she would have lost, Leigh acknowledged, if Michael had not ended the kiss at that moment.

Slipping his hand from her neck, he stepped back, singed her with a smoldering look, then smiled.

"I know you said you have a date for tomorrow," he said, "but are you by any chance free for breakfast, lunch or dinner on Sunday?"

Leigh gave a quick shake of her head. "Sorry, but I'm going out of town for the weekend. I expect I won't get back until late Sunday evening."

His smile disappeared. "I see."

Leigh was positive that he believed this a weekend lovers' tryst, and she wasn't about to correct his misconception. She met his now contemplative stare with what she hoped was cool detachment.

"Someone special?"

There was a new, rough-edged quality to his voice that sounded an alarm inside Leigh, alerting her natural instinct for self-preservation.

"You might say that," she answered, thinking not of her father or brother, but of her young nephew.

"Hmmm."

A nonreply if she ever heard one, and yet Leigh sensed his silent censure. Sensed it and resented it. "Is that sound you made supposed to have a meaning?" she asked, inserting a contrived note of amusement into her voice.

He shook his golden head. Suddenly his expression changed, grew austere, all business. "We need to get together." His voice was brisk, no-nonsense.

"We do?" Leigh pulled his trick of lifting one eyebrow, and was rewarded with a slight frown.

"Of course, we do." Impatience scored his voice. "You do want to go over the terms of the contract before signing it, don't you?"

The contract. She had completely forgotten the supposed purpose of their dinner together — getting to know each other, thus enabling her to better reflect his personality in the decor of his office.

How could she have forgotten? The commission to redecorate his office could benefit her career immeasurably. Surely the strength, the effects of one kiss could not —

"Don't you?"

St. Claire's persistence corralled Leigh's fragmenting thoughts, centered them on the question. "Certainly," she answered, frowning at him. "I was, er, mentally reviewing my schedule," she improvised, actually clueless as to her commitments.

"And?" Michael frowned back at her.

"And I believe I'm free from twelve until three on Wednesday," she said, deciding that if she wasn't, Sheila would simply have to rearrange her appointments.

"Good." Both his voice and expression

held a suspicious hint of satisfaction. "Come to the office at twelve. I'll have lunch brought in. We can discuss the terms of the contract while we eat."

Nuts. Leigh was hard put to conceal her self-disgust. When had her mind gone on strike? she berated herself. Not only had she set her own trap, she had blithely walked into it.

"Well?" This time, Michael's prompting had the sound of a contented purr.

Like a big, beautiful, golden tomcat, Leigh reflected, repressing a shocking desire to stroke his fabulous pelt — from the top of his head down to . . .

Was she losing it or what?

"Leigh?"

She bit back a groan at being caught again with her mind in turmoil. Drat the man. Looking, sounding like an intelligent human being while in St. Claire's vicinity was becoming a challenge, one she was no longer sure she wanted to accept. Now she was afraid she really was losing it.

"That'll be fine," she said in a rush, before she gave in to the urge to withdraw from their agreement. But she did allow herself to physically withdraw. Groping behind her, she grasped the knob, turned it, and pushed open the door. "Until

Wednesday, then." She stepped back, over the threshold. "Good night, Mr. . . ."

His eyebrows shot up.

She got the message. "Michael."

He gazed at her a moment, a long moment, directly at her mouth. When she couldn't control a tiny responsive quiver of her lips, he raised his eyes to hers, humor dancing in those crystal blue depths.

"Good night, Leigh," he murmured, and then he was gone, his tread fast and light on the stairs.

"Her highness called — twice."

Shrugging out of his suit jacket, Michael tossed it over the back of a white plush chair as he crossed the living room of his apartment. He came to a stop in the wide archway that led into the kitchen, loosening his tie and opening the collar button of his shirt, while eyeing the brawny man standing at the table in the center of the large room.

A grin tempted Michael's lips at seeing his disgruntled look and the incongruity of the sight he presented.

Shamus Clancy, Michael's houseman, for want of a better description, stood nearly six feet tall and was barrel chested, with muscular shoulders, arms and legs. His face was craggy, framed by an unruly mop of flame red hair. His personality was every bit as fiery.

But what struck Michael as humorous was the picture the man presented. Shamus had donned a white butcher's apron over faded jeans and green T-shirt, which would have looked perfectly normal if the man had been wielding a meat cleaver, but he wasn't. Shamus was wielding a pastry tube, in the process of creating cream puff pastries in the shapes of swans.

Shamus did love to create in the kitchen.

"She wants you to call her back," Shamus continued, his upper lip curling. "No matter how late it is."

Michael surrendered to temptation. The bright overhead light glinted off the teeth he revealed in a wide grin. "You know, Shamus, a casual observer might conclude that you didn't like my friend Barbara," he gently chided. "But you and I know better, don't we?"

Glaring at his employer, Shamus tossed the pastry tube onto the table, then slammed balled fists against his waist. "Now what the hell's that supposed to mean?" he demanded, jaw thrust aggressively forward.

Slipping the wildly expensive, conservatively patterned silk tie from beneath his shirt collar, Michael sauntered into the room before responding. "You know precisely what I mean," he said, amusement shimmering in his voice. "You're crazy about Barbara, and you know it. In fact, I suspect that you're making those delightful little swans not for me, but because she is coming for dinner tomorrow evening and adores those delectable cream puffs."

"Hah!" the beefy man exploded. "You're dreamin', man, if you think I give a damn about that nose-in-the-air broad — or care whether or not she likes my desserts. Why I . . . I . . ."

"You have the hots for her," Michael inserted into the older man's bluster. "And you know it."

"The hots for *her*." Shamus put on an expression of sheer horror. "I'll have you know I — I wouldn't give a . . . a damn if I never laid eyes on the aggravating woman again."

"Harrumph, harrumph," Michael taunted. "You know that's bull. Why bother denying it, my friend?"

Shamus bristled, his nostrils flaring like an enraged bull's. "That does it," he shouted, tearing off the flour-spattered apron. "I quit."

Michael let loose a burst of laughter. "Is

that for the fiftieth or sixtieth time now?"

Shamus held on to his indignation for a few seconds. Then, his face flushed to a shade matching his hair, and a sheepish grin spread over his lips. "Maybe the seventieth," he said, balling up the apron and lobbing it at Michael, who stepped back, chuckling as the material drifted to the floor.

"Now you went and messed up my clean floor," Shamus grumbled, bending to scoop up the apron.

"You know, my friend, I sometimes fear you're a plate shy of a full place setting," Michael retorted, leaning back against the countertop and crossing his arms over his chest. "And if you think I'm going to let you get away with changing the subject — one Barbara Saunders — live in hope."

Shamus made a sour face. "I don't want to discuss her. I don't even want to think about her."

"Sure you do," Michael persisted. "More than that, you want to be with her. So why don't you admit it?"

The Irishman took on a belligerent expression. "You hankerin' for a new houseman, or just lookin' for a whack upside your head?"

Michael merely smiled.

Shamus sighed, then shrugged. "So,

okay, the day's past when I could beat you in a rough-up. But, dammit, Mike, you're pushin' your luck here."

"Why?" Michael probed, frowning. Clancy only called him Mike when he was upset.

Shamus's gaze skipped around the spotless room, looking everywhere and anywhere but at his employer. "You know why. I'm not good enough for her."

"Not good enough?" Michael's eyes caught fire. "That's bullshit, Shamus," he snapped, incensed. "There's no woman alive you're not good enough for."

"Barbara is . . . is . . ." His gaze shifted to settle on blazing crystal blue. A sorrowful half-smile tilted his lips. "She's special, and I'm a pug, a street fighter."

"Not anymore," Michael said. "And not for a long time now. You redeemed yourself nearly twenty years ago."

"No, Michael, you redeemed me." His smile softened. "If it hadn't been for you, I —"

Michael cut him off, shaking his head. "Crap, Shamus. I can't take credit for saving you. If you hadn't wanted to save yourself, nothing I could have said or done —"

"You're wrong," Shamus put in, his voice

firm. "You showed me the way, and that's the end of it."

"Shamus —"

"I said that's the end of it, Michael," the older man growled. Pulling open a cabinet drawer, he whipped out a clean apron and put it on. "Now get the hell out of my kitchen," he ordered, moving to his former position at the flour-strewn table. "I've got to finish preparing dessert for her highness, and you've got to return her call."

Recognizing his adamant tone, Michael let the subject drop with a murmured, "You're a prize, Shamus, and at times a damned fool." With the Irishman's snort following him, and chuckling to himself, he mounted the stairs to the second level of the apartment, to use the phone in his home office.

Barbara picked up the receiver on the first ring.

"Hello, darling. You called?"

"Well, of course I did," she retorted. "You knew very well I'd call."

He laughed.

She made a rude noise. "Well?"

"Well . . . what?"

"Michael." Impatience colored her voice.

Suppressing more laughter, he teased, "What, exactly, do you want to know?"

"Oh . . . just everything," she returned, acid-toned. "You're back pretty early."

"If you didn't expect me to be here, why did you call so early?" It was evident he was amused. "Were you longing to hear Clancy's Irish brogue?"

"Get on with it, you devil," she commanded, triggering another burst of laughter from him. "And stop that damn fool cackling."

It wasn't easy, but Michael made a supreme effort.

"We — Leigh and I — had a delicious dinner," he said, when he could speak without choking.

"You really are pissing me off," she exploded. "Where did you have dinner, King of Prussia?"

"Yes." He choked again. "I'm serious. I wasn't taunting you," he assured her, grinning as he envisioned her fuming. "We ate, conversed, and then I delivered her to her apartment door."

"Did she invite you in?"

"If she had, would I be speaking to you now?"

"Struck out again," she crowed in her cigarette-raspy voice. "Chalk another one up for the wily decorator."

Not entirely, Michael thought, still suffering the discomforting aftereffects of their kiss. But he wasn't about to relay the information to her — he didn't kiss and tell, not even to Barbara.

"It's early innings yet," he said, gliding his tongue over his lower lip for any lingering taste of Leigh's mouth. The action caused a reaction, and he was hard again. Time to change the subject, divert his thoughts.

"And how was your evening?"

"Surprisingly pleasant," she answered, a smile evident in her tone. "I had a date, you know."

"Anyone I know?"

She chuckled at his probing, delighted at having the interrogation turned on her. "Not yet," she said. "But I expect you'll meet him soon."

"And who is he?" Michael asked, frowning at the thought of how Barbara's possible involvement with another man might affect Shamus.

"His name is Jake Jenson." She chuckled again. "Do you remember that I broke an engagement Tuesday to have dinner with you?"

"Jake Jenson?"

"The very same."

"Okay, but who *is* he?"

"A very nice man, as it turned out." She paused, and Michael heard her drag on a cigarette. "He's a retired army major, now in the import/export business — importing from contacts he made with merchants while serving in Europe, Asia and the far East."

"He's from Philadelphia?" Michael asked, raking his memory for any reference he may have had to the man, frowning when he came up blank.

"Originally, yes," she answered. "But he's lived all over the world, most recently New York. He relocated to Philadelphia a year or so ago."

To Michael's way of thinking, Barbara appeared to know a lot about the man after only two brief meetings . . . if there had been only two. This speculation kicked his protective instincts into high gear.

"I want to meet him." Though he was unaware of the sudden hardness of his voice, Barbara's soft chuckle brought the fact home to him. He shrugged.

"What a coincidence," she said in a raspy drawl. "Jake wants to meet you, too."

"He knows about me?" This time, he couldn't miss the hardness or the suspicion in his voice.

Barbara's steel-wool-on-metal-sounding

laughter assaulted his eardrums. "My darling, everybody in business in Philadelphia knows about you."

Michael dismissed her claim with a dry, "Yeah, yeah," then asked, "When can I meet him?"

"Soon."

"Babsy." A definite warning note.

"When we attend the open house."

Michael pulled the phone away from his ear for a moment, staring at it in confusion. "Open house? I haven't a clue as to what you're talking about. What open house?"

Her renewed laughter brought on a coughing fit, and she choked out, "I'll explain . . . tomorrow evening . . ." She drew in a deep breath. "We'll discuss it over dinner."

"Damned right we will."

Eight

Saturday morning was overcast, billowing dark clouds in the west threatening a storm.

Leigh didn't mind. She felt rather overcast and stormy, too. She hadn't slept well, hadn't rested. How could she with her mind whirling, her feelings all churned up and her body tormenting her?

Once again retrieving the music box from the far corner of the closet shelf, Leigh had wound the mechanism and lifted the lid countless times, willing the tinny-sound notes to disperse the wild sensations cluttering her mind, undermining her intellect, playing havoc with her senses.

When she could bear the sound no longer, she didn't return the box to its shelf. Instead, she set it close to hand on her night stand.

And all because Michael had kissed her.
Dumb.
Maybe.
But . . .
It was the *but* that bothered Leigh.

She had awakened early, before sunup, shivering in reaction to a vague, but extremely erotic dream in which a golden blond angel had taken licentious liberties with her body.

Her throat was dry, her feminine core wet.

Near desperation, Leigh had attempted to banish the lingering, arousing wisps of the dream and to ignore her chaotic feelings by keeping busy — as if she could outrun her thoughts and feelings.

She brewed tea and toasted a slice of bread for breakfast, then carried them into her bedroom. She drank the tea and nibbled at the toast while putting on jeans, a cotton knit sweater, and low-cut boots.

After rinsing her cup and plate and stashing them in the dishwasher, she returned to the bedroom, throwing herself into packing her overnight case and choosing an outfit for the anniversary dinner before shrugging into a canvas field jacket. Leaving her apartment, she got her car from the garage, then headed out of the city.

The mad flurry of activity worked, up to a point. But once she was free of the heavier traffic, tooling along Route 30, the suppressed aftershocks of that kiss and the subsequent erotic dream resurfaced to haunt her.

The annoying, and frankly puzzling, thing was the kiss had been very brief, lasting mere seconds.

Still, however short in duration, Michael's searing kiss had ignited the most astounding sensations within Leigh, unlike any she had ever before experienced, culminating in the blatantly sexual dream, the likes of which she had likewise never before experienced.

It was all more than unnerving.

Suffering a reflexive shiver, Leigh unconsciously tightened her fingers around the leather-sheathed steering wheel.

She ached something fierce, felt needy and wanting. And she knew full well exactly what her body was clamoring for. The inner demand was unmistakable.

Sex.

No, not merely sex, she told herself with ruthless honesty.

The inner demand was for absolute possession, the licentious use of her body by the earthbound prototype of the nighttime visitation, the glorious and golden angel — the waking, fully conscious and consenting reenactment of the dream.

There was only one explanation Leigh could credit for her inner disruption.

She had to be losing her mind.

"Damn."

The sound of her voice rang loud in the confines of the car, startling Leigh into awareness. She grimaced at the realization of a different ache and, sighing, pried loose her death grip on the wheel.

Sex.

The tiny word with huge connotations stabbed at her mind, tearing holes in the fabric of disinterest she had so carefully manufactured after her one and only fiasco with sexual experimentation while still in college.

Resentment flared to vibrant life, and in silent frustration she railed against Michael, herself, the natural physical responses of her body to sensual stimulation.

Despite the naturalness, the normality of her body's sexual reaction to stimuli, Leigh resented it like hell. She had worked too long and too hard at distancing herself, suppressing those physical demands and needs, to meekly accept the sudden quickening of inner hunger — hunger, moreover, for the touch, caress, the physical possession of the golden angel in the living image of Michael St. Claire, a man with a reputation for sensual indulgence.

It was intolerable.

It was spring.

Leigh frowned. Spring?

Spring, the season ostensibly of romance, the mating season, when the blood ran hot. Perhaps the inner disturbances that seemingly afflicted animals, humans included, were caused or connected in some way with the volatile, capricious conditions of the weather, warm one day, cold another, with rain and even snowstorms in between.

Leigh grabbed onto the excuse like a lifeline, skirting around the fact that she had survived many springs with her emotions and sexuality unscathed.

Just then, lightning streaked across the sky up ahead, followed seconds later by the deep, angry-sounding rumble of thunder, as if confirming Leigh's desperate attempt at rationalization and self-exoneration.

That's it, she told herself. The vagaries of this particular spring were affecting her balance, playing tricks on her equilibrium.

Heaving a sigh of relief, Leigh switched on the windshield wipers as the dark clouds above dumped a deluge of wind-driven rain mixed with snow onto the earth — and her car.

If nothing else, the raging storm diverted her from introspection, making her concentrate on driving on the barely visible highway. She did derive one benefit from the storm. The muscle tension caused by the deteriorating driving conditions forced the raw hunger attacking her body to retract its claws.

Leigh was thankful for small mercies.

Slowly, the roiling thunderheads continued on an eastern trek. The deluge turned to all rain before subsiding to a gentle drizzle by the time Leigh arrived at her destination.

Her tension eased a bit as Leigh steered the car into the driveway of the split-level house.

Sighing her relief, she stepped from the car and paused a moment in the now-misty rain to run a critical gaze over the brick-faced structure.

In truth, there appeared little to criticize. Her father kept the house in excellent repair.

Had she been hoping there would be reason to criticize? Leigh wondered, reaching into the back seat for her case and garment bag. Had she, however unconsciously, been anticipating some reason to find fault with her father?

Leigh winced at the mean-spirited bent of her jaundiced self-questioning.

And yet, there they were, in all their judgmental bias, as they had been since her twelfth year.

A different kind of sigh whispered from her throat, a sigh composed of despair, disappointment and — were she honest enough with herself to admit it — sheer longing for what had been and would never be again.

Until she was twelve, Leigh had adored her father.

Shaking off the conflicting emotions she always experienced whenever she visited her former home, on occasions which had grown increasingly rare over the years, Leigh shut the car door with a sideways swing of her hips, then hurried along the flagstone path and up the four steps leading to the house.

"Leigh. There you are." A hesitantly optimistic smile lighting his tired-looking yet still attractive face, Andrew pushed open the front door as Leigh stepped onto the roofed porch. "I was concerned about you driving through that storm." He reached for her case. "Was it bad?"

As she preceded him into the house, Leigh said, "It got a little hairy there for a while, but fortunately it didn't last very long."

She halted on the patch of tiled area just inside the door, her gaze darting around the familiar living room, immediately noting the changes made since her last visit.

"You've repainted the walls and had new carpeting laid. And isn't that a new chair?" she asked, merely making small talk since she knew it was.

"Yes." Andrew's smile dimmed at the contrived disinterest in her voice. "It's very comfortable. You'll have to try it out," he invited, plucking the garment bag from her fingers, then moving around her taut form. "I'll put these in your room for you."

"Thanks, but it's not necessary for you to do that." She extended a hand to reclaim the case and bag. "I have to unpack anyway." Leigh cringed inwardly at the stilted sound of her own voice. "I'll do it."

Andrew shook his head. "You can unpack later. I, er, there's a fresh pot of coffee, and I have lunch all ready — soup and salad okay?"

Leigh got a pang in her chest at noting the hopefulness, the wistfulness in the question. He always tried so hard to please her, had done so ever since she had closed herself off from him. His efforts were too little, and much, much too late.

Nevertheless, Leigh relented. "Yes, soup and salad will be fine," she said, starting for the kitchen, even though she didn't feel at all hungry.

"Good." He smiled with abject relief. "I'll

be with you in a minute." He took off in the opposite direction and climbed the five steps up to the bedroom level.

The soup was split pea with ham, home-made and delicious, unsurprising to Leigh, since her father had always been an excellent cook. In fact, he had prepared most of the family's meals for as long as she could remember. It was better so, for her mother's cooking had been uninspired and left much to be desired. Leigh recalled with bitter-sweet clarity that they used to laugh about her mother's lack of culinary skill — until she'd died.

The salad was her father's version of a common Greek salad, with a few touches of his own. Leigh had always loved it. In that respect, things hadn't changed. Andrew had also managed to bake a long, crusty loaf of French bread, which she found warming in the oven.

Leigh found her appetite, as well.

In between bursts of strained conversation, she polished off two helpings of soup, every morsel of salad and over a quarter of the slender loaf of bread. On top of everything else, she managed to consume two cups of coffee and a heavenly, if meager, slice of the Pennsylvania Dutch shoofly pie he had baked along with the bread.

"Ooooh, I'm stuffed," Leigh confessed, slumping back against the padded kitchen chair. "I haven't eaten that much food at lunchtime in . . . forever."

Andrew literally beamed in delight. "Can I assume then that you enjoyed your meal?"

"It was wonderful. You're a marvelous cook."

"Why, thank you, Leigh. I'm glad you enjoyed it." His expression was one of gratified amazement.

This open display of pleasure at her praise brought a nagging twinge of conscience, and the realization that their exchange had been the most natural and unaffected since the onset of her disillusionment with him.

"I not only enjoyed it, I appreciate the bother you went to in preparing it." To Leigh's own amazement, her voice remained free of the stilted stiffness.

"But there was no bother, Leigh." A soft, reminiscent smile curved his lips. "I remember every one of your favorite meals and desserts."

"You're kidding?" Leigh stared at him in surprise.

"No." Andrew shook his head. "Of course, your tastes may have changed over the years, grown more sophisticated, but when you were younger, your most favorite meal was chicken and dumplings."

"Mmm . . . homemade chicken and dumplings." Leigh closed her eyes, memory bringing the flavor to mind. "I haven't tasted that in years. It's so very good — and so healthfully bad and fattening."

"Nonsense," he chided. "I don't believe any food or drink is either bad or fattening, if taken in moderation."

Leigh opened her eyes to run an assessing glance over his still slender body. "Well, your cooking certainly hasn't appeared to have affected your weight," she observed.

A sparkle sprang to life in his eyes. "My blood pressure and cholesterol level are normal, too."

Leigh smiled in response to both his tone of pleased satisfaction and the sparkle in his eyes. It was an easy, relaxed smile . . . until, startled, she realized what she was doing, became aware of the sense of near camaraderie shimmering between her and her father.

A betrayal of her mother's memory?

Her smile faltered at the thought.

The sparkle dimmed in Andrew's eyes.

Guilt stabbing at her conscience, Leigh slid back her chair. "I'd better unpack," she said by way of excusing herself from the table, and his vicinity. "I need to iron and hang up my dress for this evening."

"Leigh, please wait . . . just a moment." Again, she was arrested by his hesitant, almost desperate air. "I . . . I . . . want to discuss something with you."

Leigh froze in place, all her senses alerted, afraid she wasn't going to like whatever he had to say. Telling herself to play it cool, she raised her eyebrows, prompting him to say his piece and get it over with.

Still, Andrew hesitated, eyeing her warily.

Convinced his need for discussion concerned her brother or Brett's extravagant wife, Leigh felt her hackles rise, and wondered how much it was going to cost her this time. Resentment coursed through her. Had she actually believed her bank balance was safe from the raiders for a while?

More fool she.

Tired of her father's worried look and procrastination, she heaved a sigh. "How much does Brett need, Dad?"

He started. "What? No." He shook his head. "This has nothing to do with Brett. I mean, your brother already knows about Kathie."

Leigh stared at him in blank confusion.

Kathie? Who in the world was Kathie? Leigh had never heard the name mentioned before.

Then dawn broke over her obtuse gray matter as a look of fearful consternation altered his expression.

A woman?

Her father, involved with a woman?

The mere concept stunned Leigh, though why should it be beyond her? He was a man, wasn't he?

Leigh's thinking process took a cynical left turn.

Of course he was, and what did all men appear to want from women?

Through her mind ran the old familiar refrain of her mother's bitter words.

Men will say and do anything to get sex.

Sex.

An image rose to swamp her senses, a vision of a gold-kissed man with a mind-bending mouth.

Leigh was forced to clench her teeth to contain a responsive shiver of lingering excitement.

"Leigh?" Andrew's voice, laced with anxiety, dissolved the image, diminished the churning sensation. "Is something wrong? Are you angry?"

She blinked, refocusing her image-clouded gaze on him. "Is there a reason I should be angry?" she asked, her voice roughened by another unpalatable image filling her mind, an image of her father, entwined with a faceless woman, thrashing on her mother's bed.

The bed in which her mother had suffered the death of her illusions of love, her hopes of bright tomorrows.

Disgust brought a bitter burning into her throat. Anger colored her response. "Is this woman — this Kathie — living here, with you?"

"No." He gave a quick, hard shake of his head, then stilled a moment, meeting her drilling stare head-on, before adding, "At least, not yet."

Leigh was chilled now by a different sense of betrayal. For her mother and for herself. Even while acknowledging the sensation was intellectually indefensible and immature, she found herself withdrawing inside her shell of cool, indifferent composure.

"Not yet," she repeated, her sarcasm clear. "And is there a wedding in the offing?"

Andrew sighed, suddenly looking tired, older than his fifty-five years. "If she'll have me," he said, remorse washing the sparkle from his eyes. "Would you object?"

"Why should I?" Managing a half-shrug, she stood, her facade cemented in place. For a moment there, just after lunch, she had felt a warmth, a connection to him she had not felt in sixteen years. The letdown was crushing — if she allowed it to be. Learning she was vulnerable, after all this time, was not to be tolerated. "It's your life."

"Leigh, wait," Andrew stopped her as she turned to leave the kitchen. "I wasn't finished."

Thinking he was so far as she was concerned, Leigh nevertheless turned back to face him, her composure in place.

He hesitated, swallowed, then rushed to explain. "Kathie will be at the dinner this evening." Again he paused, as if expecting an outburst, a protest — something from her. When she remained silent, he finally continued, "She will be seated at the family table, next to me."

"Whatever." This time, Leigh pulled off a full, careless-looking shrug before swinging around and heading for the hallway to her bedroom. But aching inside and confused by the hurt of being the last to know about his new, *special,* friend — an afterthought, as it were — she shot off a zinging exit line. "It's your party, Dad. Yours and Brett's and Evelyn's. Don't mind me."

"Leigh, it's not like that," he began.

She didn't pause, couldn't bear to listen to him stumble into an excuse.

"Wait, please," he called after her.

Shaking her head, Leigh strode through the living room, up the steps and along the short hallway. Entering her room, she quietly closed the door behind her, shutting herself off, away from him, maintaining the rift, the chasm of the sixteen-year status quo.

"Nothing's changed, Mother," she murmured, her bleak gaze surveying the familiar, yet somehow alien room. "Literally, nothing has changed."

She started at a gentle tap against the door, then flinched at the imploring note in her father's voice.

"Leigh, please, can't we talk about this?"

Closing her eyes and her mind, Leigh sighed. "Later, Dad," she said, raising her voice a notch to penetrate the wood door. A cynical smile twisting her lips, she echoed the long-ago, much repeated quote. "Maybe tomorrow."

"But —" Andrew persisted.

"I need to unpack, Dad." She cut him off, moving on into the room. "Then I think I'll have a nap."

Leigh wasn't even aware of holding her breath as she waited to see if he would argue. Her breath eased through her lips as, even through the closed door, she heard him sigh, then made out the slow tread of his footsteps retreating down the hall.

For several minutes, Leigh just stood there, feeling raw and defeated. Finally, bolstering herself with the reminder that it was only the same old, same old, she set about unpacking her small case and garment bag.

After taking care of her clothes, she yanked off her boots, opened the waist button of her jeans and stretched out on the bed to rest, if not to sleep.

To Leigh's surprise, when she again opened her eyes several hours later, the slanted sunrays of late afternoon bathed the room in mellow light.

Her first thought was one of gratitude, for her rest had been deep, unaffected by physically and mentally tormenting sensual dreams. Because she knew there had been something, her second thought was to wonder what had awakened her.

There came a gentle tap on her door, and then a soft call from her father.

"Leigh? Are you awake?"

Having the answer to her second thought, Leigh sat up, blinking sleep from her eyes.

"Leigh?" Andrew's voice was stronger, determined.

"Yes" — Leigh's answer was muffled by a

yawn — "I'm awake." She slid from the bed and fastened the button on her jeans. "And up."

"Dinner is scheduled for seven-thirty, so we have a couple of hours until we have to leave. Why don't you come to the kitchen? I have fresh coffee ready, and cinnamon rolls warming in the oven," he cajoled.

Leigh opened her mouth to refuse, then, shrugging, changed her mind. Damned if she'd hide out in her bedroom like a sulky kid, she thought, padding barefooted across to the door and swinging it open.

"I'll be with you in a minute," she said, actually managing a faint smile for her father. She was strangely relieved when the anxious tightness eased from his expression. "Just give me a moment to visit the bathroom and splash some cold water on my face."

"Sure." Andrew's voice quivered a bit; his eyes appeared suspiciously bright. "Take your time. I'll keep the rolls warm."

He took off along the hall, his steps a lot lighter than they had been earlier.

Leigh stared after him, her own eyes stinging. Then, telling herself to get with the program, she zipped across the hall and into the central bathroom.

Maybe, just maybe, she mused, she could

submerge her feelings, get through this blasted dinner, tolerate her sister-in-law, even endure the meeting with her father's girlfriend, Kathie, and come out of it in one piece, sane and intact.

Maybe.

Nine

The place was packed.

Leigh was familiar with the restaurant, having eaten there before during one of her infrequent visits home. The room, located in the basement of the building, was mainly used for private parties and receptions. It was tastefully decorated, but not very spacious.

As a rule, Leigh was unconscious of and unconcerned with the looks, blatant and surreptitious, sent her way whether striding along the street on her way to work or when entering public places, shops, restaurants and the like.

She was taller than average; she knew it; being neither dense nor blind, she knew she was not unattractive. She simply didn't give much credence to either her height or her exceptional looks.

But this particular evening proved the exception to the rule.

Perhaps it was her acute sensitivity, heightened by the conflicting emotions aroused by her disturbing dream, followed not many hours later by her father's mention of the woman in his life and now Leigh's imminent meeting with the lady named Kathie.

Whatever, this evening, Leigh noticed the glances, from people she recognized — friends of her brother, relatives of her sister-in-law — and from others she didn't know, overt and covert, taking her measure and, in the case of several bold-eyed men, her measurements.

Leigh was aware that she made a good appearance. She worked at it, not out of vanity, but because, as an interior designer, she deemed it a professional imperative to make as good an impression as possible.

And this evening, her possible was more than good. Leigh knew that, as well. Her assurance stemmed from the thorough and critical examination she had made of her reflected image in the full-length mirror mounted on the back of the door on her bedroom closet.

The dress Leigh had chosen to bring with her was simple yet elegant in design. It bore a famous label. She had purchased the creation for just such occasions, those requiring something dressy yet not formal.

In a deep, jewel-toned green, the high-necked and long-sleeved silk dress might have looked demure, if the mid-calf-length sheath hadn't clung to every rounded curve and indentation of her long body. Gold earrings, an intricately wrought gold chain encircling her throat and a matching chain of gold around her right wrist were the only adornments enhancing the striking severity of the cut of the garment, other than the thick and glossy mane of deeply waved auburn hair flowing over her shoulders and halfway down her back.

Where generally, Leigh wore low-heeled shoes for comfort and mobility, on certain occasions she wore higher, spiked heels. This was one of those occasions. Adding three inches to her height, the heels brought her up to an even six foot.

Leigh was fully aware of the impact she made as, head held high, she paced beside her father through the crowd of guests to the head table set at the front of the room.

Ignoring the murmurs trailing in her wake, she zeroed in on the three adults and the one child standing near the reserved table.

Holding his bright-eyed and wriggling son in his arms — most likely to contain his boundless energy, Leigh mused — her brother, Brett, at six-one, towered over the two women standing on either side of him.

Leigh skimmed a glance over the pleasure-flushed, expertly made-up face of her sister-in-law, Evelyn, noting that her eyes were every bit as bright as her son's.

At last, Leigh's searching gaze settled on the face of the woman to Brett's left. An initial sense of surprise sparked in her own green eyes. At first sight, the woman was nothing at all like what Leigh had expected.

But then, what had she been expecting? Leigh wondered. A sexpot? A scheming thirty-something looking for a free ride? A meal ticket with an older, established man? Leigh honestly didn't know, but it certainly wasn't the woman her father was moving toward in a direct line.

She was pretty, this Kathie, her skin glowing with health. She looked to be close to Andrew's age, and had made no obvious effort with cosmetics or her clothes to conceal the fact. Though not by any means fat, she was a tad overweight — some ten pounds or so, Leigh judged.

Her attire was conservative, a simple, double-breasted, coat-style dress of good quality, but not from a designer's line. She wore pearl studs in her ears and a single strand of pearls around her neck. Liberal strands of silver gleamed in her short, curly dark hair.

This Kathie had the look of a person she

could like. The thought struck Leigh as her father brought her to a stop before the woman.

Before Andrew had a chance to begin an introduction, Kathie held out a hand, almost as if in supplication, and in a soft, pleasing voice, said, "You're Leigh, of course." She laughed. "I'd have known you anywhere. You are every bit as beautiful, stunning actually, as your father claims." She flashed a sparkling glance at Andrew. "And proclaims, to anyone and everyone."

Her father? Leigh's mind boggled. *Her* father?

Her thought processes stopped cold, Leigh could only stare at the woman for a moment, utterly speechless.

"I'm Katherine Garner," the woman went on, filling what might have become a noticeable if tiny lull, while giving Leigh's hand an understanding squeeze. "But most people call me Kathie."

Nonplussed, Leigh responded in tones she knew were tight and strained. "How do you do. I, er, I'm glad —"

"An' Leigh! An' Leigh!" young Andy interrupted with a yelled demand to be noticed.

Leigh made a half-turn, a smile easing her taut facial muscles at sight of the boy leaning away from his father, his arms reaching for her.

Thinking enough to murmur an apologetic, "Excuse me," to Kathie, she took the steps necessary to pluck the child from his father's arms and into her own.

"Hello, Champ," she crooned, drawing a giggle from him with a growling bear hug. "How's my boyfriend?"

"Hunry," Andy groused.

"Know what?" Leigh whispered into his small ear. "So am I. What say we get this dinner show on the road?"

Andy blessed her with a beautiful smile and a vigorous nod of agreement.

She glanced aside to exchange grins with her brother. "His Royal Highness has spoken," she said in a solemn tone belying the amusement dancing in her eyes. "He's hunry."

"Well, then, I suppose we'd better feed the little Prince," Brett said. Chuckling, he shifted his gaze to his son. "But, would you mind very much, sir, if I say a quick hello to my sister first?" he asked, with due respect.

Andy giggled again, and shook his head.

At Brett's side, Evelyn heaved a sigh of long suffering. "Really, Brett, you're as bad as Leigh is," she said in exasperation. "Catering to Andrew's whims."

Andy looked stricken and about to wail.

The light dimmed in Brett's eyes.

It was only then that Leigh belatedly noticed the subtle changes in her brother since the last time she had visited her hometown.

He had lost some weight, which in itself would not normally alarm Leigh, especially in the current craze of eating healthy and exercising vigorously in the hope of living longer — if not forever. But in addition to the weight loss, Brett's attractive features were finely drawn into lines depicting stress and strain.

More financial worries . . . or marital problems?

Anger swept through Leigh at the speculation and at the tears gathering in her nephew's eyes, anger and a need to slap her sister-in-law, if only verbally.

Recalling where they were, she caught the scathing remark on the tip of her tongue. Wouldn't do to cause a scene at a celebratory gathering of friends and family. Instead, she raised an eyebrow and asked with sweet innocence, "Hunger is a whim, Evelyn?"

"You're so clever, aren't you?" Evelyn sniped, her lip curling. "And so superior."

"Evelyn." Though Brett's voice was low, it was forceful. "If you'll recall, this party was arranged to satisfy you. Don't start anything."

"Me? Me?" Evelyn's face flushed, and she appeared about to explode. "It's . . . it's her. She's the —"

"I think we should all sit down." Andrew's smooth tones cut through his daughter-in-law's sputter. "And calm down. They're ready to serve dinner."

"Fine." Evelyn glared at Leigh, then flounced away, leaving her son in Leigh's care.

Leigh didn't mind. In fact, she was delighted. Her arms tightened a fraction around his little body, as if to keep him warm, protected, safe.

"It's you and me, pal," she said, smiling to assure him all was well. "Let's find our seats and feed our faces."

Her teasing remark had him giggling again, giggling and wiggling. Holding him close, Leigh carried him to their places at the table. Chairs had to be rearranged — the booster seat for Andy placed on the chair between Leigh and his father, instead of on the one between his father and mother, as originally planned.

Leigh was content with the arrangement; the need to help Andy with his food gave her an excuse for not joining in with the conversation around her. To her thinking, Andy's animated conversation was a lot more enjoyable than the banal chatting from the adults, anyway.

The selections on offer were bountiful: Roast steamship round of beef, turkey breast, honey-baked ham, plus an array of vegetables, pastas and salads; insuring satisfaction for meat eaters and vegetarians alike. For dessert, there were puddings — chocolate, rice and bread — jello molds for those wishing something even lighter, and of course, a multilayered, lavishly decorated anniversary cake.

The libations were liberal, as well. Carafes of red and white wine were set at intervals on the table, and an excellent champagne was provided for toasts to the celebrating couple's continued marital success. Soft drinks were available for children and nondrinkers, as were the coffee and tea that flowed freely both during the meal and after.

Leigh couldn't help but wonder how much the affair had cost her father. And what for? To pacify a self-centered, grasping social climber. Seemed pretty much of a waste of money, time and effort to her.

But hey, Leigh told herself, apart from the brief amount of time for the short trip home, it hadn't cost her a thing. What her father did with his money, time and effort was his business.

Leigh accepted an afterdinner coffee, but declined dessert. While sipping her coffee, she sat, fascinated, watching Andy devour a dish of chocolate pudding.

Memory stirred of another chocolate lover, an image flashing in her mind of Michael St. Claire, his strong white teeth cleaving through a delicate chocolate-iced cake.

Giving memory the heave-ho, Leigh dismissed the man and focused her full attention on the boy.

Though Andy somehow managed to avoid dropping so much as the smallest glob of the sweet on his clothes, chocolate smeared his mouth, chin, one cheek and his fingers.

"More?" Andy asked hopefully, when he had scraped the last bit of pudding from the dish.

Leigh shook her head. "I think you'd better quit while you're ahead, love of my life." Laughing at the chocolate-toothed grin he gave her, she dipped her napkin into her water glass, then proceeded to make him presentable. By the time she had cleaned him up, the napkin was a mess, and the servers were busy clearing the tables.

Standing, she lifted him from the booster seat and turned, surprised to see a disc jockey setting up his stuff at the far end of the room. Other restaurant personnel were employed in rearranging the tables in the center of the room.

Dancing? Leigh frowned as she watched the tables being shoved aside to clear a small space on the floor.

Sure enough, a moment later, the DJ's upbeat voice boomed from the loudspeakers, inviting everybody to get out on the floor and have fun, fun, fun.

Fun. Oh, boy. Leigh sighed. She had thought that a short period of social chitchat would follow dinner, then everyone would go on their merry way.

No such luck. And Leigh had come with her father, in his car, which left her no choice but to wait until he was ready to leave. The nebulous hope that Andrew might choose to excuse himself, leaving the afterdinner frivolity to the younger family members and guests, was quashed at once when, practically on the heels of Brett and Evelyn, he escorted Kathie onto the floor.

Unmindful of the possibility of her dress being crushed, Leigh settled Andy on one hip, and began circulating, greeting old acquaintances, introducing herself to strangers and exchanging inanities with Evelyn's family, at which time she reluctantly relinquished Andy to his maternal grandmother, who immediately began lovingly fussing over him.

Andy ate up the attention with every bit as much relish as he'd devoured the chocolate pudding.

Smiling, Leigh drifted away to continue her rounds. She didn't get far. A hand on her shoulder brought her to a halt, and an unfamiliar voice stiffened her spine.

"I think this is my dance."

The voice was too smooth, too practiced, and much too confident. Dislodgng his hand by stepping to the side and slowly turning to get a look at the presumptuous male, Leigh raised one eyebrow. "I think you're mistaken," she said with a polite bite.

Though his voice had been unfamiliar, Leigh recognized the man confronting her. She had met him at Brett's wedding reception. A relative, a cousin, she suddenly recalled, of Evelyn. Troy? Trevor? Or a name similar, it hadn't mattered then, it didn't now. Thirty-something Troy, Trevor or whoever was an attractive man, the walking, talking representation of tall, dark and good-looking.

And he knew it better than anyone else.

"Don't tell me you've forgotten me," he said, in tones of shocked disbelief, as if the very idea was incomprehensible.

In truth, Leigh had happily forgotten him, but choosing prudence, she circumvented the truth. "Of course not," she said, dredging up a reluctant smile. "You're Evelyn's cousin, aren't you?"

"Right in one," he said, so damned pleased with himself she halfway expected to see his chest puff out. "Trevor," he obligingly provided. "Trevor Monroe."

"Yes . . ." Leigh held the smile, and shifted her gaze a fraction, searching for a means of escape. She caught a glimpse of Brett standing nearby.

"So, how about our dance?" Trevor's voice brought her gaze back to his face, his cocky, oversure expression.

No way, Leigh thought. She had danced with him the night of the reception. With his hands all over her, dancing with him had been like wrestling an octopus. She didn't care to repeat the infuriating performance.

Looking cool, feeling desperate, a dull pain running above her left eyebrow and down to her temple, Leigh sent her gaze skimming again. A strained smile on his lips, Brett was walking her way. Rescue.

"Sorry," she lied. "But I promised this dance to the anniversary boy. If you'll excuse me?" Without waiting for a response, she turned to intercept her brother.

"Maybe later," Trevor persisted.

"Maybe," she tossed back over her shoulder, thinking, yeah, maybe, at the turn of the twenty-first century.

"Leigh, I —" Brett began when she came to a stop in front of him.

"Dance with me," she interrupted, raising her arms to him. "Now, please."

"Uh, okay," he said, moving into her arms. "I wanted a moment to talk to you, anyway."

Oh, hell. Trouble. Leigh just knew it. "What about?" she asked, keeping step as he guided her into the crush on the small dance floor.

"I've . . . got a problem." His voice was low pitched, for her ears only.

"Financial?"

He hesitated, then nodded. "Yes."

Bull's-eye. Leigh smothered a sigh. How naive she had been in believing she could remain solvent.

"How much?" Even she could hear the fatalistic overtones in her soft voice.

"Fifty thousand."

Leigh's eyes flew wide. "Fif-fifty thousand," she echoed in a stunned whisper. *"Brett."*

"I know. I know." He wet his lips. "I was doing all right. I really was. But then, after Evelyn came to work in the office, things started to —"

"Hold it," Leigh cut in on him. "Back it up. Evelyn's working in your office?" At his confirming nod, she demanded, "Since when? And who's taking care of Andy?"

"It's about six months now, and only in the afternoons. Andy goes to a nursery school," he explained, then went on defiantly, "It's got excellent accreditation."

"Okay." Leigh backed off; mothers working and nursery schools had become the American way of life. Who was she to question another person's private decisions? "So, what did Evelyn coming to work for you have to do with your current financial difficulties?"

Brett grimaced, looking extremely uncomfortable. "Ummm, she . . . forgot to pay a couple of our subcontractors, and . . . ah, spent the money."

For a second, Leigh could only stare at him in astonished disbelief. Having worked in construction since his high-school days, Brett, declaring he was tired of working for another's enrichment, had started his own home-building business a few years back. He had had rough going in the beginning, as most small businesses did, her own included, and Leigh had helped him out with loans on more than one occasion. A couple of thousand here, a couple there.

But fifty thousand dollars was beyond the pale. And subcontractors frowned upon not receiving payment — understandably so. They also talked. Leigh knew that word of mouth could kill a business.

"I'm facing bankruptcy, Leigh." Though soft, Brett's cry revealed his near panic. "My line of credit with the bank is at the limit, and I owe a couple of suppliers."

While feeling impelled to flat-out strangle her extravagant, self-absorbed sister-in-law, Leigh ached for her brother. He had worked so hard to establish himself, and to have this happen, just when his business appeared to be taking off . . . No wonder he was looking thin and strained.

Growing up, she and Brett had been close, and he had always played the big brother, caring and protective. But after he had married Evelyn — a woman Leigh simply could not like, no matter how hard she tried — their relationship, the closeness, had dwindled to occasional visits and his periodic pleas for financial help.

Damn Evelyn!

The pain in Leigh's head expanded,

pounding in time to the music she no longer heard. She didn't even bother asking him how in hell the avaricious Evelyn had managed to forget something as important as paying their subcontractors, never mind their suppliers. She dreaded even asking about that. What was done, was done.

"I don't have it, Brett," she admitted, pricked by an odd twinge of guilt as if she were responsible. "At the very most, I might be able to scrape together ten, maybe fifteen thousand dollars." She didn't add, thereby putting her own business at risk.

"I wasn't asking for, or expecting you to make me a cash loan, Leigh."

He wasn't? She frowned. "I don't understand, Brett," she said. "If not a loan, then what?"

"You know Dad co-signed for my credit line?"

"Yes . . . so?"

He hesitated, drew a harsh breath, then quickly explained, "I spoke to Josh Breedy at the bank about extending the limit on the line to an additional seventy-five thousand. And Josh said the only way he could do that was if I could produce another co-signer."

He didn't need to elaborate; Leigh got the picture. A co-signer on a loan had to pledge collateral as security. And the only collateral she possessed was her business.

The pain stabbing at her forehead and temple expanded, wrapping around to the back of her neck. Leigh needed to think, and with the pain, she couldn't.

"I have a blasting headache," she said.

"I'm sorry," he said at once, dark color staining the skin stretched taut over his cheekbones. "Forget it. I understand. I'll . . . I'll find some other way."

The twinge of guilt dug deeper inside Leigh. "No." She started to shake her head, then stopped when the motion intensified the pain. "I had the headache before — you didn't cause it. It's just that . . . I need to think, and I can't right now. Can you give me some time?"

"I have until the end of the month." He gave her a helpless, apologetic look. "That's when I promised payment to both the subcontractors and the suppliers."

Leigh felt sick. The headache or . . . ? The end of the month was a little more than two weeks away. "Okay." She nodded, and immediately wished she hadn't. "I'll let you know in plenty of time." Her stomach roiled. Indigestion burned a path to her throat.

Brett studied her face. "You look terrible. Would you like me to take you home?"

Thank heaven for small mercies, Leigh thought. Still, she made a token protest. "It's your party, Brett. I don't want to drag you away from it."

He shot her a get-real look, while turning her in the direction of the door. "I won't even be missed. You go get your coat. I'll tell Dad and Evelyn."

Leigh didn't argue; she obeyed.

She was slipping her arm into her coat sleeves when a now-familiar, but unwelcome voice made her cringe inside.

"Not leaving are you?" Trevor sounded offended. "We haven't had our dance yet."

"I'm sorry," she lied, needing fresh air and pain killers followed by sleep, and wishing he'd take a hike. "I'm not feeling well."

"I'll take you home, then." His voice was eager, laced with too obvious anticipation.

"*No.* Thank you. Brett's driving me," she said, silently urging her brother to hurry.

"You're staying at your dad's place?" he persisted.

She sighed, but admitted it. "Yes."

"I'll call you there tomorrow," he said, so damned confident and sure of himself. "Okay?"

Leigh caught herself on the verge of saying no, positive he'd continue to persist, and she just wasn't up to an argument. "Yes, all right."

Still, Trevor persisted. "Maybe we could do something in the afternoon, go somewhere or —"

"Ready?" Fortunately Brett arrived, saving her from hearing what Trevor had in mind, although she suspected he had more planned than an innocent afternoon interlude.

Murmuring a quick "Good night" Leigh practically ran up the stairs and out of the restaurant.

Brett kept blessedly quiet during most of the drive to her father's house, and Leigh had just started to relax a little when he broke the silence, ratcheting up her tension.

"Ahhh . . . Leigh, what did you think of Kathie?"

With her head pounding like a maniacal drummer, Leigh preferred not to think of her at all. But as much as she longed to ignore the question, she knew by Brett's concern that she had to respond.

"I really didn't get the opportunity to get to know her, Brett," she answered. "But she seems nice." She fervently hoped that would suffice.

"She is," he said, apparently satisfied with her answer. "You know, she and Dad have been seeing each other for some months now."

"I gathered as much from Dad."

He slanted a quick, wary glance at her. "You don't object, do you?"

If her head hadn't been hurting so much, Leigh might have laughed, not in amusement, but in self-defense against a sense of betrayal. "No, Brett, I don't object." She sighed. "Would it matter if I did?"

"I guess not, but I know Dad would be upset if you, well, made a fuss about it."

Sure. Leigh swallowed the cynical thought. "I promise, I won't make a fuss."

"Good." He exhaled. "Dad will be pleased."

Men, she mused. Why were they all so transparent?

The question raised an image, an image looming as large in her mind as he was in fact. Michael St. Claire's intentions toward her were as transparent as glass, every bit as obvious as Trevor's.

Sex.

Men.

Of course, there remained one little problem with her assessment. Trevor lacked the power to stir her up, either emotionally or physically.

That power could only be claimed by St. Claire.

The realization sent the pain level through the top of Leigh's head.

When, at long last, she was back in her old room, Leigh gulped down two painkillers, made short shrift of her nightly routine, then with a silent prayer of thanks, crawled into bed in the hope of escaping into unconsciousness.

Within moments, she began to drift in the netherworld between wakefulness and sleep. The ache pounding in her head seemed to dull a little. Then her traitorous mind replayed an echo of Trevor Monroe's determined voice telling her he would call tomorrow.

She had to sleep, rest, in order to deal with the annoyingly persistent man.

That was her last lucid thought before floating over the edge and into blessed sleep.

Ten

It was after midnight. Michael had returned moments before to his apartment after seeing Barbara safely to her car. As always, he had enjoyed the evening in her company.

Propped indolently against the archway into the kitchen, he took a swallow of martini — his second and his self-imposed limit for the evening — savoring the drink's bite as he studied the anxious expression on Shamus's face over the rim of the large, bulbous, flat-bottomed glass.

"So?" Shamus demanded, further revealing anxiety alien to his nature by fidgeting with the dishcloth in his hands.

Michael grinned, he couldn't help himself; Clancy was so damned obvious, wearing his heart on his sleeve.

Shamus scowled and cursed.

"I've been instructed to convey Barbara's compliments to you for a most delicious and enjoyable meal," Michael reported, taking pity on the lovesick idiot. "And, of course, my own compliments go without saying."

Shamus heaved a sigh of relief. "She really liked the veal medallions à la Clancy?"

"Loved 'em," Michael drawled. "One might be tempted to say she rhapsodized in praise."

Clancy narrowed his eyes on his friend, his expression switching from anxious to skeptical.

"I can't help but notice that you don't seem to give a rip about the opinion of your employer," Michael observed in bone-dry tones.

"Oh, you." Shamus shrugged a dismissal. "You like whatever food I put down in front of you."

"True." Michael nodded. "For the most part. But then, I've never heard a single complaint from Barbara, either. So, why all this angst?"

"You know why. Think about it." He grimaced, then muttered, "I was right here in the kitchen, Mike. I couldn't help overhearing about this new man in her life."

"Ahhh . . . yes, the mysterious Jake Jenson."

"Yeah, him," Shamus snarled. "Who the devil is he, anyway? And what do you know about him, Mike?"

"Not a damn thing," Michael admitted. "Yet. But I'll be meeting him next Sunday afternoon."

Shamus frowned. "You've made a business appointment for a Sunday afternoon?"

Michael gave a quick shake of the head. "No. I've been invited to an open house, at which Barbara and Jake Jenson will be present. I will meet him there."

For a long minute, Shamus just stared, speechless, at Michael. "You . . . ?" he finally blurted out. "You're going to an open house?"

"Amazin', ain't it?" he said, sardonically.

"More like unbelievable," Shamus retorted. "And I don't get it. It's not your kind of thing."

"I know, but —"

"You're going to check out this Jake Jenson person," Shamus said, nodding approval. "Good."

Michael didn't voice a confirmation or denial of Clancy's conclusion, because it was only partly correct. Although it was true that Michael was more than a little curious about Jake Jenson and his purpose in cultivating Barbara, that was not his primary motivation for attending the open house.

In truth, certain he would eventually meet the other man anyway, Michael's initial reaction was to decline the invitation to the open house being given by Barbara's friend, a Mrs. Lillian Standfield, a woman he had never met.

But before he could announce his decision, Barbara had changed his mind with one supposedly offhand remark.

"She'll be there, you know."

"Who?" he'd asked, instinctively knowing the answer.

"Leigh Evans." Barbara's eyes gleamed, reflecting inner amusement. "It's the perfect opportunity for you to see a sample of her work. Lillian is having this open house to show her appreciation for the excellent job of redecorating and revitalizing Evans has accomplished."

Barbara had dangled the bait; Michael had snapped it up, as she had known full well he would.

She did so enjoy being devious at times.

But though Barbara was aware of his intent, Michael wasn't about to divulge to Shamus that Leigh Evans was his primary motivation for attending.

Leigh, who had gone out of town for the weekend, to be with someone she tacitly agreed was "special."

Michael experienced an odd, indefinable sensation in his gut. Speculating on the feeling, he raised his glass to his lips, hesitated, then lowered it again.

Alcohol wasn't what he needed.

"I'm for bed," he said, crossing to the sink

to dump the drink down the drain. "Why don't you leave the rest of the cleaning up until tomorrow?" he suggested, knowing Shamus wouldn't hear of it.

"Nah, I'm almost finished," Shamus protested.

Michael didn't press the issue. He had long since learned it wouldn't make a difference. "Your call," he said, retracing his steps to the archway. "But don't forget." He paused to level a hard look at the man. "Tomorrow's your day off. Don't bother with breakfast. I'll get something for myself."

"Yeah, yeah." Shamus grinned in the face of his employer's hard look. "Good night, Mike." His grin widened. "And don't let the bedbugs bite."

The unreal threat of biting bedbugs didn't concern Michael, but the sensation of something biting at his gut caused genuine consternation.

Dropping naked onto his bed, he stared at the ceiling, intellectualizing his unrecognizable feelings.

He had met and known many women, some intimately — though not nearly as many as the rumor mill contended. And with not one of them had he ever felt anything similar to the sensation he'd experienced at merely thinking about Leigh Evans spending an illicit weekend with another man.

He had never suffered personal discomfort from the sins of jealousy or envy. He had made his way in the world, grateful for the assistance of Barbara and a few others, but mainly by relying on himself. He had never measured by any standards but his own. He didn't covet what others possessed, be it talent, ability, personality, rewards or women.

Therefore, he deduced, the odd sensation in his gut had not been caused by jealousy of the man Leigh was very likely in bed with at that moment.

The sensation struck again, deeper; twisting, this time causing actual pain.

So much for intellectualizing, Michael thought, sighing. Intellect had damned little to do with it. His discomfort was emotional in nature.

He was jealous, goddamn it.

Michael didn't like it. But there it was.

The idea of another man touching Leigh, making love with her, made him sick.

Leigh opened her eyes, still half-asleep, to weak gray morning light filtering through the miniblinds and sheer curtains at the windows.

The pain in my head is gone.

The realization activated her memory of the dream she'd had before awakening. Whole and of a piece, the dream replayed in her mind, its events and sequences vivid in recall.

Strangely, even while asleep, Leigh had known she was dreaming, had watched the dream unfold, not as a participant but as a viewing bystander.

As many dreams appeared to do, while connected loosely to actual occurrence, the action was played out in a location unrecognizable to Leigh.

She had found herself in a large area similar to a hotel ballroom, surrounded by a crowd of unfamiliar people, all of whom seemed to know her quite well. She was dressed in the office attire she favored, gray pinstriped suit and low-heeled shoes, feeling uncomfortable and out of place, since every other person was formally attired, the men in tuxedos, the women in gowns and glittering jewelry.

Music swirled throughout the room. The unknown people around her laughed and conversed. Leigh laughed too, although she didn't have a clue as to what they were talking and laughing about.

And then a man appeared in front of her;

a man she recognized — identified — as Evelyn's cousin, Trevor Monroe. As alien and out of place as she felt, Leigh was not relieved or pleased to see him there.

"I've come to take you home," he said, curling his fingers around her wrist.

"But I don't want to go," the slumbering Leigh lied, tugging against his hold, wishing she'd wake up.

"Sure you do," he countered, as confident and persistent in her dream as he was in fact.

"No." Shaking her head, she tugged on her arm again, trying to break his hold, but to no avail. "I . . . want to dance," she improvised, beginning to feel desperate.

"Oh, we'll dance," he promised, his fingers tightening painfully around her wrist. "But not here." He smiled; it was not a nice smile. "I've got a different kind of dance in mind . . . a dance of horizontal not vertical positions."

Leigh's wrist was hurting. Still, she pulled against his manaclelike grip. Panic swelled inside her. Why couldn't she wake up? Or why wouldn't some of these dream people come to her aid? How could they stand by and watch while . . . Growing frantic, the sleeping Leigh glanced around. Where were they? The elegantly dressed people and the ballroom had disappeared. Where was she?

Moonlight slanted through the mini-blinds and sheer curtains, patterning the carpet with streaks of silver, throwing the furniture into shadowy relief.

Her bedroom? Not her bedroom in her Center City apartment, but the one in her father's house.

She was not alone. Trevor was standing beside her — next to the bed. The hard fingers of one hand were still coiled around her wrist; the fingers on his other hand were tearing at her clothes.

Rape.

Both the dreaming Leigh and the part of her that knew she was dreaming recoiled at the realization. The persistent, insistent Trevor was intent on having her, with or without her willingness. Suddenly, as if by magic, her clothes disappeared. She was naked — worse, so was Trevor. Teeth clenched and bared, he forced her down, down, onto the bed.

"No. No. No." The sleeping Leigh was unaware of crying the defiant rejection aloud.

Pain pounding in her head, she struggled against him, hating the feel of his body pressing her into the mattress. She put up a valiant battle, but it was a battle she could not win. Trevor was bigger, stronger and determined on slaking his desire. She grew tired and weak.

Dear heaven, help me. The silent plea came from both the sleeping and watching Leigh.

In the same instant, a blaze of light filled the room. There was a fluttering sound, like the ruffle made by a huge winged bird. Then a lightning flash of metal.

And he was there, the passionate angel who had taken licentious liberties with her body in her dream of the night before. The golden angel she had not resisted in her previous dream. The angel who looked like Michael St. Claire.

The angel held a long, gleaming sword in one hand. The blade flashed again, down and through the naked form crushing her against the bed.

In a twinkling, and without a sound, Trevor's dream form vanished. And the sleeping Leigh was alone with the beautiful, golden angel. Bending, he smiled and brushed his lips over her forehead, and the pain was gone.

"Sleep, now," he murmured. "I will keep you safe."

Straightening, standing tall, seemingly bigger than life, he stood next to her bed, sword at the ready.

It was at that moment Leigh had awakened.

The distinct, rattling noise of sleet striking the window penetrated Leigh's bemusement. Blinking herself fully awake, she carefully moved her head, testing.

As in her dream, when the angel's lips brushed her forehead, her headache was gone.

Shaken by the memory of the dream, and the reality of the results, Leigh lay still, wondering, wondering.

The light tap on her door was not intrusive, and yet, being off in the realm of speculation, she was startled, the sound bringing her down to earth, grounding her in reality.

Dreams. Where did they come from? What did they mean? So far as Leigh could recall, her dreams had never had any tangible or prophetic meaning.

Still, she mused, to have two similar — sort of — and back-to-back dreams . . .

"Leigh, are you awake?" Her father's soft call dissolved her thoughts, corralled her attention.

"Yes, Dad, I'm awake."

"How's the headache?"

Leigh tentatively moved her head again,

almost afraid the pain had returned; it hadn't. "It's gone." She could hear the relief in her voice.

"I'm glad." He sounded like he meant it. "I didn't want to disturb you, but I thought I'd better let you know that weather conditions are deteriorating."

"Weather . . ." Leigh echoed, sitting up to peer at the window — a fruitless endeavor, since the blinds were closed. Then she remembered hearing rain and sleet hitting the pane. "Is it still sleeting?"

"Yes," he answered. "And the latest report was for the temperature to start going down and the rain to turn to snow later this morning."

"Oh, great." Groaning, Leigh tossed back the covers and got out of bed to go to the window. Cranking the blinds open, she gazed out at a dismal, gray-shrouded day.

"What time is it?" Even as she asked, she twisted away from the window to glance at the small alarm clock on the night table beside the bed.

"A little after eight-thirty," he answered, confirming what she had just seen.

"I waited to have breakfast with you," Andrew said. "What would you like? Eggs? Pancakes?"

It was only then that Leigh realized she

was hungry. And her father had always whipped up the lightest, most delicious pancakes. "Pancakes," she answered, raising her voice. "If you can give me a few minutes to grab a shower?"

"Sure. It'll give me time to mix the batter and start a fresh pot of coffee." She could hear him move away from the door, his voice growing fainter as he walked along the hall to the stairs. "Take your time."

It was close to a half-hour later when Leigh entered the kitchen. "Sorry," she said, crossing to the countertop where the coffeemaker was set. "But I took the time to get my stuff together and pack — I think I'd better head for home right after breakfast." Leigh also had been thinking that the weather gave her a good excuse . . . if Trevor did happen to call.

"No problem — and I agree." Andrew smiled. "Even though I had hoped you could spend most of the day, it's probably wise to leave before the roads become a real mess." He flicked a hand at the table as he turned to the stove. "Sit down and have your coffee, while I get the cakes on the griddle."

The kitchen clock read nine-forty-two when Leigh placed her napkin on the table and sighed with repletion. "You've outdone yourself, Dad." She complimented him with genuine appreciation. "When did you start making the pancakes with apples and pecans?"

"Right before Christmas." He flashed a grin so mischievous it was boyish. "I stole the idea from a special holiday menu at a restaurant where Kathie and I had breakfast early in December, improvised on it."

Hmmm, Leigh mused, avoiding comment by raising her refilled coffee cup to her lips. Kathie and breakfast. In an oblique way, was her father trying to tell her something, to ascertain her feelings regarding the woman? And, if so, why bother? When was the last time her opinion had mattered?

"Ah, Leigh . . . about Kathie," he began, sounding hesitant and uncertain.

"What about her?" she countered, determined on having him lay his cards on the table.

He fidgeted with his fork, lowered his eyes, then raised his head to face her squarely, a look of resolve strengthening his features. "Our relationship is . . . serious. She usually spends the weekends here, with me."

Fax the newsroom at Channel 6 in Philadelphia, Leigh thought, resentment simmering inside her. Suspecting the woman of sleeping in her mother's bed was one thing, but he had said their relationship was serious. To Leigh, the indication was that before too long, Kathie would be taking over her mother's house, and that was something else altogether.

Aloud she murmured, "I see," not even trying to disguise her feelings.

"She's a wonderful woman, Leigh." His tone was defensive, his eyes were pleading.

For reasons beyond Leigh at that moment, his imploring look got to her. Her father, imploring understanding from her? Incredible. What could she say? It was his house, his life, after all. She had her own place, her own life, and Leigh knew exactly how she would react if he attempted to interfere with how she lived it.

She had no rights here, Leigh told herself, not even sure why his near confession upset her. Hadn't she written him off years ago?

She'd been quiet too long; Andrew's features grew pinched with anxiety. "Say something, Leigh."

"What would you like me to say, Dad?" Backing down was not easy, however inevitable it was.

He frowned, obviously not pleased with her response. "Well, what did you think of her?" he asked, repeating, almost verbatim,

Brett's question of the night before.

Leigh gave him the same answer she'd given Brett. "I really didn't get the opportunity to get to know her, Dad, but she seems very nice."

"She is," he said, eagerly. "Kathie is a lovely person, Leigh, inside and out, and" — he hesitated, then rushed on — "I'd like to give you the opportunity to get to know her." He glanced at the rain-spattered kitchen window and sighed. "I had invited Kathie to the house today, for a late lunch, to give you two a chance to really talk, but —"

"I can't stay, Dad."

"I know." He sighed again, then smiled. "So does Kathie. She called to cancel. She'd been to early Mass, and said that as there was snow as well as sleet mixing in with the rain, driving was getting bad."

Mass. Kathie was a Catholic. Andrew was not. What difference did it make? None, Leigh decided, since from the bits and pieces of information she had garnered during dinner last night, they were both widowed. Dismissing conjecture, she slid her chair back from the table.

"Then I'd better get moving," she said, beginning to clear their breakfast dishes from the table.

"Leave that," Andrew ordered. "I have all day to do the cleaning up."

Leigh didn't argue. She wanted to leave, get home to her own apartment, where she could insulate herself once again from unwanted, familial emotional tugs. Besides, remembering her dream, and Trevor's promise — threat? — to call her, she wanted to be long gone before he could make good on that promise.

She almost made it.

Her father was outside, stashing her stuff in the car, and Leigh had the front door open, about to join him, when the phone rang.

"Will you get that please, Leigh?" Andrew called to her. "It might be Kathie."

Hoping it was, afraid it wasn't, Leigh reluctantly crossed to the extension phone on the small desk in a corner of the living room and gingerly lifted the receiver.

"Hello?"

"Leigh." The now too familiar, too confident voice rang in her ear. "Hi, it's Trevor."

No kidding. Leigh grimaced, but said in the most pleasant tone she could manage, "Oh, hi, you just caught me . . ." She suppressed a sigh. "I'm about ready to leave."

"Leave?" Now his voice didn't ring in her ear; it boomed. "Where are you going?"

203

"Home. To Philadelphia," she answered. Where else would she be going?

"Why?"

Why? Leigh turned to look out the living-room picture window, at what was now more snow than anything else. "Because of the weather conditions, Trevor," she explained, projecting a patience she was far from feeling.

"Oh." A pause. "Damn. I thought maybe we could spend the day together, you know, get pizza and watch videos or something here at my place."

At his place. Or something. Uh-huh. Not in this lifetime, Leigh assured herself.

"Sorry, Trevor," she lied without a twinge of remorse. "But conditions are worsening, and I can't afford to get stuck here. I have appointments tomorrow. I'm sure you understand." She didn't give a rip if he did or not.

"Yeah, sure." He heaved what she felt positive was intended as a soulful sigh; she was not impressed. "But, hey," his tone brightened, "I'm gonna be in Philly in a couple of weeks on business, I'll give you a buzz when I get in."

Oh, goody. Leigh made a face, but said, "All right," ready to agree to almost anything, just to get him off the line so she could leave. "I'll talk to you then. 'Bye." Not even waiting for his response, she cradled the receiver and literally ran out of the house.

Driving conditions weren't nearly as bad as she had expected. For one, the rain and sleet had become all snow, which still melted upon landing, and for another, because it was Sunday, traffic was light.

By concentrating on the road, Leigh managed to shove to the farthest reaches of her consciousness all thoughts, speculations and concerns about her father and Kathie, about Brett's marriage and financial problems and about her disturbing dreams. She was successful, up to a point.

That point being an item she had dug out of the bottom drawer of her dresser, where she had stored her school yearbooks, some keepsakes and other memorabilia when she had moved out of her father's house.

That item was the picture that had hung on the wall over her bed for as long as she could remember. The picture depicted an artist's conception of the perfect guardian — the white-winged, golden, warrior archangel, Michael.

Eleven

True to the capricious nature of spring, the weather did a complete turnabout on Monday. The sunlight was bright and warm, the breeze balmy. Temperatures in the high sixties were being predicted.

Leigh felt as changeable as the weather.

Considering the state of nervous tension she had been in by the time she'd returned to her apartment, and after dropping mentally exhausted into her bed convinced she'd spend the night tossing, turning and dreaming, she had enjoyed ten hours of deep, restful sleep, unvisited by disturbing dreams — at least none that she remembered upon awakening.

Pondering her reasons for having rooted it out, the very first thing she did — before splashing water on her face, brushing her teeth, or even having coffee — was to stash away in the back of her closet the guardian angel picture.

Hoping to never again go through another one, Leigh decided the last thing she needed was a reminder of those unsettling dreams.

Brushing her hands together, as if shoving

the picture to a dark corner of her closet was symbolic of shoving the man to the darkest reaches of her mind, Leigh went about the business of preparing for work.

But a picture was just a picture. The man himself, the living prototype of the angel of her dreams, was an altogether different story. While striding the short distance to her showroom, soaking up the sunlight, breathing in the elusive but distinct scent of spring on the air, Leigh faced the reality that Michael St. Claire wouldn't be quite so easily stashed.

The conclusion recalled to mind the conveniently forgotten Wednesday appointment with him Leigh had hastily and unadvisedly and, yes, mindlessly agreed to — after he had kissed her — on Friday night.

Lord, who would have believed that one kiss — one brief, undemanding kiss, at that — could play such havoc with her mind and what she'd thought was her dormant libido?

The memory of the latent power in the kiss ignited a warmth inside Leigh that put the warmth of the sun to shame.

Breathless — from the brisk walk, Leigh assured herself — she paused, as usual, to examine her showroom window.

It was time for a change.

In more things than the window.

A strong sense of self-preservation sparking resolve, Leigh determined on the spot to decline his offer to redecorate his office and to break off all contact with Michael St. Claire, personally as well as professionally.

But her relief at having made the tough decision was short-lived, as in the next instant she remembered Brett's plea for financial assistance.

A forked road for certain, she reflected, disgruntled, for she could not, in good conscience, abandon her brother, leaving him hanging high and dry, twisting in the winds of his wife's extravagances.

Faced with damned if she did and damned if she didn't, Leigh had little option but to redetermine her attitude toward her relationship with St. Claire.

Cursing fate, circumstances, her brother's ineptitude in controlling his wife and business, *and* Michael St. Claire, she strode into her showroom, resigned to the possible necessity of having to ask Sheila to rearrange her Wednesday schedule.

The possibility proved to be a necessity.

And Sheila herself proved inquisitive with the first words out of her mouth, uttered before Leigh had shut the door.

"How did dinner go Friday night?"

"Fine." Leigh succeeded in achieving a casual, no-big-deal, attitude. "The food was exceptional."

"Food?" Sheila rolled her eyes. "Who cares about the food? I want to hear about St. Claire."

"What about him?" Leigh asked, moving her shoulders in what she hoped was a gesture of unconcern.

This time, Sheila didn't roll her eyes; she raised them to the ceiling, as if beseeching help from above. "St. Claire — arguably the most gorgeous male on the planet — and she asks, 'What about him?' " She lowered her eyes to pierce Leigh's closed expression. "What's he like? And I don't mean on a professional level, but as a man."

"Pleasant. Charming. A good conversationalist." Recalling, too vividly, the personal, almost intimate direction of his conversation, Leigh controlled a need to grimace. *Get to know each other, indeed.* "He also liked the food."

"Oh, brother," Sheila muttered. "All that sizzling masculine sex appeal going to waste."

"Not to mention all your romantic ideas," Leigh drawled, striding to her office and pushing open the door. "By the way," she went on, her voice turning brisk, "check my schedule for Wednesday and rearrange any appointments that could run into or occur just after lunchtime."

Obviously dissatisfied with Leigh's reluctance to further discuss the events of Friday evening, yet evidently deciding against voicing her curiosity, Sheila obliged, freeing the required time on Wednesday.

But being Sheila, she vented after completing the scheduling switch.

"What's up?" she asked, using the excuse of bringing a fresh cup of coffee to enter Leigh's office. "With the scheduling change, I mean."

"St. Claire wants to meet over lunch on Wednesday to negotiate the terms of our contract," Leigh said, grateful for Sheila's initial reticence, however brief in duration.

"But that's good," Sheila said, frowning at Leigh's grim expression. "Isn't it?"

"Not if it annoys a prospective client," Leigh retorted, not about to confide, even to her best friend, her resentment and trepidation regarding St. Claire.

Sheila shrugged. "Not to worry. The prospective client was most accommodating. I scheduled another appointment for her for next week. Okay?"

"Yes, thank you." Pulling her distracted

thoughts together, Leigh stared at the drapery samples strewn across her work table. "Back to work."

Taking the hint, Sheila returned to her own office.

The invitation from Lillian Standfield came midmorning, not by mail, but by phone.

Alerted by Sheila as to the intent of their former client's call, Leigh greeted the older woman, a catch of pleased surprise in her voice.

"Mrs. Standfield, hello. Sheila tells me you're planning an open house this coming Sunday to showcase my work." Leigh laughed, knowing that, uncertain but eager, blurting out her intentions to Sheila was exactly what the lovely but vague woman would do. "Is that correct?"

"Why, yes. But I did want to tell you myself," the other woman said on a fluttery sigh.

"I'm sorry," Leigh murmured, refraining from pointing out that in that case she shouldn't have confided in the younger woman. "But Sheila was so thrilled for me by your generous and thoughtful idea, she just bubbled over with the news," Leigh gently explained.

"Was she? Thrilled, I mean," the elderly

woman asked brightly. "Really?"

"Yes, really." Leigh smiled; she had grown fond of the woman during the months they had worked together. Well, while Leigh had worked, and Mrs. Standfield had fluttered. "And so am I," she went on, "both thrilled and flattered."

"Then you will come?"

Leigh was even more flattered by the woman's eagerness. "Yes, of course. I wouldn't dream of missing it. What time would you like me to be there?"

"Oh." Lillian Standfield actually giggled. "I forgot to mention that, didn't I?"

Leigh didn't answer, which was a good thing, because the woman rattled on, "I'll be serving a light lunch, you know, around two or so — catered, of course — so I posted the hours from one to four on the invitations. Would it be convenient for you to get here a little before one?" she asked, sounding rife with anxious uncertainty.

"That will be fine for me," Leigh assured her.

"Good." Lillian Standfield heaved a deep sigh of relief. "I'll send the car for you, say twelve-fifteen?"

"But that's not necessary," Leigh protested. "I can drive my own —"

Lillian interrupted, in the firmest tone

Leigh had ever heard from her. "I insist. It's the least I can do, as you'll be giving up part of your free day for me."

"Very well," Leigh conceded. "Thank you."

"You are quite welcome. Oh, and if she's free, do bring your receptionist, too," she hastened to add. "She is such a pleasant young woman."

"Yes, she is," Leigh agreed. "And how gracious of you to include her. Since Sheila has been involved with the project from the beginning, I'm sure she'd love to come and see the finished results."

"Would I like to go? And in a chauffeured limo, no less?" Sheila asked a few minutes later, after Leigh had ended the call, then relayed the invitation. "Of course, I would. I'm itching to see what you've done with the place." She grinned, her innocent blue eyes gleaming wickedly. "Besides, the Standfields are old money, and there could be some interesting, not to mention well-off, men there."

Leigh merely shook her head in despair of her friend's wishful thinking. "If you'll recall, the Standfields are both in their seventies. Try not to be too disappointed if the majority of their guests are of a similar age."

"Spoilsport," Sheila groused.

Laughing, her earlier consternation concerning disturbing dreams and her brother's difficulties, even her angst about her Wednesday lunch meeting with Michael St. Claire, relegated to the think-about-it-later compartment of her mind, Leigh returned to her work.

Still in the think-denial mode, she managed to get through Tuesday. Fortunately, her schedule was full, keeping her running between in-office appointments with prospective clients, on-site meetings with contracted clients and contentious telephone consultations with a couple of suppliers. But the weather remained springlike and warm.

By the time Leigh crawled into bed Tuesday night, she could barely think, let alone know angst.

Wednesday, it stormed.

Why not, Leigh grumbled to herself, her stomach muscles cramping as she shifted her gaze from the dark sky beyond her office window to the clock on her desk. It was almost time for her to leave. She would have to take a cab, she decided. No way would she present herself wet and bedraggled, and thus at a disadvantage, to Michael St. Claire.

Hell, she was already at a disadvantage, she reflected fifteen minutes later, dashing from the office and into the cab Sheila had procured for her. She had been at a distinct and uncomfortable disadvantage ever since he'd kissed her.

Stupid, perhaps, but there it was.

And here she was, dashing from the cab to the entrance of the tall office building, huddling beneath an umbrella battered by the deluge of rain, wincing as lightning crackled overhead and thunder rumbled, seeming to shake the pavement beneath her hurried steps.

Water dripped from the tip of her umbrella, leaving a spotted trail across the marble lobby from the doors to the security guard at the bank of elevators.

Once again, the express lift hurtled her to the rarefied atmosphere of the higher floors.

Nervous trepidation stiffening her spine, Leigh stepped from the lift, deposited the sodden umbrella in the brass container supplied for that purpose then, shaking inside though appearing coolly composed, strode to the reception desk.

It was déjà vu — all over again.

The receptionist escorted Leigh to the outer office of the inner sanctum, turned her over into the charming and capable care of the assistant/secretary/whatever, then melted away like morning mist.

Exactly as before, Rosalie, her smile open and friendly, ushered Leigh into St. Claire's sanctorum.

Delayed replay. St. Claire stood framed by the window wall, with the city spread behind for a backdrop, his golden beauty undimmed by the greenish black sky.

Rosalie retreated; Leigh barely noticed. Standing a few feet inside the office door, her legs quivering, her heart racing, but her surface composure intact, she met and returned his direct, searching stare.

The arrested tableau lasted a mere moment, yet within that instant of thrall, an ironic realization flashed through her mind. Beneath the concealment of her raincoat, donned in a moment of sheer and conscious defiance, Leigh had dressed in the very same gray suit she had worn for their previous meeting . . . exactly as before.

Déjà vu, indeed.

Unfortunately, Michael wasn't wearing the same navy blue suit or even the gray he had worn the previous Friday. But the rich, bittersweet chocolate shade of his suit, the chocolate and white striped tie, and the contrasting white on white shirt served to enhance the burnished gold of his skin with equal effect, rather than detracting from it.

Deny it as she might, Leigh felt the effect of his masculine appearance in every living molecule.

"Are you hungry?"

A leading question if she had ever heard one, Leigh thought, suppressing a sudden, unwelcome hunger completely unrelated to food.

"For lunch."

Michael's follow-up comment told her that his train of thought was running along the same tracks as her own. A collision course for certain, she acknowledged, re-solving to throw the switch separating the mental tracks.

"Yes, I am," she said, surprised to find that she was feeling the pangs of a more acceptable hunger. "I skipped breakfast," she admitted, withholding the self-condemning fact that she had been too churned up about their meeting to even dare putting anything in her queasy stomach.

"Then I'd better feed you," he said, crossing to his desk and depressing a button on the intercom. "Rosalie, buzz the kitchen now, please. Ms. Evans and I are ready for lunch. And you can bring the contract in later."

"Yes, sir."

"Contract?" Leigh frowned. "I thought you said this meeting was to discuss the terms of the contract."

"That's right." He nodded.

"But you just told your —"

"It's a form contract, Leigh," he interrupted to explain. "We'll go over it together, fill in some blanks and then the final contract will be drawn." He did his one arched eyebrow number. "Okay?"

Was she being too wary, too suspicious of his motives and intent? Leigh pondered the thought as she stared into his clear, guileless eyes. Uncertain, still wary and no less suspicious, she nevertheless gave a quick nod of reluctant agreement. "Okay."

His smile warm, Michael turned away from the desk. "I think you'd be more comfortable if you'd remove your coat. Don't you?"

"Hmmm," Leigh murmured, also reluctant to reveal the evidence of her admittedly puny and rather childish show of defiance. But she could hardly justify sitting down to lunch wearing a coat — a wet coat, at that. "Yes, of course," she finally said, quickly slipping out of the garment before he could take the steps necessary to assist her.

His smile took on a wry tilt, letting her know he was aware of her evasive tactic.

Plucking the damp coat from her hands, he tossed it over the chair in front of his desk, then swept her form with a glittering glance.

Leigh's spine stiffened and she raised her chin, as if daring him to remark on her attire.

Michael dared. "That suit looks every bit as attractive today as it did the last time we met in this office."

"Thank you," she responded with cool formality.

He looked pensive for a moment, studying her rigid expression. The moment extended, making her more rigid. Beginning to feel that her spine might snap with the tension's pressure, Leigh sighed with relief when he shifted his gaze and made a half-turn away.

"We can eat at the conference table," he said, giving a casual wave of his hand in silent invitation for her to precede him into the connecting room.

The beautifully constructed, highly polished, rectangular wood table could easily accommodate the twelve armed captains' chairs set around it.

Too restless to sit, Leigh bypassed the table and walked to the wide window, every bit as large as the one in St. Claire's office, but offering a slightly different view of the city. The spires of the tall buildings were obscured by enshrouding, low-hanging rain clouds.

"On a clear day, you can see old Billy keeping watch over the city he founded."

Leigh managed — just — not to start at the closeness of Michael's quiet voice, the nearness of his warm body. Resisting the impulse to move, put some breathing distance between them, was difficult. She managed that by concentrating on the comment he'd made, peering into the lowering angry-looking gray mist in the direction he had indicated, at the now cloud-concealed, thirty-seven-foot-tall statue of William Penn standing sentinel atop City Hall.

"I love this city."

That remark, soft as it was, did startle her into turning to look at him. She immediately wished she hadn't. His crystal blue eyes were bright, alive with the emotion he had confessed to so unabashedly.

"Come to that," he said, canting his head to meet her probing gaze, "I love this state."

If he looked like this when expressing love for a city, a state, how would he look if he were genuinely in love with a woman?

Made uneasy by the thought, Leigh dismissed it at once as irrelevant, the very idea of Michael St. Claire experiencing such a

depth of love for a woman was highly un-
likely . . . considering his track record.

"You're a native?" she asked, taking a
casual step to the side, ostensibly to get a
better look at the statue.

"Yes." There was amusement in his voice.
"You?"

Giving up the pretense of trying to see the
statue hidden by cloud cover, Leigh turned
away from the window and him. "Yes, at
least of Pennsylvania," she answered,
strolling to the table and hooking the strap
of her purse on the back of a chair. "I was
born in Lancaster, but Philadelphia has
become my adopted city."

"I was born here," Michael said, sauntering to the chair placed at the head of the
table. "Not in surroundings anywhere near
these," he went on rather drolly, sweeping a
glance around the opulent room. "I came
into the world, and the city, in one of the
less affluent neighborhoods."

"Really?" Leigh was intrigued in spite of
her better judgment, her will to remain aloof.
From everything she had read and heard
about him, Michael St. Claire had never
offered any information to anyone about his
origins. As curious about him as everyone
else, she gave in to an urge to probe.
"Would I recognize the neighborhood?"

His chuckle left her in no doubt that he was aware of her ploy, but it also revealed that he didn't resent it. "Probably." Sliding the chair away from the table, he stood beside it, waiting for her to seat herself.

Tamping down impatience, Leigh chose a seat several feet down the table, removed from him. Ignoring the knowing smile playing over his lips, she gazed at him with what she hoped was an expression of mild interest.

To her frustration, at that moment a door Leigh hadn't even noticed in the far wall opened, and a white-jacketed man pushing a food trolley entered.

"Ah. Here's our lunch," Michael said, unnecessarily as the delectable aroma announced the obvious.

"As ordered, sir." Bringing the cart to a halt next to his employer, the waiter set utensils wrapped in crisp white linen napkins in front of first Leigh and then Michael. They were followed by covered soup dishes.

"Cream of broccoli soup and" — he scooped two luncheon plates off the trolley — "breast of chicken with lettuce sandwiches." He turned back again to the cart for two cups and saucers, a small jug of cream, a container of packets of sugar and sweeteners, and an insulated carafe. "Coffee."

"Perfect. Thank you, Paul."

"You're welcome, Michael," Paul said, sparing a grin for his employer while setting out glasses and filling them with iced water. "Enjoy."

Aware of Michael watching her, Leigh lifted the lid from the soup bowl and inhaled the aromatic steam. "Hmmm," she murmured. "Smells delicious."

"I knew you liked chicken, and could only hope you liked broccoli soup."

She smiled for the first time since arriving at his office. "It's my favorite."

"Serendipity." He smiled back. "Perhaps even more interesting, it's my favorite, too, and yet another thing we have in common."

Pulling off a wry expression with her mouth full of the creamy soup wasn't easy, but Leigh gave it her best shot. She took better aim after swallowing. "I hardly think a similar taste in food portends anything of importance."

"But it could." His tone was dead serious. "I think it portends other similar tastes of major importance."

Pretty certain as to precisely what tastes he had in mind, Leigh thought it prudent to change the subject. "Immaterial. You were telling me about the neighborhood where you were born."

"Was I?" His gaze steady on her, Michael dipped his spoon into his soup, unerringly raising it to his mouth.

Suddenly feeling defensive, and hating it, Leigh shrugged again. "Of course, if you'd rather not . . ." she began, but he silenced her with a sharp hand movement.

"Have you ever been in the area around Ridge Avenue?" His tone was as imperious as his gesture.

Though she frowned at the rudeness of his interruption, she nodded. "Once, soon after I moved here. I drove along a short section of Ridge after making a wrong turn and becoming thoroughly lost. A school crossing guard directed me down Ridge to 676, and from there I was all right."

"Not exactly the scenic route, is it?"

"No." Leigh shook her head, recalling too vividly how shocked she had been at seeing what had appeared an alien place, almost like a war zone, with so many of the buildings boarded up and crumbling; the number of abandoned vehicles, some looking stripped down, others burned out. And she had felt a deep sadness for the people, especially the children, living under such conditions, with no recourse, no means of changing their situation. "It was appalling."

He grimaced. "You don't know the half of it."

"That's where you were born?"

"Yeah — not right there on Ridge, but in the area. We lived there until I was twelve . . . when my mother died."

"Your mother died when you were twelve," Leigh inserted with feeling.

He nodded. "Breast cancer."

Leigh winced. "That had to be rough, terribly frightening for her."

"Yes." The crystal blue of his eyes became cloudy, shaded by painful memories.

Leigh could sympathize, if not empathize, with the horror he had faced at such a young age. "It had to be pretty tough for you, too."

"It was." He sighed. "I adored her."

Experiencing a strange and unfamiliar sensation that she assured herself could not be envy — envy of a woman dead for at least twenty years? Leigh advised herself to back off.

"Your father?" A chancy subject, she knew, but curiosity won out over prudence.

"I never knew him — not even his name." His tone and his smile were both cynical, yet strangely there wasn't a hint of bitterness in them. "The times she mentioned him — and they were brief in number — she spoke of her love for him, never condemning him for leaving her, loving her and leaving her — without a ring on her finger, with a child to raise on her own."

"I'm sorry." Lame, she knew, but it was the only thing she could think to say at that moment.

"For what?"

"For prying," she said, apologetically. "Your history is really none of my business."

Nevertheless, with a half-shrug and a faint smile, he continued. "It's common knowledge that I'm a bastard. So, yes, even before she died, it was always rough. It was not a fun place to be a kid."

"Although I can't personally relate," she said, drawn by his openness to go on. "I can imagine that it would have been pretty awful."

"Awful precisely describes it," he agreed with a brief nod. "And yet, along with the bad elements — the druggies, dealers, hoods — we had some wonderful, caring neighbors, good people in bad straits."

Listening intently, hearing in his controlled tones as much what he didn't say as what he did, Leigh had stopped eating, arrested by a piercing sympathy for the unhappy and probably confused boy he had been then — and for the inner boy he had just revealed, however unwittingly, the twelve-year-old boy who still bore the pain.

Her feelings must have been clearly revealed in her eyes, if not written in boldface in her expression, for Michael jerked erect, as if coming out of a trance.

"Enough of strolling down memory lane." His voice held a thread of self-mockery. "Our soup's getting cold."

Twelve

"Do you have a projected starting date?"

Lunch was over. Both Leigh and Michael had declined dessert when Paul had been in to clear the table, leaving a fresh pot of coffee. Rosalie had already delivered the contract.

Michael had pushed his chair back, stretched out his long legs and, the document in hand, had fired off the question, commencing negotiations.

Too aware of, and much too affected by, the drape of fine wool material over the long, taut muscles of his thighs, Leigh shook her head, cradled her refilled cup in her hands and, standing, retreated to the wide window, putting the illusion of distance between them.

"Not a clue?" he responded to her negative head motion. "Not so much as a hint of a clue?"

Because Leigh didn't have so much as a clue, she tossed an answer of sorts from the top of her head. "Early, or possibly by midsummer."

He frowned.

"That's not acceptable?" she asked him, while wondering if she was deliberately, though subconsciously, trying to lose this contract.

"It's not that, but —"

"I do have other commitments, you know," she interjected. "Projects agreed to before —"

"Yes, I do know," he interrupted. "I wasn't questioning the time frame, but its lack of precision — a date, Leigh, to put in the contract."

How could she lose a contract when he was so easy to get along with? she silently railed, then immediately turned her ire on herself. How could she, for even a minute, think about losing this lucrative contract, especially when her brother was close to drowning in debt?

But, dammit, she didn't want to work in close proximity with this man, didn't want the feelings he aroused in her.

Thanks to her sister-in-law, though, Leigh acknowledged that her choices were limited, unless she was willing to stand by, doing nothing to help while Brett sank in a sea of red ink.

Sometimes life just wasn't fair.

Michael was waiting, watching.

Leigh surrendered. "August first?"

"Fine." He flashed a smile at her. "We're making progress." Still smiling, he bent over the table to pencil the date on the contract.

Feeling the effects of his radiant smile light up dark places inside her, Leigh averted her eyes, lowered her cloudy gaze to the base of the window.

"Now can you project a completion date?"

Leigh frowned.

"It doesn't have to be exact," he said. "Give me your best guess."

"This cries out for a bench," she mused aloud, glancing up from the base of the window to face him. "Or something."

"What?" His baffled expression was almost comical. "What the hell are you talking about?"

With a quick hand motion, Leigh indicated the empty area below the window. "This space is going to waste. The view is so spectacular, there should be a seating arrangement — some chairs, or even better, a long, padded bench seat."

"Ummm, I see." His lips twitched.

Leigh felt the movement, his amusement, to the tips of her unpolished fingernails.

An odd sensation in response to a little twitch, she reflected, frowning. She could be in big trouble here. She was unsuccessful in repressing a sigh.

"Nothing to get bent out of shape about." Silent laughter betraying his soothing tone, he set the pencil aside. Pulling his legs back, he unfolded himself from the chair with the clear intent to join her at the window.

Leigh's stomach muscles clenched in an even odder sensation. Fighting an urge to back away, run away, she stood firm, determined to at least appear unaffected by his nearness, the scent of him, the sheer sexual magnetism of him.

"If you happen to come across suitable chairs," he murmured, so close his breath feathered the short hairs at her temple, "or even better, a padded bench that catches your fancy, order one and send the bill to me."

His laughter-shaded voice stirred anger — and something else, something she refused to recognize. There were undertones here that had nothing whatever to do with chairs, benches or the contract supposedly under discussion. Sexual overtones that shouldn't — but did — stir excitement deep inside her.

Feeling threatened, but defiant, Leigh latched onto the anger, let it stiffen her spine, chill her eyes, frost her voice. "Are you enjoying yourself?"

"Not yet." Heated crystal blue speared into frosty green. "But I have hopes in that direction."

There it was, no longer an undertone. For all intents and purposes, his purposes, Michael might as well have declared his *hope* of seducing her.

If she was ever going to do it, now was the time to bolt, escape before it was too late. She didn't need to define "too late." Her rioting hormones were making the definition as crystal clear as his eyes.

Her body wanted his.

Her mind rebelled, urging her to tell him to take his contract and shove it.

Brett.

Oh, hell.

"Hello?" Michael's soft voice silenced the clamor inside her head. "Is anybody home?"

Warily eyeing the beautiful being tormenting her, conflict taxing her mind, Leigh held out for clarification.

"Exactly what direction do you mean?"

"Come on, Leigh," he chided, raising a hand to draw one long finger from her cheekbone to the corner of her mouth. "You know. For all your defensive tactics, you're as sexually attracted to me as I am to you."

"No." Her voice was a mere croak and contained little conviction.

"Yes." His finger moved again, outlining her bottom lip. "Fight it if you will, as long as you must, but sooner or later, we're going to wind up in bed together." He ignored her gasp of protest as his finger probed at her lips, seeking entrance into her mouth. "My hope is for sooner." With slow deliberation, he lowered his head, aiming for her mouth.

"You . . . you . . ." Leigh dragged a breath into her constricted chest, frantically seeking words to stop him. "This — this is blatant harassment."

"I don't think so." His breath feathered her lips; her spine, her legs weakened, went soft at the wafting warmth. "Not harassment, but blatant hunger." His lips brushed hers, once, twice. "Mine . . . and yours."

Leigh's mind, and resistance, went as soft and weak as her extremities. Her lips parted.

"Yes," Michael persisted, his lips within a sigh of hers. "Mutual hunger," he murmured an instant before taking her into his arms, then claiming her mouth with his own.

His kiss was the complete opposite of the previous Friday night's. Commanding, demanding, his mouth ravaged Leigh's lips with gentle insistence.

She resisted, stiffening her body in rejection, telling herself she was outraged at his audacity. And then his tongue laved her lips, before thrusting deep into her mouth.

Suddenly, the fight and the breath went out of her. Her senses imploded, her nerve endings quivered, her mind swam in a backwash of sensuality.

Her back tingled to the touch of his hand stroking the length of her spine. Excitement-generated warmth flared to sizzling life at the apex of her thighs in response to the pressure of his hand, pulling her up and into the heat and hardness of his body.

Sensations reigned, sensations unlike anything Leigh had ever dreamed or imagined.

Her resistence evaporated. Her body softened, molding to the hard strength of his. Her hungry lips clung to his firm, devastating mouth, surrendering to his demands, drinking in the taste of his raw sexuality.

Like a famished woman invited to a lavish buffet, Leigh couldn't get enough of him. Her mouth devoured his, her tongue raked his, her body craved —

The probing thrust of his erection speared the sensuous veil clouding her mind.

Madness.

The inner indictment restored her senses and sense, giving her the strength and impetus to tear her mouth from his.

"No," she cried, jerking back, out of his arms, away from his imposing form. "Damn you. Damn you to hell, Michael St. Claire." She stumbled in her haste to distance herself from him. "If I were a man, I'd . . . I'd . . . punch your damned lights out."

Hours later, still stunned, Leigh sat at her desk, staring into the middle distance, kiss-shocked, undone, her quivering body craving, craving.

The effects of that light brush of mouth against mouth on Friday night had been as water to champagne in comparison to the effects of the trauma incurred today.

Never could she have imagined, nor would she have believed, the power-punch possible in one meeting of two pairs of lips, the tangling of two tongues, the ramifications inherent in a serious, no-holds-barred kiss and tight embrace.

The startling experience had both thrilled and alarmed her. To the extent that she had not only flung herself away from him, cursed him, but then *had* literally bolted.

The details of her flight were fuzzy. All Leigh could recall of it was tearing her mouth from the sweet seduction of his lips, pulling out of the protective haven of his arms, damning him, not once but twice, but then scooping up first her handbag, then her raincoat as she ran from him, out of the office and past a wide-eyed Rosalie, as if pursued by demons from hell.

When in truth, Michael's kiss had been pure heaven.

The pleasure Leigh had derived from his ravaging mouth, the feel of his hard body impressed against the softness of hers, instilled in her the self-damning realization that she was not immunized, but every bit as vulnerable as every woman, any woman . . . her mother.

That was the terrifying reality.

It didn't bear thinking about, and yet, it was all Leigh seemed capable of dwelling on.

The sound of the outer office door opening, then closing, heralding Sheila's return from lunch, succeeded in drawing Leigh from her disturbing introspection.

She had no time for emotional delving, she chided herself. She had work to do.

Intent on distraction, Leigh never even thought to alert Sheila to the fact that she also had returned.

"Holy freaking hell."

Unaware he'd spoken the soft exclamation aloud, Michael stood at the window, in the exact spot Leigh had occupied such a short time ago, his body hard and aching, his senses alive and jangling, his mind rattled by the emotional fallout of a brief embrace, one kiss.

"Whoa," he whispered, laughing as he raked a hand through his hair. "Talk about the earth moving." He absently noted that the sky had cleared to a rain-washed blue. The storm had passed — outside, if not within him.

The storm raging inside him piqued Michael's curiosity as well as his intellect. It stirred him to introspection.

He had met, had known, countless numbers of women, some as acquaintances, some as friends, some as lovers. He had enjoyed knowing them, had appreciated their uniquely feminine beauty, their conversation, their willing and eager bodies.

Yet, never, had he met, known, made love with any woman who'd had an impact on him like Leigh Evans. And all he had shared with her was one near and one real kiss, one brief, wildly arousing embrace.

And Leigh had wanted him, as well. The sweet surrender of her mouth to his, of her soft body to the hardness of his, had canceled all doubt in his mind.

And, from the near violence she had revealed when she'd pulled away from him and stormed out, it would appear the lady had a temper secreted within her icy shell.

The consideration didn't deter Michael. On the contrary, it added an edge to the excitement.

He had to have her, this woman with a banked blaze inside that matched her fire-streaked hair.

Whatever it took, he would see to it that the suppressed heat inside the seemingly so cool and remote Leigh Evans would be his, to touch, to taste, to quench.

Michael was more than a trifle surprised — rather amazed, actually — by the demands of his body, the fierce determination fueling his thoughts.

A frown tugged at the bridge of his patrician nose. He had desired many things in his life, and had acquired most of them. But not since he was a kid, with his big eyes fastened longingly on a candy counter, had Michael wanted anything quite so desperately as he wanted Leigh.

A thought came to him, clearing his brow of the frown.

When Barbara learned of the depth of his desire, his determination to appease it, she would likely crow with delight.

At picturing that scene, he laughed so hard the sound bounced off the paneled walls. His mirth was swiftly stifled by the opening of his office door.

"Michael," Rosalie called from the doorway.

"I'm in the conference room," he said, strolling into the connecting office. "What's up?"

"Ms. Evans . . ." Rosalie frowned. "I mean, the way she rushed out past me. Was she feeling ill?"

"No." Michael shook his head, smiling at the thought that Leigh was not ill at all, but perhaps a bit pressured and aroused, and possibly even confused by the arousal. Well, he fully intended to increase that pressure — and the arousal — until she gave up all pretense of aloofness and freely admitted that her desire for him equaled his for her.

"She suddenly realized the time, and recalled that she had another appointment," he improvised.

"Oh." She looked relieved. "Had you concluded the contract negotiations?"

"Not quite," he said, forestalling an offer from her to take the form and have it drawn into the final contract. "But we can finish up over the phone," he said, deciding on the

spot to call Leigh the minute Rosalie returned to her desk. "I'll hand it to you
before you leave this afternoon."

"Very good." Smiling, she sent a critical
gaze around the room. "I'm anxious for her
to get started."

"So am I," he murmured, moving to his
desk. "This place is about as warm and personal as a doctor's waiting room — chic,
and attractive but clinical."

Laughing, Rosalie went back to her desk.

Laughing to himself, but for a different
reason, Michael lifted the receiver of his
direct-line phone.

"Good afternoon, Interiors by Leigh,"
the perky blond receptionist chirped. "May
I help you?"

"Hello, yourself," Michael said, smiling
as he envisioned the bubbly young woman.
"This is Michael St. Claire, may I speak to
Leigh, please?"

There ensued a brief pause. Then, in
tones of pure bafflement, Sheila sputtered,
"But . . . but . . . Mr. St. Claire, Leigh is in
your office. Isn't she?"

"No, she left a short time ago," he replied.
"I just thought of something we overlooked
during our negotiations, and I'd like to con-
sult with her about it."

"Oh, I see." Another pause. "I don't hear

anything from her office, but I'll buzz her for you."

His lips twitched. "Thank you."

A moment later, he heard a click, and then Leigh's voice, sounding a little strained and frayed. "This is Leigh Evans, how may I help you?"

"It's Michael."

She wasn't quick enough to stifle a ragged-sounding sigh. But she rallied enough to zing off a brisk demand. "What do you want, Mr. St. Claire?"

"A leading question," he dryly observed. "And the name's Michael," he chided.

"Michael," she dutifully repeated, ignoring his initial remark. "What do you want?" she bravely repeated.

He deemed it wise not to push the issue by being explicit, at least in regard to his personal wants. "We didn't complete the details of the contract."

"I don't know how long it will take me to finish," she snapped, sounding really frazzled. "There are too many variables to allow a certain date."

He was getting to her. The thought instilled in him a deep and exciting sense of accomplishment. Michael decided he could afford to be expansive.

"All right, Leigh, I'll leave the completion

date open," he offered. "Now, about your fee . . ."

"I . . . I . . ." She came to an abrupt halt for a moment, then soldiered on. "I haven't worked out the figures yet."

"Okay, maybe I can help," he soothed, before tossing caution to the wind and throwing out a figure guaranteed to blow her mind.

"Are you serious?" she asked in awed tones of sheer disbelief.

"Yes."

"But I can't accept."

"Why?" he asked, interrupting her.

"Why?" she echoed, hollowly. "Because . . . because, it's way too much, that's why." He could hear her draw a quick breath before rushing on, "And it smacks suspiciously of a bribe, an excessive payment for more than professional decorator services rendered."

Michael went stiff with affront; he had never offered a woman payment for . . .

Then he had to smile, conceding that Leigh Evans was one shrewd lady; she used well all the weapons available to her. "Not if I'm willing to pay it for purely professional decorator services rendered," he pointed out in reasonable tones. "And I am."

"But —"

"Negotiations closed." He'd again interrupted her. "Now all you need do is present yourself here, in my office, next Monday, for lunch — and to sign on the dotted line, of course."

"Really, Michael, I —"

"Goodbye, Leigh." Tingling with anticipation, Michael disconnected.

His private-line phone rang mere seconds after he had replaced the receiver.

Damned if he didn't sometimes wonder if the woman was a witch, Michael mused, chuckling as he allowed it to ring three times before answering.

"Hello, Barbara," he drawled into the receiver, settling deeper into his chair for the long haul. "What's on your devious mind?"

"You know full well what it is," she retorted. "Is it a done deal?"

"Just about," Michael answered, unsuccessful at keeping the silent laughter out of his voice.

"What does that mean, for God's sake?" Her irritation zipped along the line and into his ear. "Dammit, Michael, either you have an agreement or you don't."

Wincing, grinning, he pulled the receiver a scant half-inch away. "We have an agreement," he assured her. "Now, all that remains is for the final contract to be drawn and signed."

"Oh." Her raspy voice had lost its bite.

"Oh, indeed," Michael drawled, chuckling. "Not to worry, my darling, your plan is working," he said, trawling the motive waters to see if she'd rise to the bait.

"Plan? What plan are you referring to?"

Musing that Barbara's tone was so sweetly innocent he'd be lucky not to suffer an attack of sugar overdose, Michael held back a bark of delighted laughter.

"Ah, my beloved, it's a good thing you're a top-notch accountant, because you are a lousy actress. You know damn well what plan. I'm referring to your transparent machinations designed to arouse my interest, not to mention my libido, regarding the designer . . . one Leigh Evans."

"Michael, really!" She sounded shocked, crushed by his accusation, a sure indication that she was acting, and badly. "I never —"

"That's right, you never have." He cut her off with ruthless intent. "*Before*. And so, while the lady in question definitely has managed to arouse my respect, interest *and* my libido," he freely admitted, "you have aroused my curiosity. Forgive me for being blunt, perhaps even crude, darling, but why have you now, at this late hour, decided to stick your nose into my personal sexual life?"

"That is crude," she chastised, feigning offense but revealing amusement. "One might even say repulsive."

"Yeah?" he shot back, enjoying their little conversational war immensely. "Then I'll go you one better. Have you suddenly decided to spice up your workaholic existence by pandering for me?"

"Michael!" Barbara's burst of throaty laughter exploded in his head. "You're incorrigible."

"Cute, too," he wryly confessed, drawing another peal of laughter from her. "But that's beside the point."

Barbara's exuberant mirth had triggered a bout of coughing. When it subsided, she gasped, "What point was that?"

Michael heaved a sigh she couldn't miss hearing. "Your taking on the dubious role of Cupid."

"Oh, that." Her sigh echoed his and rang clear with heartfelt concern. "I worry about you."

"Slow news day," he countered. "You've been worrying about me, unnecessarily so, for close to, too close to, twenty years now. The claim of worry won't wash, darling. Give up the pretense and get real."

"I love you so very much," she murmured, her raspy voice thick with affection.

"I know that, Barbara," he murmured back, his own affection for her tightening his throat. "And I thank God for it, and for sending you to me to save me from myself."

"You were a good boy, Michael," she avowed. "And you've grown into a fine man."

"Hah," he hooted in ridicule. "I was a street rat, on a direct and slippery slope to the slammer, and you know it." He shook his head in remembered despair of his days on the street, dodging, scrambling to get out of there without a rap sheet if possible, and with at least a scrap of integrity intact. "If it hadn't been for you . . ." He paused to swallow, emotion clogging his throat. "If you hadn't found me, taken an interest, allowed me to clean up my act —"

"Which you have done, to the everlasting benefit of dozens of youngsters in situations very similar to those you experienced." Barbara's voice was even huskier than usual. "All of whom, thanks to your generous educational endowments and grants, have, and will continue to have the opportunity to go on to college or technical schools and to a brighter future."

Michael shifted restlessly in his chair. He

could handle and accept Barbara's praise for his business acumen, but commendation for the endowments and grants he'd funded anonymously, under the auspices of The Mary Margaret Klare Foundation for underprivileged kids, made him uncomfortable. Thanks primarily to Barbara, he had so much now, much more than he needed or could ever possibly use.

"My contributions are merely a result of, and a demonstration of, my gratitude for the interest you took in me, Barbara," he muttered, turning the focus back on her. "My small way of paying back, for all —"

"And I'm still interested, Michael," she inserted, her emotion-roughened voice betraying the tears in her eyes. "And that's why I suddenly, as you so indelicately phrased it, decided to stick my nose into your personal sexual life."

He frowned, admitted, "You lost me, Barbara. I don't understand how your interest coincides with —"

"You're not getting younger, you know," she cut in, her voice now impatient.

"Don't spread it around, will you?" he asked, injecting some humor to lighten the atmosphere.

She laughed, then immediately returned to the point. "It's time, past time, for you to settle down, Michael."

Dead stop. Astounded by the intent expressed in Barbara's statement, Michael went blank for a full thirty seconds. Then he erupted into laughter.

"You think it's time I found a permanent bed partner and got myself shackled?" he said, when he could finally speak around his laughter.

"It's not funny, Michael," she said, repressively.

"Sure it is," he insisted, shaking his head. "And that's why you steered me toward Leigh Evans?"

"Well, of course." Her cool, superior tones sent him into another fit of laughter. "And I was straight on in my evaluation of her, wasn't I?" she continued with commendable calm. "You're desperate to have her, practically pawing like an aroused bull on the ground she walks on."

Michael stopped laughing because, damned if her analogy wasn't right on target. He *was* near desperate to have her — no, he was determined to have her.

But on a permanent basis?

Orange blossoms and wedding bells and all that crap?

Michael shuddered. It didn't bear thinking about.

Then why was he doing so?

"Oh, Mi-chael," Barbara's rough, crooning voice grated on a suddenly exposed nerve. "Why so quiet, darling? Caught your attention, have I?"

"You're nuts, you know that?" he retaliated. "Marriage is the last thing on my mind."

"I know," she went on, in that same aggravating croon. "That's why I thought it was time for me to do something . . . stick my nose in, as it were."

"Yeah, well you can just retreat, Babsy," he growled. "I'll happily, thankfully, accept your guidance, your invaluable advice in anything and everything but this. I'll decide when I'm ready, and I'll pick the woman. Got that?"

"Yes, Michael," she answered meekly. Then growled back at him, "And don't call me Babsy."

"Dammit," he muttered. "Why don't *you* get married, and stop worrying about me?"

"Me?" She laughed. "To whom, for Pete's sake?"

"Shamus Clancy." Michael put voice to the image that immediately filled his mind.

Silence. Ominous silence. Michael felt contrite — mean and contrite. He braced himself for a blast of anger. He never expected, and so was both astonished and shaken by her soft sorrowful outcry.

"I'm too old for him."

"Barbara sweetheart, that's not true." He ached for her, and felt impatient with her. "There are not that many years difference between you two. And what the hell difference does it make, anyway? He cares for you."

"He doesn't. He can't." Her voice was rougher, raspier than normal. "He calls me 'Her Highness.' I know, because I overheard him say it."

"With affection," Michael insisted. "Always with affection. Do me a favor. Next time you visit me, cut him some slack . . . and see what happens. Will you do that?"

"We'll see."

"Barbara."

"Now who's sticking their nose in?" she chided him, her voice and manner back to normal. "Let's make a pact to mind our own love lives. Okay?"

"It's a deal," he agreed, grinning again. "Now, darling, I'm wrung out from this emotionally enervating conversation, so please say goodbye like a good little mentor, so I don't have to hang up on you."

"Goodbye, Michael," she said obediently, her light tones proclaiming restored humor. "I'll see you at the Standfield open house on Sunday."

"Right," he said. "See you then."

Sunday, he thought, cradling the receiver. Sunday . . . and Leigh.

Thirteen

Sunday dawned clear, bright and warm. By one-thirty in the afternoon, the indicator on the thermometer hovered at seventy, promising a perfect spring day.

Her cheeks a rosy hue in reaction to the praise being heaped upon her by Lillian Standfield's guests, Leigh wandered through the second floor of the spacious old house, pausing to chat and graciously accept accolades from individuals and groups strolling about the recently decorated bedrooms and baths.

"Beautiful woman."

The color bloomed brighter on Leigh's cheeks on overhearing the remark from an elderly gentleman as she walked by.

"Elegant, really," his companion murmured, but not softly enough to keep Leigh from hearing.

Leigh was both pleased and embarrassed by the compliments she had received, on her work and her appearance, to her face as well as indirectly.

Her work was on display, for all to see and judge. What she had not so much as considered was that she would be on display too.

After some lengthy indecision concerning her attire for the open house, Leigh was now glad she had settled on the loose silky pants, combined with a thigh-length white lacy tunic worn over a white silk camisole. Now, she was glad that, prior to leaving her apartment, and mere moments before the car had arrived to pick her up, she had kicked off her low-heeled shoes in favor of black evening sandals with spiky heels.

Finding herself near the rear staircase after making a complete tour of the rooms, Leigh descended to the kitchen, which proved to be a veritable beehive of preluncheon preparation activity.

Unobtrusively, the caterer's people moved around like a well-orchestrated dance troupe, setting out serving trays and dishes filled with delectable canapés, delicate finger sandwiches and other assorted goodies, and zipping back and forth between the kitchen and dining room.

Observing their coordinated movements, Leigh smiled. She felt surprisingly good, all things considered.

Of course, all those things concerned the inner physical and emotional chaos she had suffered every day since her meeting with St. Claire.

Stepping forward, she took a plump purple olive from a cut crystal relish plate, then quickly stepped back, out of the line of traffic. Nibbling at the olive, she contemplated her angst.

But how could she have known or so much as suspected the soft core of weakness hidden inside her? Leigh had asked herself that innumerable times over the previous days. Believing herself impervious to any masculine advances, her defenses unbreachable, she had strode forth, unafraid to meet any man on his own arrogantly claimed turf.

So how could she have guessed that she'd prove susceptible to the raging desire that blue-eyed devil in the disguise of an angel had fired in her senses, her mind, her body?

Leigh had spent those intervening days in a mental cauldron of fury, despair and frustration. She had nearly worn out the lid of her mother's music box with her continual opening and closing of it.

She hadn't dared to take so much as a peek at the guardian angel picture she'd shoved into the closet. It would have been redundant had she done so, for the living prototype of the picture made nightly visits.

And all the while, throughout her waking moments and her dreams, female hormones tormented her body, screaming in silent demand for the fulfillment of his touch, his kiss, his physical possession.

Incensed, Leigh had waged war with herself, her awakened sexuality, her vulnerability. Mentally feinting and dodging, she had exhausted herself with work, in the office and on client sites during the day, in her apartment in the evenings. Never had her clothes hamper been so empty, her living quarters so spotlessly clean.

To no avail . . . Until she got really mad, at St. Claire, surely, but mostly at herself.

Okay, she admitted, her body was giving her hell with demands for long overdue releases. So what? As she saw it, at two A.M. Sunday morning, she had two choices. She could continue to be a slave to her physical urges, or she could apply her intellect and common sense by owning up to those urges, then rising above them.

Being the person she was, Leigh set her mind on rising above the base physical demands. Come next Wednesday, she promised herself, she would make certain she kept a safe distance from the magnetic mine field of the sensual allure of the so attractive Michael St. Claire.

Having determined to be, if not stronger, at least as strong as the formidable St. Claire, Leigh had at last plunged into the restful depths of dreamless slumber.

She had awakened a little after eleven that morning, renewed, refreshed, rearmed and ready to again face the imminent open house . . . whatever life, and her rebelling body, had to throw at her, St. Claire notwithstanding.

Popping the last bit of olive into her mouth, Leigh stepped forward to follow a line of servers into the dining room, a smile curving her lips as she noticed Sheila, hungrily eyeing the food being placed on the table.

"Tempting, isn't it," she said, coming to a stop beside the smaller woman.

Starting, Sheila swung around and grinned at her. "Looks good enough to eat." She swept a quick glance over Leigh's tall form. "Come to think of it, so do you," she said, laughing. "I'm surprised you're not surrounded by a bunch of hungry-looking males."

"Males come in bunches?" Leigh asked, widening her eyes in contrived innocence. "Like bananas or grapes?"

"Past their sell date," Sheila retorted, making a face. "You were right, as usual, darn it," she groused. "I have yet to see a man here under sixty."

"But the food looks good," Leigh reminded her.

"Sure does," Sheila agreed, shifting her gaze back to the table. "Do you have any idea when they're going to invite the guests to partake?"

"As soon as they finish setting everything out," Leigh guessed.

Sheila sighed. "I'm starving."

Laughing, Leigh grasped her friend's arm to lead Sheila away from temptation. "Come along, we'll mingle, be scintillating, until luncheon is announced."

Though Sheila allowed herself to be hustled from the room, she complained all the way, through the doorway and across the foyer which — Leigh had decided this on her first day there — had more the look of a spacious reception hall found in small castles or large manor houses.

"Now we'll probably be last on line," Sheila was muttering as they stepped through the double-wide entranceway into the long living room, only to break off with a gasp.

Leigh turned to her in concern. "What is it?" she asked, anxious about the girl's wide-eyed, arrested expression. "What's wrong?"

"Oh, my heart," Sheila murmured.

"Your heart," Leigh yelped, concern escalating to near panic. "Sheila, what is wrong?"

"The only thing that ever took my breath away was a sudden, unexpected sharp pain," she answered in a strange, awestruck tone. "But I have never experienced the sensation of having my breath cut off by the sight of a man."

"A man?" Leigh demanded, relief mingling with the deflated feeling coursing through her. Frowning, she shot a glance around, noting the advanced age of the men in their immediate vicinity. "What man?"

"That one over there," Sheila murmured, her glassy-eyed gaze fixed on the far corner of the room. "The one standing by the French doors to the garden. That fabulous man talking to Michael St. Claire."

St. Claire? Here? Leigh's own breath caught in her throat. Whipping around, she stared at the direction Sheila had mentioned. As her disbelieving gaze landed none too gently on the trio standing to one side of the French doors, her eyes filled with the image of the tall man whose golden beauty was burnished by the slanting afternoon sunrays. She took scant notice of the woman with him, or the man next to him, the man who had so strangely affected Sheila.

Lord, he was gorgeous. The mere sight of him rattled her, played hell with her senses, undermined her will and her determination to resist his sensual attraction.

Breathless barely described Leigh at that moment.

"Do you know who he is?"

Sheila's eager question snagged Leigh's wandering mind, jolted her from her reverie and diverted her attention from St. Claire to the other man.

With shaming reluctance, Leigh shifted her gaze to the cause of Sheila's hyper-animation. While tall himself, the man had not attained Michael's intimidating height, and his full head of hair was more tawny than gold. In her opinion, though very good-looking, the man fell short of St. Claire's perfection of features.

"Well . . . ?" Sheila asked with avid interest.

"No," Leigh admitted, startled when her friend grabbed her arm, propelling her along as she moved toward the trio. "What are you doing?" she asked in soft protest.

"You have to ask?" Sheila threw her a quick, astonished look. "We're going to join them, of course — so Mr. St. Claire can introduce us to that delicious man."

"And what if that delicious man belongs to that lovely woman with them?" Leigh demanded, her voice lowering to a terse whisper as they drew closer to the trio.

"I just might kill myself," Sheila muttered, her bright smile belying the genuine despair in her voice.

Leigh didn't smile, she couldn't. She didn't want to approach the three people now looking expectantly at her and Sheila, either, but she had no choice, she and her idiotic assistant had arrived.

"Ah, here's the woman of the hour," Michael urbanely drawled, smiling at Leigh, then sharing the smile with Sheila. "My compliments on an excellent job, Leigh. I gather, from what Barbara here" — he inclined his head at the woman beside him — "has told us, you have turned this formally humdrum house into a showplace."

"Thank you." Leigh spared a faint smile for him before turning to the other, and as Leigh could now see, older woman. "And thank you . . . Barbara?"

"Yes, Barbara . . ." She extended her right hand.

"Sorry," Michael interjected. "Please, allow me."

Her smile wry and dry, the woman, still lovely even up close, gave him a nod of assent.

His eyes dancing with inner amusement, for reasons beyond Leigh at the moment, he said, "Our designer, Leigh Evans, and her assistant, Ms. Porter." He switched his gaze and raised a brow. "Sheila, isn't it?"

"Yes," the blonde replied, her voice thin and reedy, her blue eyes bright with expectancy as she slanted a sidelong glance at the man next to him.

Michael's lips twitched, but he soldiered on. "Ladies, my friend, Barbara Saunders." The twitch at his lips curved into a soft smile for the woman before tightening a fraction as he turned to the other man. "And her friend, Mr. Jake Jenson."

Handshakes and pleasantries were exchanged, compliments were heaped upon Leigh's head by both Barbara Saunders and Jake Jenson, Barbara's friend.

Leigh had not missed the slight tightening of Michael's lips, or the light emphasis he had used in his reference to *her* friend. His tone, in conjunction with the softness of his smile for Barbara, along with the familiar, intimate and somewhat proprietorial appearance of the woman's hand on his arm, gave Leigh pause.

Were Michael and Barbara . . . ?

Leigh banished the thought. It was none of her business. Besides, she assured herself, she didn't care. Michael's women were his . . .

Oh, God, she felt sick.

Despite her sudden attack of misery, Leigh vaguely heard the genial conversation between Sheila and Michael and his companions.

To her dismay, she did catch several remarks, which only added to her misery.

"What do you think, darling?" From Barbara to Michael.

And, a moment later:

"An excellent suggestion, sweetheart." From Michael back to Barbara.

After that, Leigh blocked out distinct words and voices.

Her first indication of the current crux of the discussion came to her as a verbal nudge from the young woman she had believed was her friend.

"Ready, Leigh?" Sheila's voice shimmered with unsuppressed excitement.

Ready? For what? Keeping her cool with applied effort, Leigh turned a questioning look on the blonde.

"Luncheon is served," Sheila explained, a tiny frown drawing her pale brows together. "We're going in together to get on line. Are you ready?"

They were entering the dining area as a party of five, Michael and his friends, her and Sheila?

No, Leigh thought at once. But then, gazing into Sheila's sparkling eyes, she thought again.

"Of course," she answered, nearly choking on the brief words of acceptance.

Shelia's smile was brilliant.

Though sorely tempted to advise her to get real, Leigh knew her advice would fall on her smitten friend's deaf ears, she heaved a silent sigh of despair and fell into step with the group as they moved to join the other guests making for the dining room.

The appetite that had induced Leigh to snitch an olive earlier had completely vanished. When the forward-inching queue brought her to the table, she viewed with disfavor the lavish array of finger sandwiches, canapés, fancy cookies and desserts, the trays of fresh vegetables and fruits with accompanying dips and sauces.

"Not hungry, Leigh?" Michael murmured from behind her — too close behind her.

Braving a look at him, Leigh found him musing on the scant contents of her luncheon plate: three purple olives, two shrimp canapés and one small wedge of Havarti.

"Not very," she replied, raising her shoulders slightly. Then, taking notice of his own sparsely filled plate, she observed, "It appears you aren't, either."

"Oh, but I am." He grinned as he speared a fat red strawberry from a tray, dipped it into a deep dark chocolate sauce and, with obvious relish, sheared the sweet in two with a snap of his perfect white teeth. Then, catching her off guard, he popped the remaining half into her mouth.

Leigh was left with two choices. She could eat the damn thing, or embarrass herself by spitting it out.

She ate the chocolate-coated fruit. It was delicious and tasted like more. But nothing short of a direct command from the Almighty would have compelled her to secure and dip another strawberry.

"Temptation is . . . tempting . . . isn't it?" he murmured, his silky voice shivering down her spine.

Choosing not to respond, to either the tingling sensation, his comment or his suggestive tone of voice, Leigh moved forward along the table, then paused to deliberately select another canapé.

"Don't overdo," he murmured, sticking close to her side. "You wouldn't want to ruin your dinner."

Dinner? Leigh shot a frown at him, but before she could question the remark, he grasped her arm to draw her out of line and away from the table.

"What are you doing?" she demanded, bristling at this presumptuous action.

"Saving your appetite," he said, smiling as without breaking stride he urged her from the room.

Leigh dug in her heels in the foyer, refusing to take another step until he explained. "Okay, what's this all about, Mr. St. Claire?"

He gave her a chiding smile and a soft, patient reminder, "Michael."

If Leigh hadn't been holding the plate, she would have planted her hands on her hips in sheer exasperation. Come to that, she railed in silent frustration, if they hadn't had an audience of milling guests, she might have screamed at him. As it was, she made the feelings known by glaring at him.

"What, precisely," she hissed through gritted teeth, "did you mean by your obscure reference to dinner and saving my appetite?"

He pulled a patently fake expression of surprise. "Why, don't tell me you've forgotten our collective decision to go on to dinner from here?"

"Collective decision?" Leigh repeated, confused and agitated. "What collective decision?"

Michael made a tsking sound, and shook his head, as if in despair of her inattention.

Fighting against an impulse to slug him, Leigh was reduced to conveying her escalating aggravation by tapping one foot on the parquet floor.

He got the message. A suspicious tremor on his lips, he finally explained, "The decision reached before lunch was announced, the agreement made for all of us to go on to dinner together after we leave here."

Leigh's stomach sank, while her pulses leaped. She recalled no such agreement, but then, consumed by her physical reaction to his proximity, and the dreadful sense of dejection she'd suffered from hearing the endearments exchanged between him and Barbara, she hadn't been paying much attention to the discussion.

Damn.

Michael was smiling benignly at her.

Leigh targeted her curse. *Damn* him. She couldn't go. Hadn't she determined to distance herself from him? she asked herself. She had. Besides, how could she endure witnessing the obvious affection shared by Michael and Barbara?

That settled it. She simply wouldn't go, and that was that.

"Jake has made the restaurant reservation," Michael appeared happy to inform her, as though he had tapped into her thought process.

"When?" she asked, her tone charged with skepticism. "I didn't see him leave the room to make a call."

"Really?" he drawled, arching that one blasted brow. "But then, by your own admission, you didn't hear most of the conversation either, did you?"

Leigh was beginning to feel conspicuous, standing there in the center of the foyer, holding a plate of untouched food, and yet she wouldn't back down. "Even so, I couldn't have missed seeing him leave the room."

"Granted." He nodded in agreement; then he smoothly continued to demolish her argument. "But Jake didn't leave the room or even move away. He used his cell phone."

Had her earlier distraction been that intense? Though it riled her to acknowledge it, even to herself, Leigh silently admitted it probably had been, thanks to the disturbing man now doing his male manipulation game and the older but depressingly still lovely woman he called his *friend*.

Well, she thought, resentment simmering inside her, she wasn't playing along, her senses, her emotions, couldn't take the strain.

"I see." She was proud of the cool tone she'd managed. Casually stepping aside, she set her plate on the credenza against the wall, gliding her fingertips over the smooth, glossy surface. It was a beautiful piece of furniture, hand crafted and carved. Leigh had found the piece in an out-of-the-way shop in Lancaster County. In a strange way, touching the wood put her in touch with herself, as an interior designer and as a person. It renewed her strength, her conviction.

Her smile was serene when she turned back to face Michael. "But as you noted before, I'm not hungry, so I'll give dinner a skip."

Moving in on her, Michael set his plate next to hers. "Too bad," he said, his tone matching hers for coolness. "It's really a shame for your young friend, though."

Conviction wavered, as did her cool. "What are you talking about?"

"Sheila, naturally," he answered, with a quick, sorrowful-looking shake of his head. "She was all for the idea. Delighted actually."

"So?" Leigh prompted, knowing it was a mistake.

"So, didn't she accompany you here today?"

"Yes, we both came in the car the Standfields sent," she reluctantly admitted. "But —"

"Pity." His gleaming eyes telegraphed his intent. "Under the circumstances, I feel certain she'll feel constrained about joining us for dinner, if you don't. And I'm afraid she's going to be disappointed."

Fourteen

Leigh agreed to dinner.

They all, Michael, Barbara and Jake, lingered, waiting along with Leigh and Sheila until the last guest departed the Standfield house.

"I'll ring the garage for the car," Lillian graciously offered, starting for the house phone resting on the very same credenza on which Leigh had set her untouched plate of food nearly three hours before.

"That won't be necessary," Michael said, halting the woman in midstep. "Mr. Jenson and I will see that Leigh and Sheila get home safely."

Leigh didn't want to join the group for dinner. She wanted to go home. Having had some time to reevaluate her compliance, she longed to demur, yet knew she couldn't. She didn't have the heart to shoot down Sheila's soaring spirits.

A moment of animated discussion ensued after they took their leave of the charming and grateful elderly couple. The discussion revolved around the two cars available, Michael's Cadillac and Jake's equally roomy

Lexus, and who was going to ride with whom.

In the end, Michael again decided the issue by imperiously assigning bodies to vehicles.

Against her better judgment, and feeling outshuffled by a pro, Leigh found herself belted into the gray, glove-leather seat next to St. Claire.

She had argued for staying close to Sheila, preferably in Jake Jenson's car, figuring there was safety in numbers, even if the numbers amounted to a scant two.

She had lost the argument to the decisive dictates of the devil with an angel's visage.

"Sulking, Leigh?" Michael asked, in a soft, infuriating purr of satisfaction.

Fuming, Leigh now had an urge even more compelling than her earlier impulse to strike out, smack him or better yet punch him, right in the mouth.

She didn't, of course. Because, not only was she morally opposed to physical violence, but she wasn't stupid enough to endanger her own safety by physically attacking him while he was behind the wheel of a moving car — a swiftly moving car, at that.

But her prudence didn't extend to avoiding a verbal attack, which she commenced at once.

"Over your feeble machinations?" she retaliated, in tones dripping with disdain. "Not likely."

He gave a quick bark of laughter. "I really must take exception to the term 'feeble.' Personally, I deem my machinations quite effective . . . since they worked."

She angled a scornful look at him, and immediately wished she hadn't. The late afternoon sunlight bathed his head in a blazing aureole of burnished gold, cast his near perfect profile in sharp relief, sparkled off his blue eyes, delineated his sculpted, grinning lips.

Zing, bam, the sexual tension was back, humming like a live wire between them, creating havoc in her body and deep resentment in her mind.

"Well, personally, I think you're a piece of work — an annoying piece of work," she sniped, dragging her gaze away from his too masculinely beautiful face, only to have it snagged by the inherent strength of his long, slim fingers curled around the gray leather-sheathed steering wheel.

How many women have thrilled to the touch, the caress, the stroke of those long, slim fingers. And is the still-lovely Barbara one of those women?

Leigh stiffened against the thought, the

thickening tension and the resultant burst of heat, at once angry and sexual, inside her generated by both unsettling factors.

"You have a temper," he observed, threads of amusement and an odd note of tenderness evident in his tone.

She dared another haughty look at him. "Every normal person has a temper," she retorted.

"True." Michael slanted a knowing smile at her. "But you suppress it better than most — your temper, as well as your normal sensuality."

Indignation warring with the damning excitement inside her, Leigh snapped, "You're offensive."

"Maybe so," he softly conceded, then canceled the concession by adding, "But I'm also right."

The hell of it being, he *was,* Leigh acknowledged to herself. She had with cool and deliberate forethought suppressed her natural sensuality. She had had ample reason for doing so. But now, finding her fortitude tested to the limit by Michael's blatant sexual appeal cut the ground of just cause from beneath her.

While her physical response to him enraged and frustrated her, Leigh honestly, if secretly, admitted to a never before experienced heady stimulation, a glorious sense of an almost combative flow of energy.

Like it or not, to all intents and purposes, it appeared she had stumbled into the fray in the war between the sexes.

"No rebuttal, Leigh?"

"If you want a rebuttal, join a debating team." Oh, Lord, she couldn't believe she had actually said that. Leigh winced.

He laughed.

She shuddered, but quickly rallied to change the subject by demanding, "Where in the hell are we going, anyway?" She glanced out the window, just in time to catch a glimpse of a road sign for the Gulph Mills exit. "It seems like we've been driving forever."

"Or at least twenty minutes," Michael drawled, his expression rife with now repressed amusement. "But not to worry," he said, in soothing tones. "We're almost there."

Leigh heaved a sigh of relief and long suffering. "And precisely *where* might *there* be?"

He mentioned the name of a restaurant she had never heard of. "I've never been there myself," he went on. "It's in the general vicinity of Jake's place. He highly recommends it, said they have superb cuisine and an excellent wine list." He smiled at her. "For myself, I can only hope the bartender can mix a perfect martini."

Leigh turned back to him with a puzzled frown. "I've heard of a perfect Manhattan but what is a perfect martini?"

Michael's smile grew into a wicked grin. "You pour gin over ice in a container, whisper vermouth over it, then gently stir and pour into a glass containing two olives."

"No bitters?" She controlled an urge to smile.

He pulled a horrified expression, and an exaggerated shudder. "No bitters. Very dry."

The beginnings of a smile slipped by her control. "In other words, your perfect martini consists of straight gin."

"Don't forget the olives," he reminded her, his voice solemn, his lips twitching.

"I wouldn't dream of it," she assured him, her smile growing.

"You'll have to try one."

"Your version of a perfect martini?"

"Hmmm," he murmured, nodding.

"I wouldn't dream of it," she managed to repeat in the instant before her laughter escaped.

Michael's laughter blended with hers, lightening the atmosphere, easing the tension crackling between them and inside her.

Leigh was in a more congenial frame of mind when, a few minutes later, her appetite restored by the tantalizing aromas wafting on the air, she and Michael were escorted through the stylishly appointed restaurant to the table where the others were already seated and waiting for them.

She didn't even mind — too much — that the only two empty chairs at the round table forced her to sit next to Michael. She consoled herself with the fact that Sheila was seated on her other side.

The waiter arrived to take their order for drinks. Leigh chose wine, as did Sheila and Jake. Both Barbara and Michael ordered martinis, mixed to his specifications.

That show of togetherness Leigh did mind, although she assured herself she didn't care, jealousy being anathema to her, especially jealousy of any other woman.

Apart from that one instance when Leigh suffered a jolting sensation too close to jealousy to be examined, the evening was surprisingly congenial.

While sipping her wine, listening to the easy flow of conversation around the table, Leigh surreptitiously studied the older woman, concluding that for her age Barbara Saunders was in excellent condition.

She was of average height, and her figure

was good, not too thin, not too rounded. Her age was more evident up close. Though her skin was still soft, her complexion creamy, there were telltale lines around her eyes, nose and mouth, a slight natural sagging under her chin. And, while it was apparent the woman applied cosmetics, and expertly at that, it was obvious to Leigh that she had not employed the enhancing services of a cosmetic surgeon.

In addition to her striking attractiveness, Barbara proved to be a good conversationalist, knowledgeable on a variety of subjects. To top it off, the woman was likable, pleasant and exquisitely mannered.

Despite her age, Leigh could both see and appreciate her appeal to the opposite sex, to men of almost any age.

Jake, though of a similar age, deferred to her.

Michael, her junior by at least fifteen years, teased and indulged her.

Sighing into her wineglass, Leigh mused that the attention Barbara commanded by her presence alone was enough to demoralize Miss America, never mind Leigh Evans. And she didn't even want to delve into why she felt demoralized.

It was a relief when their dinners were served, greatly curtailing the round-table conversation, to which she had contributed next to nothing.

The quality of the food, expertly prepared and presented, lived up to Jake's high recommendation. Leigh thoroughly enjoyed, and consumed every morsel of, the wine-glazed prawns, lightly herbed potatoes and pear and avocado salad she'd ordered, topping the meal off with the smoothest, most delicious lemon-lime sorbet she had ever tasted.

Michael, naturally, chose a chocolate mousse for dessert.

Pitching his voice low, beneath the discussion between their companions on the excellence of the meal, he murmured, "Want a taste?" He offered his spoon, mounded with the chocolate confection, to her.

"No, thank you." Leigh tried to deny the thrill caused by the almost shocking intimacy involved in accepting a taste of dessert from the spoon he had moments before placed in his own mouth, closed his lips around.

"Coward."

His soft taunt intensified the thrill into a delicate shudder, and Leigh was relieved when Sheila inadvertently came to her aid with a question she heard only partially.

". . . isn't that right, Leigh?"

"What?" Leigh smiled and offered an apology. "I'm sorry, I didn't catch all of that."

Sheila shot a glance at Michael, then a knowing look at Leigh. "I was just telling Mr. Jenson —"

"Jake," he interrupted in gentle insistence.

Color bloomed on Sheila's cheeks. "Jake, then," she murmured, her eyes soft and revealing.

Leigh experienced a twinge of alarm for her friend, afraid Sheila was in the throes of serious infatuation, and way out of her depth with the older man.

"You were just telling . . . Jake . . . what?" Leigh prompted her starry-eyed assistant.

Jolted from the realm of romantic dreamland, Sheila blinked herself back to reality. "Oh, yes." Her smile was bright, her cheeks were even brighter. "I was telling him that you've been commissioned by a client to decorate a new condo," she explained. "Isn't that right?"

"Yes, but . . ." Leigh broke off, frowning in puzzlement at why Sheila had offered the information.

The answer was forthcoming, not from Sheila, but from the man under discussion.

"I've recently purchased a new townhouse," Jake explained, blessing Sheila with a gentle smile. "And being impressed with the job you did on the Standfield place, also hopeful of acquiring your services, I queried Sheila about your schedule."

"Leigh's schedule is full." Though soft, a strain of menace ran through Michael's voice.

Unable to believe she had heard correctly, Leigh glanced at him in astonishment. "I beg your pardon?"

"Well, isn't it?" He shrugged. "How many commissions have you contracted for — in addition to my office?"

Leigh was suddenly so incensed she could barely articulate. "Are you presuming to . . . to . . ." she sputtered, allowing him an opportunity to cut in.

"Is your schedule not full?" he persisted.

Disregarding the truth of his assertion and furious at his interference, his chilling, repressive tone, Leigh glared in icy censure at him. "That is beside the point. How dare you presume to answer for me?" she demanded.

"I simply stated a —" he began.

"Ummm, look, I'm not in a hurry to begin the work," Jake interjected, shifting an alert and strangely amused look from one to the other of the two combatants.

Her expression a combination of alarm and confusion, Sheila wailed, "What's going on?"

"Is your schedule not full?" Michael repeated, his cool blue gaze steady on her cold stare.

"Yes," she hissed, seething.

He didn't speak; he didn't need to utter a word, his smile conveyed supreme superiority.

That did it for Leigh — she lost her cool. "Might I remind you, Mr. St. Claire," she said, instead of succumbing to a compelling urge to slap the self-confident smile from his face, "I have not yet signed your contract."

Her implied threat got his attention and wiped the superior look from his face.

It was Leigh's turn to smile; she made it a nasty one.

"Now, now, children." The calming voice of reason came from Barbara, who appeared about to choke on suppressed laughter. "Please remember where you are."

Brought to her senses, Leigh glanced around the table at the rapt expressions of her companions — all except Michael. She didn't dare risking a look at him, for fear of flying apart and actually attacking him.

Appalled at her violent reactions, she returned her gaze to Barbara. "You're absolutely right," she said, her eyes narrowing on the tremor playing over the woman's lips. Holding her explosive emotions in check, she carefully slid back her chair and stood up, propelled by an overwhelming need to escape, from the embarrassing situation in general and that overbearing devil, Michael, in particular. "If you will excuse me?" Not waiting for a response, she grabbed her purse and turned to walk away.

"Leigh!" Sheila blurted. "Where are you going?"

Without breaking stride, Leigh lobbed the answer back over her shoulder. "Home."

Under a full head of indignant steam, she sailed through the restaurant and out the door. The cool evening breeze quickly swept the wind from her sails.

Idiot, she berated herself. In performing the grand exit, she had completely forgotten that she was without transport. She should have thought to call for a taxi.

There was nothing for it, she'd have to go back inside. Sighing, she moved to make an about-face, just as a hand curled around her upper arm.

"Waiting for me, green eyes?"

Leigh went stone-still, stiff with repudiation of Michael's possessive hold, his seductive tone, the meltdown of her anger, her resentment, her will.

Finding speech difficult, and looking at him impossible, Leigh shook her head.

"How were you planning to get home then?" His voice was low, soothing, exciting. "Walk?"

She shook her head again, in denial of both his question and the bone-weakening coil of excitement, and commanded her vocal chords to function. "I'll call for a cab."

"I don't think so." Tightening his grip a fraction, Michael began walking, impelling her forward with him. "I brought you, and I'll take you home."

"But wait," Leigh protested, stumbling in an unsuccessful attempt to halt his progress. "What about Sheila? How will she get home?"

Michael slanted a wry look at her. "Jake brought her, and Jake can take her home."

"Michael, stop," she ordered, concerned for her friend. "What do you know about Jake?" she asked, her imagination conjuring lurid images.

"For God's sake, Leigh," he snapped. "Sheila's not a child. And I think it's pretty damned obvious she's more than a little attracted to him."

"For God's sake, Michael." Leigh flung

his words back at him. "That attraction is what has me worried. The man is much too old for her."

"And this is your business?" he demanded, seemingly unconcerned that they were standing there, arguing, in the middle of the restaurant parking area.

"Sheila's my friend — my best friend," Leigh said defensively. "I don't want to see her hurt by an aging, if charming, predator."

His smile was chiding. "Jake's a predator?"

Without a thought, Leigh gave voice to her conviction. "Aren't all men?"

Michael went taut for a moment, his eyes probing hers; then he smiled. "I see," he murmured, nodding his head. "Yes, now I understand."

"What do you see?" Leigh had trouble keeping her voice steady, certain she had revealed too much of herself, her inner self, to him. "What do you understand?"

Just then, a car turned onto the lot, the sweep of its headlights startling both of them.

"Later," Michael said, applying light pressure on her flesh with the fingers still curled around her arm. He moved; she had little choice but to move with him. "We'll talk about it later, in a less conspicuous and dangerous location."

"But Sheila —" she began.

"Is on her own," he said, pulling her along as he strode to his car. "Besides, you forget, Barbara's there. She'll look out for Sheila."

Standing next to him as he unlocked the car, Leigh felt a sinking sensation at her sudden recall of the overbright sheen of expectancy in Sheila's eyes as she'd gazed at Jake. "But what if he drops Barbara off first?" she worried aloud, absently sliding onto the seat.

Michael rolled his eyes. "Then, I suppose, Sheila will have to look out for herself." Swinging the door, he shut it with a solid, punctuating, thunk.

Though still uneasy with the situation, Leigh had secured her seatbelt by the time he'd circled the car to unlock the driver's side door. Responding to the unappeased qualm, as he slid behind the wheel, she released both the belt and the door lock next to her.

"I'm going back for Sheila," she muttered, pushing the door open.

"*Dammit, Leigh!*" Michael exploded, grabbing hold of her shoulder as she turned to step out of the car. "Stay right where you are." Leaning forward, he reached across her to pull the door shut, then quickly and efficiently connected the ends of her seat belt.

Fuming, Leigh heatedly objected, "You have no right to —" She broke off at the click of his seat belt, immediately followed by the starting of the engine. "Damn you, let me out of this car."

"Oh, Leigh, will you please shut up?" Concentrating on backing the car from the slot, Michael didn't spare her so much as a glance.

Indignant, rigid with anger and fully aware he would simply ignore any demand or argument she might launch, Leigh turned away to glare through the side window as she railed to herself about his enraging arrogance.

Michael didn't utter a word all the way back to the city, which was fine with Leigh, because she wouldn't have responded, anyway. She was too incensed to speak coherently.

Her disposition wasn't improved when, after turning onto her street, Michael again found a convenient parking space one building down from her apartment building.

Damned if she wasn't tempted to believe the man led a charmed existence.

He cut the engine, then turned to her. "Now, if you want to fight, let's go inside and thrash it out."

"Fight . . . with you?" Leigh met his gaze with the coldest stare she could muster. "You've got to be kidding. I don't even want to talk to you." Her shaky fingers fumbling with the seat belt, she finally managed to unfasten it and reach for the door release. "And I'm not inviting you in."

He reacted exactly as he had before, but this time both of his arms shot out to grasp her by her shoulders, hauling her around to face him.

"Let go of me," Leigh ordered, shaken by his audacity and by the tingling of her flesh beneath his hands.

"This is ridiculous." Michael gave a quick shake of his head. "You're reacting like an overprotective mother hen with a newborn chick. But Sheila is not a baby; she's a mature adult, fully capable of making her own decisions."

Leigh mirrored his motion with a shake of her own head. "But that's the problem. She wasn't consulted about either decision concerning transport, to the restaurant or from it."

"Of course she was."

His assertion caught her up short. "She

was?" Leigh eyed him skeptically. "When?"

Michael's expression said reams about her recent propensity for distraction. "Both before we left the Standfield house," he answered, "and again later, before I followed you out of the restaurant."

"I didn't know."

"No kidding." His smile took the sting from his chiding tone. "What are you so afraid Jake might do to her?" His fingers flexed, tightening his grip before drawing her resistant body to him. "This?" Lowering his head, he captured her parted lips with his ravaging mouth.

That was exactly what she had been afraid of, for Sheila . . . and herself.

This was the last rational thought Leigh had for some wildly arousing minutes, for Michael's commanding mouth was so compelling, the spear of his tongue so seductive, her mind closed up shop, surrendering without protest . . . as did she.

The sexual tension that had been humming between them, even during the previous angry silence, expanded into a full-throated roar. Michael's mouth was voracious, a sensual weapon he used with ruthless intent against her dwindling defenses.

Unequal to the power of his magnetic

attraction, the electrical impulses leaping along her nervous system, Leigh gave in to the demands of his mouth and of her own desire.

Curling her arms around his neck, she arched into the warmth of his solid chest, thrilling to the abrasive friction against her hardening nipples. Abandoning senses for sensations, she moved with restless craving.

Michael groaned into her receptive mouth, his tongue plunged deeper, initiating a rhythm evocative of a more complete possession. Releasing his hold on her shoulders, he wrapped his arms around her, crushing her breasts to his chest.

Drowning in a crashing sea of unimagined pleasure, she tangled her fingers in his hair, holding him fast to her starving mouth.

Loosening his hold, he insinuated one hand between them to cup her breast. Caressing her lace-covered flesh, he teased the hard, aching tip. Leigh shuddered in response to the lightning streak of pleasure from her breasts to the moistening core of her femininity.

Tearing his mouth from hers, Michael trailed biting kisses over her face, along her jaw. Trembling with need, she tipped back her head, exposing her arched throat to the suction of his greedy lips, the glide of his tongue.

"Damn . . . Leigh . . ." Michael's voice was raw, ragged. "You smell so good . . . taste even better," he muttered, gently sinking his teeth into her skin.

Consumed by the fire of rampant desire, Leigh bowed her spine, arching her breast in invitation to his foraging mouth. She whimpered, deep in her throat, at the incredible sensations generated by his tongue wetting the delicate lace and silk materials shielding her nipple.

Where it would have ended, how it would have ended, Leigh was beyond thinking or caring about. But it ended a moment later, when the blare of a car horn shattered the silence, restoring her mental faculties.

Appalled at herself, shaken by her near complete surrender to the temptation of Michael's allure, she pulled away from him and groped for the door release.

His hand snaked out to catch her by the wrist. "Don't even think about trying to bolt again."

"Let me go." Shocked by her loss of control, Leigh gave a quick, unsuccessful tug against his grip; it held firm. "Michael, please," she pleaded, cringing inside at the incipient panic edging her voice.

"For God's sake, Leigh, calm down," he said in soothing tones. "It's not as if you haven't been kissed before. I don't understand why you're so upset."

Choosing to ignore his gibe about her having been kissed, Leigh lashed out at him for his insensibility. "We're in the car, for heaven's sake, on a public street, and while it may not bother you, it embarrasses me. I've always considered public displays of this sort distasteful. Do you understand that?" She yanked against his hold again — to no avail. "Let go of me. I want to go inside."

Michael stared at her a moment; then he sighed. "Okay, Leigh." He released his grip and turned to open his door. "I'll see you safely inside."

"That's not necessary," she said, scrambling out of the car. "I'll be perfectly . . ." she broke off, saving her breath; he was already standing next to her.

In mutinous silence, she stormed off.

Playing her shadow, Michael followed along.

"I suppose you're not going to invite me in for a nightcap or coffee," he said, raising his brows in amusement at her third attempt to jam the doorkey into the lock.

Gritting her teeth, Leigh slotted the key

on her fourth try, then condescended to reply. "You suppose correctly." She turned the key and pushed open the door.

"Not even if I promise not to jump you the minute we're inside?" Laughter danced in his eyes.

Damning his undeniable attraction, and her weakening resistance, Leigh shook her head. "Thank you for dinner," she said politely. "And, good night."

"Not even just to talk?" he persisted, his lips curving into a seductive smile.

"No, Michael." Leigh was proud of the firmness she'd injected into her voice despite the softening inside her. "Now . . ." She stepped inside.

"Okay, okay, I give up." He exhaled. "I'll see you Wednesday. For lunch. Right?"

Leigh hesitated, precariously poised on the edge of a dilemma. If she signed the contract, she could back Brett with the excessively generous fee Michael had offered, but if she followed her instincts, and turned down his offer, broke all contact with him, she'd be risking her business in backing her brother.

"Leigh?" Michael's voice was sharp, his eyes intent.

She sighed with defeat. "Yes. Wednesday. For lunch. Now, *good night*, Michael."

Fifteen

Michael laughed all the way home. It was either laugh or curse a blue streak.

Good Christ. He had actually been about to seduce Leigh in the car, like an overeager teenager caught up in the fallout of hormones gone ballistic. And now his body and mind were paying the price for his juvenile behavior.

Never before in his adult life had he been so frustrated — sexually, emotionally and intellectually.

What was it with this maddening woman, anyway? Michael asked himself. Leigh Evans was unlike any other woman he had known. Of course, he reflected, though her beauty had aroused his interest and his libido on first sight of her, it was her uniqueness that kept him interested — and aroused.

And stupidly jealous. Like it or not, and he definitely did not, he was jealous of the man she had spent the previous weekend with, whoever that might be; he was jealous of any man she had ever spent intimate time with; hell, he had even been jealous of the interest Jake Jenson had shown in Leigh, however professional in intent.

Acknowledging the unpalatable truth, he reflected that his feelings were a muddled combination of emotions, the uppermost being jealousy and possessiveness.

Dammit. Leigh was his. Or would be. All the sensual fire smoldering inside beneath her cool facade, the fire of desire that blazed to vibrant life in response to the flame of his own unbridled passion, belonged to him.

Michael uttered a half-laugh, half-grunt of pain as he drove the car down the ramp to the complex's underground parking area. Those few wild moments spent with Leigh in the car, the feel of her, the taste of her, had made him as horny as a stallion with the scent of a frisky filly flaring his nostrils.

And deny it though she might, her desire, her passion, had betrayed her by equaling the passion consuming him. Oh, yeah, she was in denial, he concluded, waging a losing battle against her natural physical demands. By her own actions, Leigh gave evidence that she was fighting the physical attraction between them tooth and nail.

The thought brought a feral grin to his lips, and an anticipatory spasm to his groin. Tooth and nail. Hmmm. Kinky. Exciting. Though he had never been tempted to indulge in the kinky stuff, Michael mused that it could be fun, so long as the teeth and nails were Leigh's.

Shaking his head at himself, his runaway imagination, he stepped from the car and headed for the elevator. On the ride up to his floor, Michael told himself that, if he didn't come to some kind of agreement with her, and soon, the tempting Leigh would drive him to distraction . . . or would make him completely nuts.

Pondering the pros and cons of a number of approaches he could employ in his pursuit of Leigh, and thus save his sanity, Michael didn't hear the murmur of voices until he came to within a few feet of the kitchen.

Pausing, frowning, he immediately identified the speakers. Shamus and . . . Barbara? Jake must have dropped her off first for her to have gotten here so quickly. But why had she wanted to come here? Curious, but interesting, he thought, sauntering into the room.

"You're having a tea party?" he drawled, indicating the teapot, cups and saucers, the sugar bowl and plate of cookies on the table. "And didn't invite me?"

Barbara's head jerked up, and she stared at him in blank surprise. "What are you doing here?"

"I own the joint, remember?" Michael said, smiling into her flushed face. It wasn't often that he, or anyone else, for that matter, caught the formidable Barbara Saunders in an embarrassing situation. Although why she would be embarrassed about having a cup of tea with Shamus escaped him.

"Dammit, Michael, you know what I mean. I thought you'd be hours with Leigh, if not all night." Her voice was rougher, raspier than usual. Nastier, too. "Losing your touch, my poor darling?"

"Could be." He smiled. Used to her hooked barbs, he still felt the sting from the jab to his ego.

"Better lay off, Your Highness," Clancy advised in dust-dry tones. "I do believe the boss is ticked."

Michael winced, fully expecting Barbara to verbally tear a strip off Clancy's back in the same way she played him whenever he called her Babsy. Instead of a tongue-lashing, to his delighted amazement, she smiled at the big Irishman.

"Last I knew, you two were at daggers drawn." He shifted a glance from one to the other. "Have I missed something important here?"

"Uh . . . hmmm . . ." Clancy paused,

found a soft smile for Barbara and a cocky grin for Michael. "We've . . . ah . . . been talking some the last coupla days."

It was a couple of days ago that he had urged her to talk to the man. Controlling an urge to laugh, Michael murmured, "Must have been some conversations."

Barbara lowered her eyes, fiddled with her cup. "Yes, they were," she murmured, looking, sounding shy.

Barbara? His Barbara? The lady with the shrewd mind and caustic wit? Shy? Michael lost it; his roar of laughter bounced off the tiled walls and floor.

"What in hell's so funny about us talking?" Clancy glared at him, bristling with affront.

"It's . . . not . . . funny." Michael had to push the words out between gasps for breath. "It's . . . hilarious." He was off again, laughter pealing from his throat.

"Dammit, Mike," Clancy erupted. "Knock it off."

"I've got a better idea," Barbara said. "Why don't you knock him down, Shamus?"

"An excellent suggestion, Your Highness. Shoulda thought of it myself," Clancy complimented, shoving back his chair. "Who knows?" He stood to confront his employer.

"It might even knock some sense into his hard head."

Choking on another bout of laughter triggered by Clancy's revealingly quick defense of the lady, Michael stepped back, raising his hands in surrender.

"I give up, I give up," he said, dragging in deep, hopefully calming breaths. "But after all these years of listening to you two snarl at each other, and doing my damnedest to get you talking to each other" — he drew in another deep breath — "I can hardly stand the shock of it."

"Annoying, devil, isn't he?" Barbara tilted her head back to look at Shamus.

"More like a royal pain in the ass, I'd say." He scowled at Michael, and smiled for Barbara.

"True." She nodded. "Good thing we both love him," she opined. "Otherwise, we might be tempted to kill him."

"Cut him up in little pieces," Shamus suggested.

"Stuff him down the garbage disposal," she elaborated.

"Works for me," Shamus said, grinning.

"You're both a little flaky, you know that?" His laughter reined in, Michael stood there, deriving pleasure, satisfaction and a pang of envy from their affectionate glances, the lack of strain in their droll exchanges.

"Yes." Barbara's voice was soft, her expression softer, younger than he'd seen it in years.

"Yes," Clancy echoed, his gaze a tender caress of the older woman.

A sudden feeling of dejection stole the last of Michael's amusement. He had no idea what dynamic had been brought into play to bring these two former adversaries together, but he longed for the power to activate it, get it working for Leigh and himself.

"You want a cuppa tea, boss?"

Tea? Michael started to grimace, then, shrugging, turned it to a grin. "Sure, why the hell not?"

Square one. She was right back to the sleepless state she had suffered from through the previous four nights.

Heaving an impatient sigh, Leigh tossed back the tangled covers and got out of bed.

It was no use, nothing worked; and she had tried everything she could think of, from submerging her sexually aroused and throbbing body in a tub of soothing warm water, to repeatedly playing and rewinding the music box, to supposedly mind-calming meditation, to relaxing every muscle in her body, starting with her toes.

Nothing had worked. None of her efforts had borne the fruit of desired slumber.

She had been left with nothing but desire.

As a last resort, Leigh trailed through the apartment to the kitchen, hoping, praying a cup of herbal tea would prove to be the magic formula.

It wasn't. Though she drained the fragment brew in her cup, twice, the result she derived from the liquid was not the dousing of the inner fire, but merely a necessary trip to the bathroom.

Laying the blame for her discomfort on Michael proved counterproductive. Her innate honesty rose to remind her in vivid detail of her active participation in the scene enacted earlier in his car — in his arms. Every cell in her body retained the memory, clamoring for more of the same, aching for completion.

Though Leigh battled these impulses with intellect, her weapons were defeated by the age-old instinct.

Resolution in the form of surrender came late Sunday night, and with it an inner peace . . . of sorts. It came with a notion she would have dismissed out of hand mere days before.

She wanted Michael St. Claire. Her body demanded him. So why shouldn't she have him and put an end to this hormonal rebellion?

At first shocked at herself for entertaining the notion, the more she thought about it, the more convinced she became of its validity.

Of a certainty, there were ramifications to be considered. Leigh examined them, one by one.

There was the demeaning surety of publicly having her name added to the long list of Michael's conquests. Definitely a blow to her pride, but Leigh assured herself she could withstand being the cynosure of gossip.

There would be the natural interest of friends and family. She told herself she could grin and bear it.

There were other probable consequences, minor in importance, however annoying, all of which she decided she could handle.

But, by far the most serious consideration for Leigh was the effect a sexual liaison with Michael might have on her business and her professional life, as well as her personal life, her carefully guarded independence.

Her mind clicking with surprising clarity, Leigh formulated guidelines she planned to present to Michael the next time he made a move on her. She didn't feel in the least overconfident about believing he would make that move at some point during their Wednesday appointment.

At long last, she was granted the blessing of deep and restful slumber.

"Morning, coffee's ready," Sheila sang out the minute Leigh walked into the office on Monday. "Isn't it a gorgeous day?"

"Lovely," Leigh agreed, her friend's bright smile and exuberant manner a belated reminder of her anxiety over Sheila's safety the previous evening.

Since it was obvious that Sheila was not only safe, but in even higher spirits than usual, Leigh presumed her friend had enjoyed herself while in Jake's company.

And that worried Leigh, enough to prompt her in the name of friendship to abandon reticence and delicately probe into Sheila's personal life — and while she was at it, perhaps to learn something about Michael's friend, Barbara, as well.

"Did you and the others linger over coffee at the restaurant last night?" Her expression one of mild interest, Leigh crossed to the coffeemaker on the credenza and poured a cup for herself.

"No, we left right after Michael followed you out, after you as much as told him to get stuffed." Sheila laughed. "Jake had found a space closer to the restaurant, but we saw you and Michael confronting each other in the middle of the parking lot. I was concerned about your getting home, but Barbara assured me you'd be fine with Michael."

"She must know him well to feel confident about offering assurances." Feigning disinterest, Leigh raised the cup for a tentative sip of the steaming drink.

Sheila nodded. "From the little she did say, I gathered they were old friends."

And possibly old lovers, too, Leigh thought, steeling herself against a pang she refused to identify.

"And they must be," Sheila continued on, unaware of the envy assailing her employer, "because Barbara had Jake drop her off at Michael's apartment complex."

Leigh was both devastated and alarmed; alarmed at hearing that Jake had dropped Barbara off first, devastated at learning where he had dropped her off.

"So you were alone with Jake, then," she said, dealing with the alarm, concealing the devastation.

Sheila gave her a droll look, and unknowingly echoed Michael's assertion. "I'm an adult, Leigh, perfectly capable of taking care of myself."

"I know, but Jake is —"

Sheila cut in. "A lot older than I am I know, and I don't care." Her voice held a new, unfamiliar note of determination. "I'm attracted to him, Leigh, very attracted, more than I've ever been to any other man."

While Leigh could relate to Sheila's claim, having the same compelling attraction to Michael, it did not relieve her anxiety concerning the extensive age difference between the two, nor did it alleviate her suspicion of Jake's motives. She feared he saw Sheila as a trophy rather than a person.

"Has Jake indicated an interest in you?" she asked, hoping against hope the attraction was one sided.

"Yes, a strong, unmistakable indication." Her blue eyes sparkling, Sheila wrapped her arms around herself, as if hugging close her excitement. "And I'm going to see him again, on Saturday morning." She laughed. "We're going running together. Can you believe it, Leigh, Jake runs several mornings a week to keep in shape, just like I do."

Leigh refrained from reminding her that, at his age, Jake had more reason to run to keep in shape. And it struck her, on second thought, how much hassle could Jake give Sheila if he was panting for breath after running?

Comforted by the thought, Leigh relaxed enough to smile at her friend. "Well, have fun," she said, suppressing a shudder at the mere idea of running to have fun. To her mind, working up a sweat by running was tiresome, not entertaining.

"I can't wait." Sheila laughed.

To each his own, as the saying went, Leigh reflected, moving to her office door. On the other hand, why was she squandering her angst on this? she asked herself, pushing open the door with unnecessary force. As Sheila had been quick to point out, her friend was an adult capable of taking care of herself. Besides, I have man problems of my own, Leigh reminded herself. A big problem she had to confront in just two days.

Despite her resolve regarding her game plan for dealing with Michael on Wednesday, a feeling of dread coursed through Leigh, instilling doubt and trepidation.

"Time to get to work, time flies and all that," she said, grasping at the straw of work for distraction from her fears and uncertainties.

Time flew too quickly over the next two days for Leigh's peace of mind. But then, how could she attain peace of mind, when her muddled thinking process was the direct cause of her mental conflict.

Brett called her at her office on Tuesday, adding more weight to her mental gyrations.

"Leigh, I don't want to apply pressure here, but . . ." He paused a moment.

Of course he wants to apply pressure, Leigh thought, sliding her hand over the mouthpiece so he wouldn't hear her tired sigh.

"I'm under some heavy-duty pressure, myself," he rushed on, his attempt at a firm tone unsuccessfully concealing his frantic center. "I need an answer by the end of this week at the latest."

"I have talked to my accountant about this, Brett." That much was true; Leigh had talked to him, and she winced at recalling his reply.

"Are you crazy?" The refined, normally quiet-voiced man had actually raised his tone to a shriek. "Risking your personal finances is one thing — but to put your business at risk would be sheer madness."

Well aware of the risk involved, Leigh had responded to the man with the only answer she had: "He's my brother."

"Well," Brett demanded, impatient with her brief hesitation. "What did he say?"

"He was not enthusiastic." A real stretch there, Leigh conceded, but it was all her rattled mind could come up with under the circumstances.

She could actually hear Brett grind his teeth before exclaiming, "The man works for you, Leigh, not the other way around. It's your decision."

No kidding Dick Tracy. Leigh contained the impulse to lob the outworn retort at him. "I know that, Brett," she said instead, smothering another sigh. "And I'll have a definite answer for you by Friday," she promised, thinking of the meeting with St. Claire on Wednesday.

"Okay," he agreed, sounding strained. "I can hold the creditors off until then."

Talk about strain, pressure. Brett had four more days; she was down to one.

What to do?

As the hours ticked away, Leigh kept changing her mind, swinging back and forth between yes, she would go through with her plan to no, she simply couldn't do it.

With the exception of her attire, Leigh was still in a state of flux upon entering the now-familiar stylish reception area of Michael's suite of offices on Wednesday.

She hadn't vacillated a moment over her

clothes. With cool deliberation, she had dressed to annihilate. Instead of her accustomed working-day trouser suit, she had chosen a deceptively simple-looking, white-jacketed, sleeveless sheath dress, accessorized with a small, slim-strapped black patent leather purse, spike-heeled shoes and a filmy neck scarf splashed with the spectrum of spring pastels.

The looks of unmasked admiration she received from both the receptionist and Rosalie bolstered her ego and her flagging courage.

Leigh was, in a word, scared.

Steeling herself, gathering her composure, she literally swept into Michael's office.

Her composure was immediately tested when she saw the man waiting for her, for it appeared that Michael also had dressed to annihilate.

He had discarded the jacket of his navy blue suit, and his necktie. The top two buttons on his blazing white shirt were open, the sleeves rolled midway on his forearms. He looked . . . he looked . . .

Devastating.

Appearing unaffected, while the steel in her spine melted, Leigh decided it was simply unjust for any one man to look that good, that golden blond, that handsome, that blatantly sexy.

She could only thank heaven he didn't smile.

"I was afraid you'd call it off." The low, masculine resonance of his voice hastened the melting process in her spine.

Certain her own voice would betray her if she spoke, Leigh arched a brow in response.

"After my . . . er . . . precipitous actions Sunday evening," he explained, slowly walking to her.

Stock-still, Leigh defeated an urge to back up.

"In all candor, I feared you'd change your mind about doing my office."

However unwittingly, Michael had offered her the perfect opportunity to state her counterproposal. But with her heart racing, her breathing erratic, Leigh stared at him, unable to force from her constricted throat the admission that she *had* changed her mind . . . at least about the commission.

But, damn, how can I think, never mind speak, with him closing in on me? Leigh asked herself, tamping down a compulsive impulse to take to her heels.

"Can't we talk later?" She was amazed at the unruffled sounds she'd wrenched from her tight throat. "After lunch, perhaps?" she suggested, in a desperate bid for time to collect herself, her wits.

He paused in midstep, less than two feet from her, his eyes alert, wary, as if probing for a possible hidden meaning woven through the fabric of her request.

"Certainly," he agreed, turning abruptly to walk to the intercom on his desk.

Lunch was a repeat of the previous Wednesday, prepared and served with quiet efficiency, the menu the only exception, a deliciously blended shrimp and pasta dish replacing the soup and sandwiches of the week before.

Determined not to betray her trepidation by picking at her meal, Leigh ate every bite of it, drank every drop of coffee in her cup and congratulated herself on her ability to engage in cursory conversation with Michael during her nerve-wracking performance.

But she couldn't procrastinate any longer. With the table cleared of everything but the coffee carafe and their cups, Leigh's moment of truth was upon her.

In the still quiet of the room, she sat at the table, contract in hand, pretending to read, while not absorbing a single word of the document.

The lengthening silence finally broke through the fragile shield of Leigh's dwindling control. Setting the contract aside, she rose and walked to the window. The measure of her distraction was revealed by her lack of notice of the tall, impressive statue of William Penn keeping guard over the city from its perch atop City Hall, clearly visible in the bright spring sunshine.

"There's a problem?" Michael's soft purring voice seemed to stalk her.

A problem? Leigh was sorely tempted to laugh, tempted to tell him that he was the problem, tempted to demand he explain why he seemed intent on derailing her admittedly shaky plan by thus far not making a move on her.

The hell with it, she decided, at the end of her endurance. The time was now, fish or cut bait. Acting before she could change her mind yet again, she stiffened her spine and her resolve, and turned to confront him.

"Do you want to have an affair with me?" Blunt and stark, perhaps, but effective, she thought, if his reaction was any indication.

Michael froze in his chair, his lazily relaxed appearance belied by the sudden tautness of his long form. For endless seconds, not a muscle twitched, not one eyelash flickered, not a breath moved his chest.

Leigh didn't twitch or flicker or breathe, either. She couldn't. His eyes, glittering with an inner fire, cauterized her motor skills.

When he finally did move, an instant, an hour, an eternity later, he startled Leigh so badly, she swung around to stare blindly out the window.

She didn't hear him cross the thick carpeting, but she knew when he came to a stop next to her. She felt the heat of him, smelled his tangy cologne, the musky male scent of him.

"Yes, I want to have an affair with you." Michael was so close to her his warm breath ruffled her hair, sending a delicious thrill skittering through her.

Her shoulder brushed his chest as she made a half-turn to look at him. "I . . ." She paused to wet her parched lips with the tip of her tongue, the thrill inside intensifying when his glittering gaze fastened on her mouth. "I have conditions," she said in a rush.

"Of course." A sigh of acceptance whispered through his lips, and he raised keen eyes sharpened with cynicism. "I'm a fairly wealthy man, Leigh. Within reason, you may have anything you want."

Money. *Things.* He was offering to buy

her — her services. Leigh closed her eyes to conceal her hurt, the pain of disappointment. And why not? she asked herself with savage fury. Money for services rendered was, had ever been, the rate of exchange between the sexes, hadn't it?

"I'm referring to ground rules, Michael." Opening her eyes, Leigh derived pleasure from setting him straight, and from the puzzlement that wiped away the cynical expression.

"Ground rules?" He frowned. "Be specific. What sort of ground rules?"

"First and foremost," she said, hanging onto her composure for all she was worth, "I want nothing from you. Nothing, Michael. I will accept no gifts of any kind from you, personal or professional. None — including the commission to decorate your office."

"*What?*" He stared at her in astonishment. "But that's ridiculous. What does the commission have to do . . . ?"

A quick shake of her head silenced him. "Ridiculous or not, that's the way it must be. I mean it, Michael, and nothing you can say will change my mind." Tension spiraling inside her, tying her nerves into twanging knots, Leigh dragged a breath into her constricted chest, then told herself to get it over with. "Yes or no."

"Yes," he said at once, a flame springing to life in his eyes. Then softly, so softly, he asked, "When?"

When? The bottom fell out of Leigh's resolve. She hadn't thought that far ahead. But she had started this, she reminded herself. He deserved an answer, however strained.

"Whenever you wish."

"Tonight," he again answered at once, his tone adamant and free of strain. "I have a late appointment. I'm meeting here with a group of engineers to finalize plans for the installation of air conditioning in a high-rise pending construction," he surprised her with the courtesy of an explanation. "They're on a tight schedule, so we'll eat in here, work through dinner. I hope to conclude by eight."

Eight. The number rang inside her head like a death knell. Leigh repressed a shiver.

"I'll come to you directly from here," he went on when she remained silent, that one eyebrow arching. "Agreed?"

"Yes." A whisper, but a commitment nonetheless.

The deal was struck, and she was stuck with it.

Sixteen

Seven hours to wait, possibly longer.

"Damn —"

Curses rolled off his tongue in muttered growls as Michael prowled his office, not unlike a big, golden cat impatient for the keeper to arrive and toss him a large chunk of meat.

Hell, he hadn't even kissed her.

Why hadn't he? he railed at himself, all the while knowing the answer. He hadn't kissed her, hadn't so much as touched her, simply because Leigh had seemed so coolly composed, so utterly remote, so removed from the distasteful necessity of discussing the terms and conditions of a physical alliance between them. Damned if he hadn't been afraid to touch her, never mind kiss her. It damn sure hadn't been because he hadn't wanted to touch her, kiss her — every inch of her.

What was it with her, anyway?

It wasn't the first time he had taxed himself with the baffling question.

He had never met a woman quite like Leigh.

It wasn't the first time he had contemplated the difference between her and the other females he knew. And there had been plenty of them.

Sensitive to that very difference, he had observed — with an unusual and uncomfortable twist of possessiveness — the sly and overt looks of admiration and barely concealed lust cast on her by men of all ages on the two occasions he had escorted her into restaurants.

Though annoyed by those speculative, covetous masculine glances, Michael had been more impressed by Leigh's reaction to them, simply because she had evinced no reaction at all, as if she hadn't even noticed.

Impervious barely described her demeanor, her attitude, or the lack of same, to men in general.

Yet, Michael reminded himself, Leigh had raised the subject, boldly asking if he wanted an affair with her.

He wanted . . . Lord, how he wanted.

Michael couldn't recall the last time he had wanted something quite so badly. Hell, he couldn't remember ever wanting anything that much.

He had been wanting since the day he'd walked into her office, so damned confident and thus unprepared for the devastating effect the mere sight of her had on him.

With wry self-understanding, Michael acknowledged that he had been practically panting after Leigh ever since that fateful first meeting.

And when she'd walked into his office today . . . At the thought, his mind recreated the scene.

Her auburn hair gleaming, her tall willowy form striking in the elegant jacketed sheath, her long, gorgeous legs displayed to advantage below the hem of the narrow skirt, Leigh had swept into his office like a swirl of fresh spring air, taking his breath, blowing his mind free of every thought but one.

God, she is magnificent.

Michael inhaled a ragged breath, his body hard and hurting, as it had been . . . No, it was worse now.

Seven hours.
Seven hours.
Possibly longer.
Probably longer.
If I survive.
Dammit.

By eight-twenty Wednesday night, Leigh knew exactly how many steps it took to traverse her apartment from one end to the other, and she had only been home from the office a little over two hours.

Counting to herself, she had paced off every one of those steps at least four times, and every one of those steps had been fraught with disturbing and conflicting feelings of anticipation and apprehension, with a scintillating dash of excitement tossed into the mix.

In between her agitated pacing trips, Leigh had heated a can of soup for her supper, which she'd barely touched, and had brewed a pot of tea, which she'd cradled in her hands and sipped while making her pacing trips.

She also had had a shower, had shampooed her hair and changed clothes — twice.

What did one wear for a night of cold-blooded sex? she'd asked herself, staring into her closet after rejecting her first two selections. Were there specific garments considered de rigueur for the occasion? Or did one simply greet one's intended partner swathed in plastic wrap or merely in one's birthday suit?

Deciding she was getting perilously close to the edge of hysteria, Leigh pulled from the closet a silky at-home palazzo ensemble with wide pants and a loose flowing top in a shimmery emerald green shot through with slashes of silver.

For one mad moment, before slipping into the outfit, she even toyed with the idea of wearing nothing but skin under the pants and top — to precipitate matters and get the deed done — but quickly rejected the notion when her heart began palpitating and she broke out in a cold sweat. Instead, she stepped into sheer black briefs and front-clipped a lacy black bra, which was the next thing to her birthday suit.

Her breathing shallow, her fingers trembling, she masked her pale face with a light application of makeup and gave her hair a vigorous brushing until the gleaming mass crackled around her taut shoulders.

Deciding she was as ready as she'd ever be to join the ranks of the initiated, Leigh resumed her pacing barefooted, but that was not a concession to the ultimate intent of the evening; she always went barefoot at home.

At eight-thirty-six — she knew the exact time, because she glared at the clock — beginning to feel seriously ridiculous and more than a little funny in her stomach, she curled up in the corner of the sofa and picked up the paper she'd bought at a stand near the State store, where she'd purchased a bottle of Bombay gin on her way home from the office, hoping a reality check of local and world news events might lend perspective to the events soon to unfold in her personal life.

She lasted all of five minutes. Churned up as she most definitely was to begin with, that was all Leigh could devote to the accounts of murder, mayhem, drugs and politics at one sitting.

She was plumping the sofa toss pillows, for the tenth or eleventh time, when the doorbell chimed somewhere around eight forty-five.

Expecting it, listening for it, the sudden ring still startled her so badly, she jumped. The toss pillow went sailing over the arm of the sofa, missing the table lamp's shade by a fraction and landing on the floor with a soft plop.

For an extended moment, Leigh froze in place, her heart racing, her lungs refusing to function as she stared at the color-splashed pillow on the floor.

The bell rang again, quick, sharp, as if activated by the impatient jab of a finger. The startling sound of it effectively broke the thrall, setting her into a flurry of motion.

Zipping around the end of the sofa, Leigh scooped up the pillow, dropped it into place as she retraced her steps around the sofa. Heart thumping, she walked to the door and peered through the peephole, not for the first time wishing the building had some form of security system, however rudimentary, at the least an intercom.

Even with the distorted view afforded by the convex lens, there was no questioning the distinctly masculine figure in the hallway near the door.

She drew a deep breath, and then another, trying to calm the flutter in her chest.

For a moment, an extended instant, tendrils of incipient panic swirled, rooting her to the floor; Leigh squashed them just as instantly. Composing herself, her features, she deactivated the three security locks, and swung open the door.

And there he was, the beautiful devil in the disguise of a glorious angel, attired in a navy blue suit and white shirt, the top two buttons undone, the end of a gray-and-red-striped tie sticking out of his pocket. He indolently leaned against the door frame, his expression hinting at mild boredom, looking for all the world like a man making a duty visit to a casual friend.

Leigh was seized by, and nearly gave in to, a compelling urge to slam the door in his handsome face.

"Am I too late?"

Too late? *Too late!* Leigh railed to herself, anger now swirling into the mix of emotions racketing inside her. His bland tones held a faint shading of chagrin, as if he had been invited for an evening of dinner and conversation, rather than a coldly agreed-upon night of debauchery.

The very idea of a night of debauchery, the exact meaning of which she hardly comprehended, dashed her anger while igniting her sense of humor and had Leigh fighting an impulse to laugh. Controlling the tremor on her lips with supreme effort, she shook her head, more to clear and collect her jumbled thoughts than in answer.

What, precisely, did occur during a night of debauchery? she mused, wondering if Michael knew the answer.

"Then" — he lifted a brow — "may I come in?"

Reining in her mind's tendency to wander into erotic realms, Leigh conquered another spurt of laughter and stepped back, dragging the door along with her. "Yes . . ." — she flailed the air with a hand — "of course."

Giving her a strange look, he walked by her, from the dimly lit hallway into the bright lamplit room, giving Leigh her first clear look at his eyes.

In contrast to his bland expression, Michael's crystal blue eyes were backlit by a flame of rigidly controlled desire. His searing gaze stole her breath, her dwindling strength and her meager store of caution.

Warmth stirred deep inside Leigh, a molten warmth unlike anything she had ever experienced, not even during their heated kiss in the car the previous Sunday. For a moment, she feared she lacked the coordination to shut the door, never mind cross the room to a chair on which to collapse.

She managed the door, slamming it shut with a jerky shove. Then she stood there, as if transfixed to the spot, staring in mesmerized bemusement into the flame leaping even higher, hotter in his eyes.

Michael returned her stare for a moment; then his gaze slowly lowered, drawing chillbumps to the surface of her skin with his glittering perusal of her body.

"You looked beautiful in the white outfit you wore to my office today — beautiful, and remote, and untouchable." His voice was soft, rough edged, exciting. "But I like this outfit better," he murmured, moving to close the short distance between them. "In this" — he raised a hand to stroke a finger over the silk covering her shoulder — "you look beautiful and sexy and very touch-able."

Leigh stopped breathing, her heart racing, as his finger glided to the neckline of her top and followed the vee opening down to the valley between her breasts.

"You're trembling." He lifted his gaze from her breasts to sear her eyes with the blue flame in his. His voice went lower still. "Are you afraid of me, Leigh?"

"No." She matched his stare while raising her chin a notch. "But, I feel I must tell you, I'm —"

"Uncertain?" he inserted, interrupting.

"Inexperienced," she finished, despairing at hearing the dry rawness in her voice, at feeling the visible shiver rippling through her.

His smile was tender, knowing. "I figured that out for myself." His finger moved down to her waist. His hand flattened against her, the warmth of his palm making her skin tingle through the sheer material. His palm slid around her waist and was joined by his other hand, caging her with his arms in a loose embrace. "Were you afraid I'd pounce on you the minute I crossed your threshold?"

Feeling oddly both trapped and protected, Leigh shook her head in answer and lowered her eyes, her breathing catching as her gaze settled on his beautifully delineated yet utterly masculine mouth.

"I promise, I will not rush you into anything. I will be careful, go slowly."

That mouth drew closer to hers as he slowly lowered his head. Leigh's heart thrummed, her throat dried, her tongue snaked out to wet her parted lips.

Michael sighed, touched his mouth to hers . . . and wet her lips with a slick glide of his own tongue.

Leigh had formulated a vague plan to offer him a snack and a drink — which was why she had bought the Bombay gin — and to engage him in conversation, before . . .

The plan went out of her head, everything, every thought went out of her head — every thought but one. Michael's mouth and the incredible sensations it stirred to life inside her. She was on fire from the instant of contact.

Leigh was a strong woman, a self-determined woman, and she had made a conscious decision. She was not vanquished by the fire he alone had the power to ignite within her. She did not surrender to it. She reveled in it.

Disdaining being careful and slow, she raised her hands to clasp his head, deliberately deepening the kiss.

Michael's response was immediate and electrifying. His arms tightened compulsively, crushing her softness to the muscled hardness of his body. The gentle touch of his lips turned savage with demand, his tongue thrust deep, staking a claim to her mouth.

Leigh couldn't get close enough to him, *feel* enough of him. Needing more, she arched against his taut hardness, pressing into him with her starving body, and spearing the silky thickness of his golden mane with her fingers, tugging him closer, closer to her hungry mouth.

She was never sure afterward who initiated that move into her bedroom, nor did she care. All she later recalled was that they were there, next to her bed, tearing at each other's clothes, tossing garments aside in a mad frenzy to touch, caress, feel flesh against flesh.

After flinging back the covers, and sliding next to her on the bed, Michael quickly proved to her the truth of his reputed expertise.

Moving with mind- and nerve-wracking slowness, he proceeded to drive her to the edge of sanity with excruciating pleasures.

He began by learning every inch of her

face with the butterfly touch of his lips.

"Your hair . . ." he murmured, lightly kissing her temple, while coiling strands around his forefinger. "Your hair is fantastic, like dark chocolate–hued silken threads, shot through with shimmering streaks of fire." He sprinkled quick moist kisses from her temple to the corner of her eye. "And you know how much I love chocolate."

Leigh might have answered, if she could only have found the strength to lift her mouth from the enticing, slightly salty taste of the warm skin at the curve of his neck.

"Your eyes . . ." He closed them with a soft kiss. "I dream about your eyes . . . the green so deep, so mysterious, like a shadowed forest glen, cool and inviting."

This time Leigh managed to respond, in a way, to his touch, his low voice, his words — and to the riot of sensations they sparked along her nervous system. She sighed a breathy "Hmmm" against the hard edge of his jaw.

"Your skin . . ." Michael paid homage to her cheeks with his lips and his tongue. "Your skin is so soft, like warm satin, and it smells so damn good."

Leigh trembled a reply, and skimmed her own lips up to his squared, rock-solid chin.

"Your mouth . . ." His breath feathered over her lips; she parted them on a sigh. "Your mouth has been the object of my erotic fantasies since the day I walked into your office. I wanted it then, on the spot. I'll have it now." His lips brushed hers. "I wanted you then, on the spot, on your desk." He groaned into her mouth. "I'll have you . . . soon."

Leigh felt boneless, weightless; shivering with anticipation on the outside, burning with need on the inside. Her mouth captured his on the second brushing pass and settled, clung, surrendered to the mastery of it.

His lips and tongue thoroughly explored her mouth, until her lips were red, swollen, sensitized to the feel, the exclusive ownership of his caress.

Her mind drenched in sensuality, her body aching for yet more, Leigh palmed his shoulders and back, sank her nails into unyielding muscle. Undulating, her body slid against his in a silent demand for something, something.

Only then did Michael transfer his attention from her mouth to her squirming form. Leaving a moist trail with his lips and tongue, he surveyed the arch of her throat, blazing a path to her quivering breasts.

His tongue flicked first one, then the other nipple.

A gasp was wrenched from Leigh's throat as a hot streak of sensation zinged from her nipple to her feminine core. Reflexively, she arched her back.

"Beautiful, so beautiful," he murmured, tonguelashing the tightening peaks into throbbing arousal.

Leigh moaned, deep in her throat, then cried out at the unbelievable sensations tearing through her as his lips closed around a stinging nipple, drawing on it, greedily suckling on her flesh.

A moment later, his hand stroked down to cup her mound, long fingers raking through auburn curls. Leigh cried out again when his fingers parted the folds to find, caress, the aching heart of her heated core, and yet again when one finger delved, testing the desire-moistened passageway into her body.

On fire, a raging flame burning for his possession, Leigh arched her hips against his hand, wanting, needing, desperate for the fullness of his body inside hers.

She whimpered when he pulled back, away from her.

"Soon," Michael whispered, bending to kiss the insides of her parted thighs. "You're so beautiful," he murmured, dropping tiny wet kisses up the length of one trembling thigh, to the apex of her legs.

Startled, shocked, Leigh stilled as his breath bathed her an instant before he bestowed on her the most intimate of kisses.

"Michael . . . no." But even as she refused him, her needy body arched into his kiss.

His tongue touched her.

The fire inside Leigh blazed out of control, incinerating her resistance. Twining her fingers into his hair, she clung to the solidity of him, riding the waves of unimagined pleasure pounding her into submission to his will.

When the final wave crashed, Leigh collapsed, shuddering in the aftermath of shattering release, absently aware of the faint sound of ripping foil.

Her breathing was beginning to level when Michael moved into position between her thighs. Her eyes widened in surprise, excitement stirred to renewed life again when he slid his hands beneath her and raised her hips off the mattress.

"Michael," she whispered his name.

"Yes," he whispered. "You're ready now." Grasping her hips, he leaned forward, took her lips and thrust his tongue into her mouth, his body into hers.

Leigh had known what to expect, had

known there would be a moment of pain. Still the sudden tearing inside caught her off guard. She cried out; her muscles clenched.

Michael froze. He blinked in disbelief. Then he cursed.

"Jesus Christ, Leigh, why didn't you tell me?"

She stared up at him, into the amazement shading his eyes, into the rigid set of his features. The pain had dissipated. Her muscles were slowly relaxing. It really hadn't been all that traumatic, or off-putting. She shrugged. "I didn't think it mattered."

"Not matter?" He muttered another curse. "Dammit, I wouldn't have put my mouth to you — not for your first experience. And I would have taken more care if I had, I'd have realized — You're so tight." Heaving a sigh, he began to withdraw. "I wouldn't have hurt you so much."

"No." She clutched at his hips, holding him inside her. "Michael, it's all right now. The pain's gone." Her claim was true, so far as it went; the pain was gone. Still, there remained a slight discomfort, a stretching caused by her body's adjusting to the fullness of him.

"You're sure?" While his eyes expressed concern, his tone betrayed a hint of expectancy.

"I'm positive. I didn't come this far to back off now." She enforced her assertion with a tentative movement of her hips against his.

It was Michael's undoing. His chest expanded in a sharp inhalation that shuddered out on a sigh.

"Oh, hell, Leigh, do that again . . . please."

A sense of feminine power stormed through Leigh, fanning the flames of desire to a roaring demand. But instead of merely granting his plea with a gentle movement of her hips, she slid her hands to his buttocks, and thrusting forward, forced him deeper into her.

"Yes." Michael shut his eyes, only for a moment, and when he again opened them, unbridled desire glittered in those crystal blue depths. "Ahhh, Leigh," he said in a feral-sounding near growl. "I knew you were hiding strong passions behind that cool exterior you wear."

Leaning down to her once more, he kissed her with breathtaking intensity, and began moving in a rhythm dating back to the first man.

And like the first woman, enthralled, beguiled, Leigh drank the wine of sensuality from Michael's intoxicating mouth and followed his lead in the waltz to fulfillment.

It was a wonderful, muscle-clenching, nerve-twanging, mind-shattering whirl.

Michael was magnificent, driving Leigh to the edge, then easing her back, only to resume the process. Writhing, her body sheened with perspiration, each breath a sob wrenched from her heaving chest, Leigh matched him thrust for thrust, parry for parry, taking as well as giving, driving him as relentlessly as he drove her.

In the instant before cataclysm, Michael reared back, spine bowed, throat arched, eyes closed, features stark; taut with strain. Then, drawing a quick, shaky breath, he drove deep, gasped, and trembled with the force of release.

Leigh cried out his name in the throes of ecstasy.

How long they lay, replete and exhausted, Leigh hadn't a clue, it could have been seconds or minutes or hours. She didn't know; she didn't care. For that length of time, however long it might have been, all she knew was the delicious weight of Michael's spent body pressing her into the mattress, his ragged breaths rasping in her ear, his palm soothingly caressing her side from her shoulder to her breast to her waist, over the curve of her hip and along her still quivering thigh to her knee, then back again.

He murmured his appreciation as she reciprocated, the gliding movement of her hand reflecting the soothing downward stroke of his.

"Perfect." He gently sank his teeth into her earlobe. "You're perfection." The swirl of his tongue against a spot behind her ear drew a responsive shiver from her. "We're perfect together . . . I knew we would be."

Leigh sighed, and wriggled beneath him; she hadn't known the ear and surrounding area were so sensitive. Then she gasped, surprised at feeling him quicken inside her; she hadn't known that was possible so soon, either.

"Yesss . . . pure perfection," Michael crooned, tickling her ear, and her fancy. "Let's do it again."

Too startled by her own immediate resurgence of desire to articulate, Leigh laughed in glorious abandon, curling her legs around him in enticing response.

It was past two A.M. when, yawning and half-asleep, Leigh walked Michael to the door. And it was past two-thirty, when, clinging to him after one last kiss — the fifth — she found the strength to open the door.

But it was two forty-five when he finally left.

Seventeen

Considering how late it was when she'd crawled into bed — to at last sleep — and the vigorous exercise she had engaged in with Michael in the preceding hours, Leigh felt amazingly good when her alarm rang in the morning.

The sun was shining, and the air was balmy. What was not to feel good about?

Maybe there was something to the claim about the tension-easing benefits of sexual satisfaction, Leigh mused, as she strolled to the office — a stroll being the best she could manage, since she was too tender in too many places for her normal brisk stride.

A soft smile of well-being curved her kiss-sensitized lips. Who would have thought she'd turn out to be a sensualist? Rather than upsetting her, the idea amused Leigh, had her wondering why she had waited so long to indulge.

The answer was right there, in the forefront of her mind. She had waited, had planned to continue on a course of abstinence because of her mistrust of men, of their motives. The clumsy groping and the ineptitude during her one and only previous attempt at sexual experimentation, with that idiot who couldn't handle two beers — or one woman — had merely reinforced her determination to give sex a pass.

Of course, that was before she had crossed paths, and verbal swords, with Michael St. Claire.

Thinking his name conjured his image, evoked vivid memories of his passion, caused a thrilling inner quiver.

Michael was . . . Descriptive terms and phrases assailed her mind, banged together, became tangled, but one phrase stood out, bold and clear.

Michael embodied everything any woman, every woman, fantasized about in a lover: tender, gentle, caring, yet masterful, aggressive, powerful in turn.

Leigh caught her breath on a muted gasp as corresponding images flashed through her mind, arousing her, tingeing her cheeks with color. The warmth of sensual excitement converged in the most sensitive part of her body.

Heavens, she thought, quickly glancing around at the faces of the crowd to see if anyone had heard her soft gasp, taken note of her sudden flush, wondered at her faltering step. Fortunately, intent on their own thoughts and pursuits, no one appeared to have paid attention.

Damned if I'm not in lust, Leigh thought, laughter at her self-betraying reactions tickling her throat.

She lusted after Michael's body. And why not? she reflected. It was worth lusting after. And he used it so well to her advantage.

Leigh was still laughing to herself when she swept into her two-room office suite.

"Morning, Leigh. Coffee's just about ready," Sheila greeted, flashing a quick smile over her shoulder from her position at the credenza.

"Good morning." Leigh flashed a smile back. "Isn't it a glorious day?"

Her assistant nodded in agreement. "Perfection."

Perfection. The word reverberated inside Leigh's head, but the echoing voice was deeper. Michael had said she, they, were perfection together. Remembering sent shards of anticipation of the recreation of that perfection splintering through her.

"You look . . . different this morning."

Sheila's observation effectively doused the spark of desire kindling in Leigh. Trying to appear her normal self, she raised her eyebrows. "Different in what way?" she asked, as if she didn't know.

"I'm not sure how to explain it," Sheila said, a puzzled frown scoring her smooth forehead. "It's just . . ." She shrugged. "You look — Oh, I don't know . . . content, maybe."

How about sated? Leigh thought, a smile teasing her lips as she taxed her mind for a suitable reply.

Fortunately, Sheila spared her the effort. Snapping her fingers, she exclaimed, "I know — the contract. You signed the contract with Michael yesterday."

"Ahhh . . . no." Leigh shook her head, rather amazed that she didn't feel so much as a twinge of regret over her decision. "I turned down the commission."

Sheila stared at her in astonished disbelief. "You did what?"

"You heard me." Leigh took a sip of coffee.

"But" — Sheila set her blond curls jiggling with a sharp shake of her head — "why?"

Leigh considered offering an excuse, a bald-faced lie, but immediately rejected the idea in favor of the truth, which Sheila would likely learn anyway, and more likely sooner rather than later.

"Simple, really." She moved her shoulders in a light shrug. "I chose not to mix business with pleasure."

There was the briefest hesitation before Sheila proved she was quick on the uptake. Her blue eyes flew wide, and she gave a burst of delighted laughter. "You . . . and Michael St. Claire? *I love it.*"

"I thought you would," Leigh drawled, recalling how often Sheila had predicted that she would someday be swept off her feet by some special man.

Well, sure enough, Leigh mused. That day and that special man had finally arrived, and he had swept her right off her feet . . . and into bed. It was wonderful.

Sheila stopped smiling smugly to resume frowning. "But, Leigh, don't you think rejecting such a lucrative commission is a little extreme?"

"No." Leigh shook her head, but suddenly reminded of the financial situation, both her own and Brett's, she turned to her office door. "By the way," she went on, opening it, "I won't be in the office tomorrow, so I need you to rearrange whatever appointments I have."

"Okay." Sheila didn't bat an eyelash. "You're meeting with Michael again?"

Leigh smiled and shook her head. "No. I'm meeting with Brett — a business matter."

Fully aware of Brett's continued dependence on his sister in times of financial strain, Sheila frowned, but knowing it would fall on deaf ears, she kept her opinion to herself.

Grateful for her friend's hard-fought reticence, Leigh smiled her approval and thanks. "So, under the circumstances, I do think I'd better get to work." She crossed the threshold, then paused to again smile back at Sheila before entering her office. "I can't afford to lose the commissions we do have by displeasing our clients."

The phone rang as she was closing the door.

Circling around to the front of her desk, Sheila said, "Hopefully, this will be another prospective client. I have a feeling you'll need all you can get."

His mind a distracting jumble of thoughts and impressions, all related to the incredible hours he'd spent in Leigh's bed, Michael held out as long as he could — all of five minutes after entering his office at nine — before giving in to the need to call her. But, before he could tell Rosalie he had an important call to make and didn't want to be disturbed, his direct-line phone rang.

Certain of the caller's identity, and feeling a flicker of impatience for the first time ever, he grabbed the receiver on the second ring.

"Good morning, Barbara," he said, surprised at how hard he had to work at keeping his tone normal.

"Damn you, Michael." Her tone was far from normal, the raspiness abraded by emotion.

"I love you, too," he drawled, frowning over what crisis could have occurred to cause such an unusual effect on her. "What's the problem, darling?"

"It's all your fault." Her harsh accusation was followed by the distinctive click of a cigarette lighter, her deep inhalation of smoke.

"More'n likely," he agreed, in soothing tones. "Want to tell me about it?"

"I'm in love." She didn't tell it, she wailed it.

Michael laughed . . . to himself. "Anyone I know?"

"Oh, cute," she growled. "Really cute. You know damned well it's that blasted houseboy of yours."

Dumping tact, he laughed in her ear. "Not much of a boy, though, is he sweetheart?" he chided.

Barbara sighed.

Michael could have sworn he felt it. He felt a tug at his heart, as well; her sigh spoke volumes about the vulnerability and uncertainty she was feeling. Unused to, and not particularly liking the unfamiliar helplessness her sigh conveyed, he hastened to offer assurance.

"It's all right, Barbara, you can trust him. Shamus is one of the good guys."

"Oh, Michael, I know. I suppose I knew it all along." She sighed again, but with a different note that reassured him. "He's, he's . . . incredible."

"I coulda told you that, dear friend." He was relieved. Devilment danced in his eyes, in his voice. "Wait till you taste his Yankee pot roast."

"I'm not referring to Clancy's culinary expertise, and you know it, smartass."

"No?" He affected shock. "What then?"

When it came, her voice was a satisfied, raspy whisper. "We spent the night together."

Hmm, he thought, the urge to merge must be contagious. Michael didn't offer his conclusion aloud, he offered his congratulations, instead. "Good for you. And I mean that in more than the obvious way."

"Which is?"

"I believe you're good for Clancy and Clancy's good for you."

The hesitant note crept back. "But, Michael, what about the age difference?"

"Bunk," he retorted. "For Christ's sake, Barbara, think about it. You're less than ten years older than Clancy. Big deal. I didn't notice you frowning over the interest your new acquaintance Jenson evinced for young Sheila . . . and I do mean young; Sheila has got to be close to, if not more than, twenty-five years his junior."

"I know, I know, but still, I —"

"Hold it," he cut in without compunction. "You're talking to Michael, re-member, the man who knows you, possibly, probably better than any other person. And I know you to be a singularly independent thinker. So think, will you, before you smother your chance for a mutually satis-fying relationship by sinking into the quag-mire of the double standard." Protective anger nearly choking him, he paused for a quick breath.

When she didn't jump right in to dispute him, Michael charged ahead. "Barbara, I have never known you to follow the path of convention. Why start now? Screw conven-tion. If you want the man, if he can fill the empty corners of your life, for God's sake, grab him."

"You aren't into mincing words, are you?" Her soft, raspy chuckle soothed his ruffled feathers.

"Was I ever?"

She laughed. "Come to think of it, no.

You've always been a straight shooter."

"Right," he agreed. "And I'm not about to change at this late date. In fact, I'll fire off another straight shot, aimed at your heart — the man's crazy about you, honey."

"Ohhh . . . Michael." Her voice melted like chocolate left out in the summer sunlight. "I do love you. That's something Shamus and I have in common; he loves you, too."

A tender smile curved Michael's lips, for the woman who had had such a profound effect on his life and the man who had devoted himself to him ever since Michael had saved Shamus's life.

As a young man, Shamus had had real potential in the square arena called a ring. A light heavyweight, Clancy had lowered the boom on many opponents on his way up through the ranks. He had a wicked left jab. Problem was, Clancy also had a wicked temper, and a voracious appetite for booze and women — broads, as he called them.

Overindulgence in the booze and broads took a toll on Clancy's health and stamina. Indulging his temper led him down the path of self-destruction.

Shamus had been near the end of that path, trapped in a dark alley, outnumbered and having his brains rearranged by the fists of three thugs when, still in his late teens, Michael passed by the alley on his way to the tiny rented room he wouldn't have considered referring to as "home."

Michael had hesitated, every instinct he possessed urging him to move on, to ignore the unmistakable sounds of raining blows, the grunts and groans, the weak moans for help from the injured party. But, in good conscience, he couldn't ignore the reedy-voiced plea.

Figuring attack was his best, possibly his only, chance of any success at all, Michael had pulled off the heavy lid from an old metal trash can and charged into that alley screaming like an ancient warrior gone berserk. The element of surprise, along with the wildly swinging lid proved effective. The thugs gave up the field of battle, scurrying away into the night like the rats they were.

Then, once again, Michael had hesitated. But he just couldn't leave the injured combatant lying there in a spreading pool of his own blood. Coaxing, heaving, cursing, Michael had managed to get the man upright; then, bearing most of his weight, he had stumbled and staggered to his room.

He had shared that tiny room with Shamus for a couple of years, through the Irishman's period of recovery from the wounds inflicted by those thugs and through an even longer period of detoxification.

Claiming Michael had literally saved his life and his soul, Shamus had served Michael ever since, both as houseman and by remaining clean and sober.

Nothing Michael said to the contrary could change Clancy's mind. When Michael started to reap the rewards of the long hours and hard work he devoted to his fledgling business, relocating into a succession of ever larger quarters, Shamus moved with him, forgoing the boxing arena for the role of houseman, learning to keep house by trial and error, how to prepare food by attending night-school cooking classes.

They bonded, became as close as natural brothers, with one difference. To Shamus Clancy, Michael was and would always be the undisputed boss.

To Michael, Shamus became not only the brother, but the father he had never known. And now his sense of satisfaction was great at hearing about the budding relationship between his mentor and his friend.

"I know, and I love you both." Michael swallowed against a tightness in his throat. "So make me happy by being happy together. Okay?"

"Yes." A mere whisper. "Thank you, darling."

The minute he had disconnected, still holding the direct-line receiver, Michael buzzed Rosalie to tell her he was not to be disturbed until further notice. He was dialing Leigh's number as he issued his instructions.

"Good morning." Sheila chirped in his ear like a spring hatchling. "Interiors by Leigh. May I help you?"

"Good morning," Michael responded, smiling at the chipper-bright sound of her. "This is —"

"Oh, Mr. St. Claire," she exclaimed, finishing for him. "Just a second, I'll connect you to her."

Michael grinned. Last night he had been connected to Leigh, and he ached to repeat the performance, which was precisely why he was calling.

In the brief moments required to transfer the call, Michael's mind whirled with memories of their night together. His senses clamored a demand to again experience the incredible sensations derived from being with, inside, Leigh.

Never before in his sexual life had Michael scaled such physical and emotional heights, exploded in climax with such mind-

and soul-shattering pleasure, as he had known, not once but twice, while lying between her thighs, embraced by her long, gorgeous legs.

And she a virgin, at that.

Incredible.

He shuddered in reaction to the memories.

"Yes, Michael?"

He shuddered again at hearing her soft voice — an echo of her voice in the night, not in questioning of but in surrender to him.

"How are you feeling this morning, Leigh?" he asked, wanting, needing her reaffirmation of her commitment to him, if only of their physical union.

To his utter relief, she did not play coy.

"Surprisingly good," she said with wry humor. "Considering the exercises we indulged in last night."

He laughed, softly. "Wanna do it again tonight?"

She hesitated.

Alarm blanked his mind, stopped his breath.

"I . . ." She sighed. "Yes."

He resumed breathing.

"But it must be earlier, Michael. I have to go out of town early tomorrow morning, and I must get some rest."

Sheer, unadulterated jealousy erupted like a volcano inside him, astonishing in its intensity. He inhaled a deep breath, then slowly exhaled before attempting a response. "Will you be gone for the entire weekend?" Asperity tinged his voice; he didn't care, figuring it was better than the anger tearing at his gut.

"I don't know." Her tone had cooled somewhat, implicit with a warning against crowding her.

Michael heard, understood and resented the implication, the unstated command to him to back off. Suspicion blended with jealousy into a bitter-tasting concoction.

Was there another man in Leigh's life?

The very thought enraged him.

The last time she had gone away for the weekend, he had tormented himself with wild imaginings of her with another man, in the way she had been with *him* the night before.

But she had not been with another man, he reminded himself. At least, not in the same manner she had been with him.

He had been the first.

The sensation that realization instilled far outweighed his earlier feeling of satisfaction, which was odd, as he had never subscribed to the double standard regarding a woman's sexual experience.

Atavistic? Maybe.

"Michael?"

Leigh's voice nudged him from his reverie, into the here and now, the frustration of spending the weekend alone, edgy and wondering about . . .

"Will you tell me where you're going?" he asked, denying an urge to demand the name of the individual she'd be seeing. He had no right to question her. One night of great — no, fantastic — sex hadn't given him proprietorial rights over her actions, her choice of companions.

Dammit.

"Lancaster." Her response came after a brief hesitation, granting him at least the right to press her further.

"You're going home? To your parents' home?" Michael barely succeeded in concealing his relief.

Once again, Leigh hesitated, then conceded with a soft sigh. "Yes, but primarily I'm going to see my brother."

"There's a problem?" Michael's protective instincts went on alert. "A family problem?"

"Michael . . ." A definite warning there, cautioning him against overstepping the line.

Chafing against the boundaries she had

set, and he had agreed to abide by, regarding their association, Michael stewed in the simmering juices of frustration and impotence. He wanted, needed, to be allowed to offer her his help and support, moral, financial, emotional — whatever she might require.

"Leigh . . ." Michael was amazed and slightly shocked by the note of pleading in his voice, the levels of meaning in that one spoken word.

"I can handle it," she said, her tone softening with appreciation for his concern. "I'll be fine."

He gave in with reluctance. "All right." Then defiance flared. "If you're certain?"

"I am."

Michael stilled at her tone. Was that a thread of tender amusement woven through her voice? Tenderness? For him? God, he hoped so. Deciding to test the waters of her restrictions, he cleared his throat.

"Uh, Leigh, does dinner come under the heading of gifts in your book of strictures?"

She laughed.

He drew a deep, relaxing breath.

"What did you have in mind?"

"Any restaurant you fancy." Michael was envisioning a quiet off-the-beaten-path place he knew.

"Oh, Michael, how about take-out?" Her tone became sultry, sirenlike. "We could be more comfortable, eat at our leisure, then . . ." Her voice trailed away.

He got the picture, or rather, the picture got to him. He was hard already, and it wasn't midmorning yet. "How about Chinese?"

"I've got the tea."

Michael shot a glance at his appointment book. "I've got a conference call at four. It shouldn't last longer than an hour and a half. I'll pick up the food after I leave the office and come straight to your place. Okay?"

"Perfect."

And it was perfect, Michael reflected later that night as he slid between the cold sheets on his suddenly too large and much too empty bed.

All of it, the laughter, the sheer enjoyment they'd derived from delving into the array of foods he had chosen, because he didn't know her preferences — perfect.

The heated, sensuous glances they'd exchanged while sipping the green tea she had brewed — perfect.

The heights they had attained later, lost to the world while loving each other — perfect.

But, for Michael, in his eyes, in his thoughts, Leigh was the most perfect of all.

A sigh whispered through his lips as he settled into the huge bed, a sigh of utter contentment.

Leigh was everything he had never expected to find with a woman. He felt comfortable, at home with her, whether in the office, seated at the kitchen table, or lying between her thighs, buried deep inside her.

Home.

Perfection.

A wry smile twitched at the corners of Michael's mouth.

Damned if he didn't suspect he was falling in love.

Strange thing was, the idea didn't scare him at all.

Eighteen

It was done.

Leigh affixed her signature, not with a flourish but a sigh, to the last of the pile of documents.

Who would have dreamed co-signing a line of credit would require so much paperwork?

"That's it." Shuffling the papers together, the young bank official Brett had introduced as "something" Vogel — she'd missed the first name — glanced up, displaying an impressive row of white teeth in a smile both self-satisfied and insincere.

Suppressing a grimace at the elation reflected in her brother's expression, and the sinking sensation in her stomach, Leigh hooked the strap of her purse over her shoulder and stood, absently smoothing her skirt over her thighs.

Quickly rising also, the young man extended his right hand. "It's been a pleasure Ms. . . ." He paused, his eyes gleaming with lascivious intent in a bold perusal of her tall, slender figure. "May I call you Leigh?"

Not anytime soon, Leigh thought, gazing

at him with cool disdain, and wiping his name from her memory, while giving a brief, negligent nod of assent.

The young, self-important would-be Lothario, preened and beamed, as if she had issued an open invitation into her bed, instead of a get-lost look.

Strange creatures, men, she mused, giving his hand a quick shake. Of course, there were exceptions, Michael St. Claire to name one. Thinking his name brought him to mind, him and a host of memories, every one of them exciting.

Suddenly anxious to be gone, from that cramped office and the bank, on her way back to Philadelphia and Michael, she turned to her brother. "Ready, Brett?"

"Yeah, sure." He also shook hands with the young man. "Thanks for all your help, Ralph."

Ralph? Ralph! Leigh controlled an impish urge to laugh — just. She must have been distracted to have missed his given name. Her expression bland, nearly choking on the amusement tickling her throat, she strode from the tiny office and headed for the exit.

"Hey," Brett yelped, trotting after her. "What's the rush?"

Leigh halted. "Since Dad's away for the

weekend, I thought I'd just head back to Philly."

He shot a sharp look at her. "Are you annoyed because Dad went away with Kathie for the weekend?"

"No." She was somewhat surprised to realize that she meant the forceful denial.

"That's a relief. I was kinda afraid you might be."

She took his hand and gave it a squeeze. "I'm not, Brett." Grinning, she raised her other hand to draw an *X* on her chest, as she had so often done when they were kids. "Cross my heart and hope to die."

Brett grinned back at her. "Okay, but at least let me buy you lunch before you leave," he pleaded. "If only in that small way, let me thank you."

She laughed. "Brett, you've been thanking me ever since I arrived this morning."

"I know, but I'll never to able to thank you enough." He smiled. "Come on, Leigh, let me buy you lunch."

Of course, she couldn't refuse. How could she? "Sure. I am a little hungry, now that you mention it. Where do you want to go?"

"There's a place out on the highway, not too far from here." He flicked a hand in the general direction. "It's not fancy, but the food's good and the coffee's great."

Deciding that, after Ralph, she really needed coffee, great or lousy, Leigh agreed.

She followed behind him, frowning in disapproval when she saw him raise a cell phone to his ear. When Brett pulled onto the parking lot she saw that the restaurant was larger than she had expected from his description, low and sprawling, the sign above advertising homestyle food.

Leigh parked in the spot next to Brett and lit into him the minute she slid from her car.

"Don't you know it's not safe to talk on the phone while you're driving?" she scolded, in much the same way she had been scolding him for his own good since they were kids.

"Sure." Brett grinned, in exactly the same way he always had before. "But traffic was light, so I figured it was safe to call Evelyn, tell her where to meet us."

"Evelyn's joining us for lunch?" Stupid question, Leigh chided herself. Hadn't he said she was?

"Of course." He laughed. "She's gotta eat, too."

Wonderful, Leigh mused. "Yes, of course," she said, forcing a smile.

"We don't have to stand here waiting," he said, taking her arm and starting for the entrance. "She'll find us."

"I'm sure," Leigh murmured, her tone wry, her smile plastic as she loped along beside him.

True to Brett's words, the place wasn't fancy. But it was clean and bright, and the aromas wafting on the air did smell like home cooking.

Evelyn arrived soon after their coffee was served. Although she looked fashionable as always, the picture of upper middle-class chic, there was something about her appearance that puzzled Leigh.

She seemed . . . subdued. The word sprang to mind, startling Leigh by its antithesis to Evelyn's usual bold self-confidence.

"Darling . . ." Evelyn murmured, bending to brush a kiss over Brett's cheek before taking the seat next to him. An uncertain smile trembled on her lips. "How are you, Leigh?"

"Fine, thank you," Leigh answered, frowning in confusion as she studied her sister-in-law's anxious expression.

"Everything settled?" Evelyn asked, flicking a nervous glance between Brett and Leigh.

Aha. Mystery solved. Obviously, Evelyn was anxious about Brett's financial situation and its effect on her own spending ability.

Brett patted his wife's hand. "Yes, every-thing's settled." He turned a grateful look on Leigh. "Thanks to Leigh, I know I can now make a success of the business."

With a long sigh, Evelyn slumped back in her chair. "We'll make a success of it," she said, her voice gaining strength. "I swear I'll do my part, Brett."

He smiled and grasped the hand he'd been patting. "I know you will, darling. You've already begun by seriously applying yourself to the bookkeeping and other pa-perwork, freeing me for the on-site details."

Well, well, will wonders never cease? Leigh mused, hearing much in her brother's gentle tone and his spoken praise. Could it be that self-indulgent, self-centered Evelyn had finally smartened up and realized her own well-being was tied to her husband's, Leigh reflected.

Apparently it was so, for Evelyn outdid herself being pleasant throughout the meal. To her amazement, Leigh actually enjoyed herself. Understandably, her pleasure was enhanced by the glimmering of hope con-cerning her own financial situation. For if Brett succeeded in salvaging his business, the risk she had taken by securing his credit line with her own firm would be minimized.

All things considered, she felt a lot more

optimistic after parting company with the couple. She felt so good, in fact, that she did what she had so recently scolded her brother for doing. She used her cell phone while driving to dial the direct-line number Michael had given her.

"More questions?" Michael answered with the mystifying question on the first ring.

"I beg your pardon?" Leigh said, her tone reflecting her frowning confusion.

"Leigh." He sounded gratifyingly pleased at her call. "Where are you?"

Mollified, she smiled. "I'm in the car, breezing along Route 30," she told him.

"I thought you said you were leaving early this morning." His voice reflected his frown.

"I did — leave early, I mean." She laughed. "I'm on my way back, and decided to call you to invite you to dinner. I'll do the cooking," she added as an inducement.

"Oh, damn," he muttered. "I can't, Leigh. I agreed to have dinner with Barbara, just moments ago."

Moments ago. Had Michael thought it was Barbara calling to ask more questions? Leigh wondered, shocked by the searing sting of jealousy she felt and hating it.

"Oh . . ." She faltered, not quite sure how

to respond, afraid she'd revealed too much.

"May I stop by your place later in the evening?" Michael asked, taking advantage of her hesitation.

After being with another woman? The very idea sent a shaft of hot resentment through her. She didn't entertain any doubts about why he wanted to stop by later. Though she wasn't on the dinner menu, she felt certain he intended having her for dessert or a nightcap.

She opened her mouth to deliver a blistering no. But the single word that whispered past her lips was a pitiable defeated, "Yes."

Leigh spent the rest of the day straightening up her apartment, and upbraiding herself for her lack of pride, her spinelessness, her need for him, to be with him, if only for a few, passion-motivated hours.

When she ran out of things to wipe, dust or vacuum, and derogatory names to call herself, she dialed her office to check in with Sheila before her assistant left for the day.

"Interiors by Leigh," Sheila answered in her accustomed bubbly voice. "How may I help you?"

"You could beat the bushes for some new commissions," Leigh said dryly. "I'm afraid I'm going to need them."

"Leigh." Sheila sounded startled to be hearing from her. "Where are you?"

"Here, in my apartment."

"How come?" Sheila was surprised. "I mean, I thought you'd be away until to-morrow."

"Yes, well, we finished our business before noon, and I decided to head for Philly right after lunch." Leigh wasn't about to confess to having anticipated dinner and spending the evening with Michael.

Damn his faithless soul.

"So everything went smoothly, then?"

Leigh grimaced. "For sure. When they saw my books, my current client list, they were delighted to accept Interiors by Leigh as collateral for Brett's line of credit."

"Kinda scary, huh?" Sheila sympathized.

"No, very scary," Leigh admitted.

"I guess I shouldn't say this, but I really think you should have grabbed Mr. St. Claire's offer. It would have secured your business." Sheila gave a half-laugh. "Hell, his name alone would have offered secu-rity."

Leigh bristled, possibly because she knew her friend was right. "I don't trade on names, Sheila," she said, her voice cool.

"I know, I know," Sheila said. "You and your darned, rigid pride."

Leigh was hard put to keep from laughing — hysterically. Pride? What pride? Fat lot of good it had done her to stand on pride and principle in turning down his commission. What of pride and principle now? She had just tossed both aside in ignoring his blatantly admitted dalliance with another woman. And all because she was in lust with him.

Disgusting.

But there it was, like it or not.

Leigh didn't like it. She didn't want to think about it. She changed the subject.

"So, is your date still on to run with Jake Jenson tomorrow morning?" She amazed herself with the lightness she managed to infuse into her voice.

"Rain or shine," Sheila said, in shimmering tones of enthusiastic excitement.

Leigh made a face at the receiver. "Are you serious? You'd really run in the rain?"

"With Jake? You'd better believe it." Sheila giggled. "To be with Jake, I'd run in a hurricane."

Madness, Leigh thought. No question. Both she and Sheila were stark, raving mad.

She had to laugh; it was either that or cry.

"I really, really, like him, Leigh."

"Obviously. Well, have fun."

"I will." Sheila giggled again. "And, hey,

it's spring, too early for hurricanes."

Leigh gave a fatalistic shrug after they hung up. She was still concerned about the age difference between her friend and Jake Jenson. She was also skeptical about Jake's motives — was he looking for a trophy? But, in truth, Sheila's romantic life was none of her business. Sheila was a mature adult, as Michael had pointed out.

Michael.

Having dinner with Barbara . . . an older woman . . . an attractive older woman.

Were Michael and Barbara just friends?

Or . . .

She shuddered. Envisioning Michael with the older woman, the way he had been with her, sickened and angered Leigh at one and the same time.

Nevertheless, she still wanted him.

And she had set the rules. Hadn't she? she ruthlessly reminded herself. An affair. Nothing asked, nothing given. Sex and only sex.

So, then, why wallow in misery because he seemed so willing to abide by her terms? she asked herself, even though the answer was there, tormenting her mind.

Dammit. She'd never said she was willing to share the wealth, of his company or his body.

Shamus had outdone himself. The dinner he had prepared had been an Epicurean's delight.

Michael could only wish he had been able to relax enough to enjoy it, as Barbara most obviously had. She was lavish in her praise for Shamus's culinary talents.

As for himself, Michael longed for the extended meal to end, freeing him to go to Leigh.

Leigh. Absently, he brought the dessert spoon to his mouth, barely aware of what he had scooped from the delicate stemmed-crystal dish. Distracted, he swallowed the cool, smooth stuff, whatever it was.

Leigh. A thrill trickled down Michael's spine, curled around to gather force in his loins. Even now, hours later, he tingled with the pleasure and satisfaction he had felt when she'd called after lunch. And now, so many hours later, he suffered the pangs of regret and disappointment he had felt at having to turn down her invitation to dinner.

She had actually offered to cook for him, this woman who was so cool and composed on the surface, this self-contained woman he strongly suspected harbored an aversion to any kind of endearments, even the very word "love" . . . this same woman who was so sexy and hot for him while making love with him in the dark privacy of the bedroom.

Did her offer signify anything? Dare he hope that Leigh was beginning to care for him? Michael thrilled at the mere thought.

"You don't care for the dessert?"

"What?" Michael frowned, first at Barbara, then at Shamus, the questioner.

"The chocolate pecan pudding is my own concoction," Shamus said, indicating the barely touched sweet in front of his employer. "You don't like it?"

Michael peered at the sweet. He had no recollection of having tasted the pudding, yet he must have done so, as a spoon's scoop gave evidence of the fact.

"Michael not like anything chocolate?" Barbara gave a throaty laugh. "Not in this lifetime."

Michael shot her a quelling glare.

Unquellable, Barbara laughed harder.

"Do you think, maybe, our Michael has something more important even than chocolate on his mind?" Shamus wondered aloud. "Something . . . or someone else?"

"A female someone, you mean?" Barbara played coy. "Perhaps a female someone with red hair and green eyes?"

Michael maintained his cool, it wasn't easy, considering the heat generated inside him by the mere mention of Leigh's beautiful eyes and glorious hair.

Shamus chuckled. "Sure and if I don't suspect the boyo's hot to trot, Babsy, me girl."

Michael winced, dreading an eruption from Barbara at being called the detested nickname. He blinked, staring at her in disbelief when she simply smiled instead of screaming at the big Irishman.

Clancy looked smug. Then, with a jerk of his thumb at the dining-room doorway, he ordered, "Go on, Mike, get moving. The pudding will keep. The lass might not."

"Right." Shoving back his chair, Michael stood and blessed his two best friends with a devilish grin. "I'm outta here. Have fun, and don't do anything I wouldn't do."

"Well, darling, that does give us plenty of leeway," Barbara said drolly. "Since I can't think of anything that you wouldn't do."

"That's true," Michael drawled, turning and striding from the room.

He could hear Clancy's booming laughter echoing inside his head all the way to Leigh's apartment.

Standing at the stove, Leigh tapped her

foot, impatient for the water in the teakettle to come to a whistling boil. The tea she had spooned into the pot was herbal, supposedly calming, soothing.

Leigh needed both. Ever since she had spoken to Michael after lunch, a poisonous mixture of anger and jealousy had tainted her thinking, having a devastating effect on her emotions, her nervous system.

Although she hadn't eaten, had felt too churned up to even think about food, it was past dinnertime, long past, raising doubts and questions that haunted Leigh.

Were Michael and Barbara quite innocently lingering over dinner, perhaps discussing business or old times?

Had they run into some close acquaintance, gotten caught up in conversation?

Or . . .

Leigh shuddered, but couldn't block the destructive, pride-shriveling thought.

Or were Michael and Barbara, their dinner long over, indulging an even more basic appetite?

It didn't bear thinking about, yet Leigh's repeated attempts to banish it had failed miserably.

She had considered seeking inner strength from her cherished music box. But what good would that do? She knew, as well as her mother had, that there were no bright tomorrows, no maybe about it, simply because tomorrow never came. With each successive new dawn it was always today.

No bright tomorrows, no maybes and no honest men.

Users. Hadn't she known all men were users? Leigh railed, glaring at the kettle, the tempo of her foot-tapping increasing. They were all the same.

Even her own brother didn't have a qualm about using her whenever he found himself in trouble, usually financial in nature. Without hesitation or scruple, Brett took cavalier advantage of her love for him, as her father had used and abused the love her mother had had for him.

Of course, she was not in love with Michael St. Claire, Leigh assured herself. Fortunately, she was merely in lust.

Leigh hoped the condition would be short-lived.

The doorbell rang at the exact same moment that steam trilled through the whistle on the teakettle.

Leigh stilled, stood hesitant and uncertain for a moment; then she switched off the burner, shifted the kettle to the coil opposite and turned away from the stove just as the bell rang again.

Telling herself she really should send him packing, she hurried to the door. Intending to cite the lateness of the hour as a reason for refusing to see him, she peered through the tiny security peephole.

Even with the distorted view, Michael looked handsome and urbane, demoralizingly appealing to the eyes and senses.

Leigh's resolve to offer him short shrift melted, along with the steel in her spine, the stiffness in her body.

Damn his attractive hide.

Springing the locks, she pulled open the door, determined to tear a verbal strip off him. The first angry word of her tirade never made it past her lips.

Michael pushed by her, kicked the door shut behind him, and pulled her into his arms.

"God, I'm starved," he muttered, compulsively tightening his hold on her.

"But, Michael, didn't you just have —" she began, barely able to breathe, let alone speak around his chest-constricting embrace.

His mouth claimed hers in a hungry kiss, answering her aborted question with greedy intent; he wasn't hungry for food, he was hungry for her.

Leigh raised her hands to his shoulders to

push him back, give herself breathing, and thinking, space. But, fool that she was, hungry for him, her hands kept moving to tangle in his hair, and she returned his kiss every bit as greedily.

Michael moved with sudden intent. The room seemed to spin as she was swept up, cradled against his chest and carried into her bedroom.

"I thought Shamus would never be done with serving courses," he muttered into her hair.

"Shamus? Who's Shamus?" she murmured into the curve of his shoulder.

"My cook. My houseman. My friend," he answered, giving a quick shake of his head between designations.

"Oh," she said. *Oh,* she thought, her agitation pacified to some degree by the realization that he and Barbara hadn't been entirely alone together.

They reached for each other the moment Michael lowered Leigh's feet to the floor beside the bed. Their breathing ragged, hands eager, they tossed their clothing helter-skelter about the room. Leigh sighed as Michael lowered her to the mattress, shivered at the delicious sensations caused by his heated skin gliding against hers, surrendered to the beguilement of Michael, his kisses, his touch, his possession.

"Perfection." Head thrown back, the tendons taut in his arched throat, his features stark with strain, Michael expelled the word through gritted teeth as he shuddered in the throes of orgasmic ecstasy.

Caught up within the glittering nerve-piercing shards of her own cataclysmic release, beyond the power of speech, Leigh could only sigh and nod in response.

He collapsed onto her, his bronzed body glistening with the sheen of dedicated physical exercise.

Unable to resist the allure, Leigh touched her lips to his shoulder, tasted his sweat with her tongue.

"Hmmm . . . delicious," she murmured against his heated skin. "I love the salty taste of you."

Turning his head, Michael gently nipped her earlobe, stroked his right hand down her body, from her face to the curve of her hip.

"Satin." He rubbed his forehead along her jawline, his palm over her thigh. "You're satin, warm satin." His fingers found her, delved. "Hot satin . . . and sheer perfection, love."

Leigh stilled for an instant at his last whispered word, then relaxed again, telling herself that Michael had meant nothing deep and personal with the endearment.

Her momentary fears allayed, she gave in to the exquisite sensations his lips and fingers were again arousing. And while he murmured many exciting, erotic words, he did not call her love, or any other endearment, again.

His transgressions, real or imagined, were forgiven by the time Michael left her in the early hours of the morning.

Still, although sated and besotted, Leigh had not forgotten. The remembered pain of possible betrayal was too raw.

Nineteen

Saturday evening, a week later.

Leigh and Michael were having dinner with Sheila and Jake, at Jake's invitation.

It was early, not yet six; Michael wasn't due until six-thirty to pick up Leigh.

Already showered and partly dressed in black satin panties and bra, and sheer black hose, Leigh had plenty of time — too much time.

Standing before the bathroom mirror, blow-drying her hair, she slipped into introspection about the previous week.

Except for a few hours grudgingly given over to the need for sleep, she had spent the entire weekend, and the majority of her nonworking hours the last week, with Michael; dining with Michael, arguing with Michael, laughing with Michael, making love with Michael.

Their intense concentration on each other, Leigh reluctantly admitted, if only to herself, could be likened to a serious courtship, even a honeymoon.

He is becoming necessary to me.

The idea scared Leigh so badly, she

nearly dropped the blow-dryer. Her heart thumping erratically, she pushed the thought away, to the darkest reaches of her consciousness, refusing to acknowledge that she could be, in any way, becoming vulnerable to him.

She liked him . . . a lot.

She was *not* falling in love with him.

She was in lust, Leigh reminded herself, allowing that, for now, her lust was rampant, possibly even a little out of control, which could be expected, even forgiven, considering how long she had waited to indulge.

But she did like Michael — quite a lot. More and more, with each passing day, he had revealed new, appealing facets of his character to her, his keen intelligence, his wry humor and, most surprising, his humane compassion.

A complex man.

An exciting man.

A passionate man.

Leigh felt grateful for their time spent together, for she knew it could not last, that excitement, passion, even lust were fleeting conditions of the senses and thus subject to reversal.

Eventually, Michael would revert to type, becoming a predator on the prowl for the next sexual conquest.

Leigh told herself that, when that day came, she would go on as she had before, her sensuality appeased perhaps, but her beliefs confirmed.

Her almost dry hair a gleaming mass flying around her head, she stared into the anxiety-clouded green eyes reflected in the mirror.

Why the hint of ambivalence revealed in them, when she should be feeling comforted by her acceptance of life and men as they really were?

The answer teased at the back of her mind. Leigh blocked it out, unwilling to face the truth of the feelings swirling inside her, making her edgy and uncertain.

Switching off the blow-dryer, she picked up a brush and went to work on smoothing her hair. Dodging the mental issue, she steered her thoughts to her friend.

Sheila seemed to be having no problems at all with doubts and introspection. Unequivocally, she had announced that she was flat-out crazy about Jake, despite the over twenty years difference in their ages.

Though distracted by the intensity of her affair with Michael over the past week, Leigh couldn't avoid noticing the way Sheila fairly glowed from the effects of her serious romantic infatuation.

Come to that, Leigh thought, setting the brush aside and reaching for her makeup foundation, she would have had to have been deaf not to have noticed; Sheila had talked of little else all week but Jake. How handsome he was. How gentle he was. How considerate he was.

Leigh was reserving judgment until she knew the man better, starting with dinner that evening.

The doorbell rang as she was replacing the few cosmetics she had used in the makeup case. Six-thirty already? she wondered, frowning as she walked to the bedroom to glance at the bedside clock.

No . . . It was only five after six. Now who . . . ?

Shaking her head, Leigh pulled on a robe, tying the self-belt as she made her way to the door. A quick look through the peephole brought a smile to her lips and her hands to the locks.

"You're early," she said, swinging open the door.

"I know." Michael grinned at her, one hand held behind his back as he strode into the room.

Leigh didn't notice; her eyes were feasting on the sight of him, attired in a dark suit and a pale blue shirt that enhanced his golden handsomeness.

"I wasn't sure if your rule of no gifts included flowers," he began, eyeing her warily, "but I felt certain you'd object to masses of them."

"I would," Leigh concurred, her attention drawn to the arm he was concealing. She arched a brow. "So, what are you hiding there?"

"I . . ." He brought his arm forward with almost boyish hesitancy. "These are for you."

These were two pink rosebuds and a tiny spray of baby's breath, the stems tied with a blue satin ribbon.

"Michael, I . . ." Leigh's voice sounded harsh, abrupt, only because her throat suddenly felt achy. Her eyes stung from a rush of salty tears.

No one had ever brought her rosebuds before.

"You're not angry, are you?" His eyes darkened with an anxious expression. "It's no big deal — only two little buds. This guy was selling them on the street corner." He shrugged. "Hell, he was trying to earn a couple of bucks."

He looked so uncertain, so concerned, Leigh had to laugh.

"They're beautiful," she murmured, taking them from him and sniffing for the buds sweet scent and from the moisture caused by the rush of tears.

"You're not mad?"

"No, Michael, I'm not." Afraid he wouldn't understand, she didn't explain that, to her, the two buds were more precious than gemstones. Even more afraid that she'd lose control, fling herself into his arms and cry all over his beautiful, expensive suit, she turned away. "I'll put them in water, then finish dressing."

"Must you?"

He spoke very softly, but Leigh heard him. Puzzled, she cast a backward look at him. "Put them in water?"

The smile he gave her was so sexy, it sent exciting shivers dancing down her spine. "No," he murmured, slowly moving to her. "I meant, must you dress?"

He reached for her; she raised her hand to his chest. "Now, Michael, we have a dinner engagement." Though she tried to make her voice stern, it came out in a breathless quiver. "Remember? Sheila? Jake?"

"Oh, right," he said dramatically. "Well, then, I'll have a drink, instead." Laughing, he grabbed her hand and strolled with her to the kitchen.

After arranging the buds in a slim crystal vase, Leigh left Michael to his martini mixing and started back to the bedroom to finish dressing. She was almost to her bedroom when the doorbell rang.

"Now who?" she muttered, pivoting to return to the door. She groaned with dismay on peering through the peephole. The very last person she wanted to see was her sister-in-law's cousin. The bell rang again. Sighing in resignation, she opened the unlocked door.

"Hi, Leigh." Trevor Monroe stood there, looking as if he still believed he was God's gift to women and favoring her with a toothpaste-bright smile. "I promised I'd stop by when I got into Philly."

"So you did," she murmured, gritting the teeth she'd bared in a tight smile. She did not invite him in.

But he invited himself. His step jaunty, he brushed past her into the room. "I thought we could grab some dinner, then go on to a place a friend told me about, to hear some jazz, maybe do a little dancing." The hot-eyed stare he ran over her satin-robed body made her flesh crawl.

"I'm sorry, Trevor, but I can't." An impish impulse made her add, "I have to clean my oven, and —" She broke off, gasping, when he reached out to grasp her waist and pull her tightly against him. Michael, help, she thought, revulsion washing through her at the feel of his bulging hardness pressing into her pelvis.

"I can think of a lot better things to do," he said in a suggestive tone, rotating her hips in a grinding motion against his erection.

Simultaneously, Leigh curled her fingers into a fist and opened her mouth to blast him. Before she could accomplish either, another presence made itself felt.

"Would one of those things be picking up your teeth?" Michael asked in an indolent-sounding drawl, coming to a halt next to Trevor.

Trevor started in surprise. Releasing Leigh, he whipped around to stare at Michael. "Who the hell are you?"

"I'm the significant other," he answered, curling one arm around Leigh's waist to draw her close, protectively, to his warmth, his strength. "And you're trespassing."

Leigh stilled, struck by the similarity of the scene unfolding between the two men and her dream on the night of her brother's anniversary party. The difference being, instead of a sword, Michael wielded a sharp tongue.

"Leigh never said anything about any significant other." Trevor sneered.

"No?" Michael arched one toasted-gold brow and curved his lips in a serene, yet deadly smile.

"No," Trevor said belligerently, while at the same time proving he was ninety-five percent bluster by taking a cautionary step back.

"Understandable, if you think about it." Michael continued to smile, but his eyes acquired a warning glitter, not unlike sunlight dancing off crystal. "Why would Leigh mention anything of a personal, private, nature to an insignificant creature such as yourself?"

Trevor drew in a sharp breath. His gaze shifted to Leigh. "Is it true, Leigh? Is he your significant other?" His lips curled, his tone got nasty. "Your . . . lover?"

"Careful, friend," Michael said with soft menace.

Trevor took another step back, edging closer to the still-open door.

"Yes." Leigh proudly raised her chin, and with cool deliberation, wrapped her arms around Michael's waist. "He's my lover."

Trevor's eyes narrowed, glowed with a sudden calculating light. "Oh, I get it." His sharpened gaze gleaned the value of

Michael's attire, then shot to Leigh. "Evelyn told me you had risked your business by securing a line of credit for Brett to save his ass." He let loose a short burst of denigrating laughter, then pointed an unsteady finger at Michael. "He's the reason you felt safe in doing that. Right? You sold yourself to the highest bidder, didn't you?" he accused. "Does your father know about him?"

Appalled and sickened, Leigh stiffened, her fingernails digging into Michael's jacket.

"You have two options." Michael's voice had lost all traces of softness, leaving only hard menace in it. "You can walk out of here — now — or be carried out of here later." He shrugged. "Up to you."

Though he made a rude noise of bravado, Trevor walked.

Michael quietly shut the door after him, then turned laser blue eyes on Leigh. "Was he telling the truth? Did you put your business at risk for your brother? Is that why you had to go to Lancaster?" he demanded, rapid-fire.

"Yes." Leigh met his piercing stare head-on, proud of the composure she had managed to project. Inside, she was a quivering mass of nervous outrage.

Michael looked baffled. "Why?"

"Brett's my brother," she snapped, stunned that he felt it necessary to ask. "He needed help."

"Not that." He shook his head. "These things don't happen overnight. You knew about this before. Dammit, Leigh, why did you turn down the commission to do my office?"

Damning Trevor and his big mouth, Leigh held on to her composure for all she was worth. "I told you why."

"You put your very livelihood in jeopardy, and still . . ." Michael raised a hand, then let it drop to his side. Frustration scored his handsome features. "I don't understand you."

"Yes, you do," she countered, desperately wanting this discussion to end. "You understand pride and honor and independence, don't you?"

He gave a quick, disbelieving laugh. "But I offered you a legitimate commission." Angry color heightened his sun-kissed cheekbones. "My offer did not include sex on demand."

Although Leigh felt relieved by this assertion, it really didn't change anything. "Nevertheless, I could not accept your offer."

"Or gifts of any kind." A wry smile of

acceptance shadowed his lips. "Other than two rosebuds."

"Precisely."

Michael shook his head again, but the light of humor glittered in his eyes. "I think you're nuts."

Leigh controlled an impulse to laugh, but her amusement shook her voice. "Does that mean you no longer want to take me to dinner?"

He raised his eyes, as if seeking help from a higher authority. "Go finish dressing, you crazy woman." Removing her arms from his waist, he gave her a gentle shove in the direction of her bedroom. "Meanwhile, I'll go fortify myself with my by now warm martini."

Considering the trauma caused by Trevor's unpleasant visit, the rest of the evening went surprisingly well.

The restaurant Jake had chosen was known to Leigh, so she had expected the meal to be excellent. What she had not expected was to so thoroughly enjoy Jake's company, or the rapport that quickly sprang to life between Michael and the older man.

That evening set something of a precedent for the four of them. They then got together on the average of once a week, to dine, see a movie or show or to attend some function — a gallery opening or social gathering.

Before the month was out, they had become as close as longtime friends, which, of course, Leigh and Sheila had been for over twenty years.

Leigh was reasonably content, or at least as content as she had ever hoped to be.

She was busy as, within those weeks, she had signed contracts with four new clients, and had made appointments to confer with an equal number of interested parties.

Michael was an exciting, considerate lover, giving to Leigh every bit as much of himself in the physical act as he vigorously extracted from her.

It wasn't long before Leigh was forced to reevaluate her opinion concerning her friend's association with an older man. She concluded that Sheila, rather than being infatuated, was head over heels in love.

Indeed, her friend was blooming, frank in her admittance of enjoying a blissfully satisfying sexual relationship with Jake, and dreaming of a more permanent union with him.

But, since life was never perfect, there were glitches, some more troubling than others.

One of them concerned Jake.

Though Leigh wasn't envious of the growing camaraderie between Michael and Jake, she was puzzled by the keen interest evinced by Jake in every aspect of Michael's life, both personal and professional.

She couldn't help but wonder if Jake had a hidden agenda.

Another glitch concerned her sudden influx of clients. Had she, Leigh wondered, achieved enough recognition with her work to draw these well-heeled clients to her, or, and it was a big or, had Michael decided to lend a hand to minimize the risk she had placed on her business by steering clients her way?

But Leigh's most troubling glitch concerned the seeming dancing attention Michael continued to confer on Barbara Saunders.

At each and every summons from Barbara, Michael dropped everything, including Leigh, to hasten to the older woman's side, do her bidding.

Although she concealed her feelings, it made Leigh furious, because deep down it frightened her.

Were Michael and Barbara more than friends, possibly even long-standing, if secret, lovers?

The destructive thought would not be

banished, however hard Leigh tried to eradicate it. Like a poison dart, it pierced her mind, punctured her emotions, tainted her life.

While she feared the answer, Leigh knew she could not long continue on with Michael without demanding the truth from him concerning his near slavish devotion to Barbara.

Twenty

Leigh broached the subject of Jake's overt interest in Michael on an evening, becoming steadily more infrequent in number, when they were on their own, with no arrangements made with the other couple.

She had cooked dinner, a simple shrimp and pasta dish she particularly liked, and she hoped he would too. He did, and didn't hesitate in saying so.

"That was superb," he praised, raising his wine-glass in silent salute to her. "Too bad Sheila and Jake missed this. Shrimp is one of Jake's favorites."

Recognizing an opening when she saw one, Leigh took the plunge into personal waters. "Michael, I know it's none of my business, and I don't want you to misunderstand, because I really like him, but doesn't it seem a bit odd, I mean, the way Jake appears to have insinuated himself into every corner of your life?"

"Funny you should mention it," he said, his brow furrowed in consternation. "Because I've been thinking along the same line lately. I have a theory." He paused, a self-derisive smile slanting his lips. "Actually, a suspicion sparked by a casual comment, a slip of the tongue I picked up the other night when I had dinner with Barbara."

Barbara. Leigh tensed, a vivid recollection of the jealous anger she'd endured the other night coloring her emotions a sickly green for a moment. Breathing deeply, she reminded herself, as she had repeatedly done that night, that she had no claim on Michael's time or activities.

"A suspicion?" she asked, in a reasonably normal tone. "A suspicion about what?"

"No. It's too ridiculous." He made a quick, deprecating move of his head. "Too soap-opera scenario."

"What is?" Leigh said on a half-laugh. "Come on, Michael, you can't toss out a teaser like that and then not explain. Tell me," she insisted.

"You won't laugh?"

She shook her head.

He inhaled, then expelled the breath in a rush. "I suspect he believes he's my father."

"Your father." Leigh's voice was rife with incredulity.

He shrugged. "I told you it was ridiculous."

"But . . ." She broke off, her mental wheels

whirling. Could it be possible? Other than Michael and Jake being tall, and fair, there were few similarities, and yet . . . They did share a few like traits: a sharp business sense, a wry humor, an almost old-fashioned gallantry toward the opposite sex. "I'm not so sure it is ridiculous," she said at length.

"No? Hmmm," he murmured, contemplatively. "Of course, there is one way to find out."

"Ask him outright?" she said.

Michael nodded. "The very next time we see him."

As it turned out, they saw Jake two nights later, not by accident, but by Leigh's design. Curious as to the outcome, she had invited Sheila and Jake to dinner that Friday evening.

All three of her guests heaped accolades on Leigh for the rather plain fare of chicken and dumplings — her father's recipe. Nervously conscious about the discussion to follow the dessert, Leigh had barely tasted the food herself, but had graciously accepted their compliments.

They were having after-dinner coffee in the living room when, apparently as anxious as Leigh to have the matter settled, Michael went right to the crux of the question.

"Jake, because of something Leigh said to

me last week, I feel I must ask you a delicate question."

Jake gave an expansive wave of his hand. "Feel free."

"Okay." Michael nodded. "Now, if it's utter nonsense, you may laugh in my face, but, if it's true, I'd appreciate a direct, honest answer."

"Sounds serious," Sheila said, looking worried.

Turning to smile at her, Jake patted her hand, in a calming yet possessive way. "Not to fret, honey," he soothed, before turning back to Michael. "Fire away."

"Are you, or do you think you might be, my father?" Michael bluntly asked.

Sheila gasped.

Leigh stopped breathing.

Michael stared into Jake's eyes, and coolly took a careful sip of his hot coffee.

"Yes." Not a shred of doubt shaded Jake's voice. "At any rate I'm almost certain that I am."

Total silence . . . for all of ten seconds.

"Huh?" Her eyes wide with shock, Sheila shifted an astonished glance from one man to the other. "But, Jake, what makes you think you're Michael's father?" she asked, stealing the initiative from Michael.

"I have reason," Jake answered, never

taking his eyes from Michael. "As a matter of fact, I've been girding myself to ask if he'd consider taking a blood test, even a DNA profile if necessary, to prove paternity."

"I will." Michael inclined his head, his manner cool, remote. "On the condition you explain your reasons for believing you could be my . . . father."

"Fair enough, since I was planning to do so, anyway." Jake smiled. "It's a long story."

"I'm not going anywhere." Michael didn't return the smile. He reached out to grasp Leigh's hand. "Story on."

Feeling the tension in the grip of his fingers, Leigh squeezed his hand, waiting with bated breath. She didn't have to wait long; Jake launched right in.

"Mary Margaret Klare," he murmured, his eyes taking on a faraway shadow, while Michael's gaze sharpened. "I met your mother at a teen club dance when I was seventeen, recently graduated from high school. I had enlisted in the Army that afternoon, and was bent on celebrating.

"She was eighteen, an orphan, with no known living relatives. She was working as a waitress in a neighborhood Italian restaurant and living in a run-down boarding house in south Philly. She was so beautiful, Michael, as you are yourself, with the same spun gold hair, shimmering blue eyes, and fine, one might say aristocratic, features . . . though hers were softer, more feminine."

"I remember." Michael's voice was low, ragged with rigidly suppressed emotion.

Leigh's throat went dry, became tight, thick.

"So do I." Jake smiled. "I immediately fell head over heels in love. She said she loved me, too, and in my heart, I believe she did."

"She did," Michael confirmed in a whispery rasp.

"Thank you for that." Jake sighed, then went on. "Anyway, we had two wonderful weeks together before I had to leave her, report for boot camp. I promised I'd write, and I did, every day, but" — he winced — "I genuinely liked boot camp, and got so caught up in the regimen, I didn't mail the letters until nearly a month had passed. Then I mailed them all together in one packet. The next week the packet came back stamped No Known Address." He paused once more, his feelings of long ago reflected anew in his expression.

"Oh, Jake," Sheila whispered.

"Go on," Michael instructed.

"I came to Philly to find her when I got

leave after finishing boot camp. I went straight to the boarding house. The woman who ran the place told me Mary Margaret had moved, leaving no forwarding address. She told me something else, as well, something that both thrilled and terrified me. She told me she suspected Mary Margaret was pregnant."

"She was," Michael growled, his fingers tightening reflexively around Leigh's.

"I didn't know what to do, where to turn," Jake said, starkly. "I didn't know where to look for her. She had left no trail to follow, had simply lost herself, yet I felt she was here, somewhere in the city."

"She was," Michael repeated.

Jake nodded. "I knew it. That's why I kept coming back here every time I had leave. I had done the figuring, come up with probable dates, and when I had leave ten months later, I came back, checked through the birth records." He grabbed a breath. "I found a birth registered for one of my probable dates. A son, to Mary Margaret Klare, father unknown. I wept, Michael. I had a son — a *son*." Tears trickled unnoticed down his cheeks. "I located a copy of the birth certificate, learned the child had been named Michael J. Klare, but I couldn't find him or his mother."

Michael's features were set, locking out any show of emotion. "How did you conclude that I was that son?"

"Process of elimination." Jake dashed the tears from his face. "I made a career of the Army, rose through the ranks, did tours of duty in many different countries, but I always kept coming back here to Philly. I don't know why. I never found a trace of her or you in all those years."

Sheila interrupted him, her own face wet with tears. "But, Jake, you just said —"

"I'm getting to it," he cut in, offering her a reassuring smile. "After I took retirement from the service, I started my export-import business in New York, still, I continued to return here. Five years ago, I suddenly felt compelled to examine the death notices. I became obsessed with the need to know something — anything — about her and my son."

He paused again, swallowed, his eyes studying Michael, as if memorizing every nuance of his face. "I pored over those notices, starting from the day you were born. A little over a year ago, I found the notice of your mother's death the year you were twelve. I thought that, at last, there would be a trail for me to follow to you. And I did find that trail, in the social services records, only to come to another dead end the last time you ran away, when you were fifteen." He shook his head, smiled sadly. "You're as good as your mother was at getting lost, Michael. I've been searching for a Michael J. Klare ever since, here and in other major cities."

"You still haven't connected the dots," Michael said, seemingly unmoved by Jake's recitation.

"I'm getting to it," Jake promised, forging on. "Early this spring, while I was looking around for space to open an office here in Philly, I met Barbara — and hit pay dirt."

Michael went still at hearing her name.

Leigh cringed.

"How precisely?" Michael's tone was frigid.

Leigh felt the ice chill her heart.

"I needed a local accountancy firm; an acquaintance recommended Barbara Saunders. During our first interview, I happened to catch sight of a designation on a label on a thick folder on her desk. It read The Mary Margaret Klare Foundation. Naturally, I immediately questioned Barbara about it — who had endowed it, who supported it, etcetera." He chuckled. "As I suppose you know, Barbara is one tough lady. No matter how much I demanded and pleaded, she refused to give me any information, said it was strictly confidential."

"It was," Michael said through clenched teeth. "How did you pry the information out of her?"

"Simple, really. As I'm sure you also know, while tough, Barbara has her soft spots. You in particular. I related my story to her. *She* connected the dots. But before you damn her betrayal, I must tell you she never actually told me anything. She merely mentioned you, suggested I meet you, hinted it could be to my advantage."

He was quiet a moment. Everyone was. Then he smiled. "Ahhh, Michael, the minute I saw you I knew. You must realize you're the masculine image of Mary Margaret, your mother." His smile vanished, his tone grew stern. "Now, tell me why in hell you changed your name?"

A pall fell, brought on by the abrupt harshness of his voice. Three pairs of eyes were fixed on Michael, and the expressions of all three showed curiosity. Would Michael answer or deny? As if carved from solid rock, he sat, crystal blue eyes staring at Jake. The humming tension was fractured by the dryness of his words when at last he responded.

"I changed my name because I had sworn

I would never be taken back, that for me there would be no more orphanages, no more foster homes." His voice was soft, his eyes were hard. "I preferred the mean streets."

Leigh's heart ached for Michael, for the boy he had been, and the man he now was. For she knew beneath the polished, self-confident and yes, at times arrogant facade, the boy still lived, still grieved, still hurt.

She ached to go to him, hold him, comfort him. But Leigh didn't move, didn't even speak. She felt she couldn't — she was only his lover, his current fancy, after all.

While she was hurting for him, with him, her eyes misty with unshed tears, numbed by misery she couldn't allow herself to examine, she caught only bits and pieces of what transpired between Michael and Jake.

". . . that I am your father?" She caught the last part of Jake's question.

"Yes. You see, I had suspected . . ." She sniffed, and that was all she heard of Michael's reply.

Then, hearing Michael laugh, she blinked away the mist, only to feel the sting of tears again at the sight of Michael enfolded within his father's embrace.

They celebrated with champagne. And it was only after Michael had eased the cork from the distinctive bottle without losing a fizzing drop of the wine, that Jake proclaimed the celebration two-fold.

"I have two toasts," he said, raising the glass Leigh passed to him. "First, to my son, the child of my youth, who was lost to me and now is found." He took a sip of the wine.

Smiling, Leigh sipped from her flute and glanced at Sheila, her smile turning quizzical at the flush tingeing her friend's cheeks, the sparkle in her eyes.

"And," Jake continued, once again holding his glass aloft. "To my wonderful Sheila, for the child of my . . . er, more mature age, for the child that she is now nurturing in her body."

A celebration, indeed. And one glitch resolved.

Twenty-one

Throughout the following week, Leigh felt she was living in two opposite worlds. In the office, Sheila was ebullient, giddy with the excitement of planning a small, intimate wedding, thrilled to be pregnant with Jake's baby.

It was a different story in the private world of Leigh's apartment. Michael was strangely subdued, almost moody, always attentive and courteous to her yet oddly pensive, seemingly deep into his own, not always palatable, thoughts.

Was Michael distracted by the enormity of discovering his father after all this time? While this explanation for his distraction was reasonable, it wouldn't wash, simply because the advent of Jake into his life was one of the subjects he openly discussed with her.

That left the question uppermost in her mind: was Michael growing tired of her, of their affair? Leigh pondered the probability, her anxiety mounting with each passing day. Could his interest in her be beginning to wane, even though his ardor during their lovemaking appeared to be, if anything, growing stronger?

It didn't make any kind of sense to Leigh. Michael seemed to be distancing himself from her, while at the same time, there was a near desperation in his lovemaking.

Uncertain, feeling like a trapped animal not sure which way to jump, Leigh grew increasingly more remote, self-contained, cool and withdrawn.

What would she do if he called a halt, walked away as he had reputedly done to so many other women?

Tormented by these questions and doubts, Leigh's stomach was in a constant clench.

The situation could not be maintained, and she knew it. Something or someone would have to crack.

The something did on a late Saturday afternoon.

The someone was Leigh.

They had reservations for an early dinner, tickets for a concert later at the Mann Music Center. Leigh was looking forward to the evening, the first Saturday in weeks that she and Michael would be going out alone together.

Michael called an hour before he was due to pick her up. Leigh had a sinking sensation that something was wrong, the minute she heard his voice.

"Leigh, I'm sorry, but I'm afraid I have to cancel our plans for this evening," he said, then hurried on before she could respond, "I promise I'll make it up to you with something special at a later date."

"Business?" Leigh asked, certain it wasn't, just as certain he had begun withdrawing from her.

"No," he said, surprising her with his frankness. "Barbara called me a little while ago and said she needs to talk to me. It's important."

Barbara was important, which meant that she was not, Leigh concluded, controlling a need of her own, a pressing need to rant, rave, scream. Instead, gripping the receiver until her knuckles turned white, she managed a cool, "I see."

"You're sure you don't mind?" His voice contained an odd thread of strain.

And why not? Juggling two women would naturally cause him to feel strain, wouldn't it? Leigh reflected. Aloud, she lied through her teeth. "No, I don't mind."

"If it's not too late," he went on, sounding even more strained, "maybe I'll stop by after Barbara and I finish our discussion."

Maybe not, Leigh silently railed, fury at

his audacity roaring through her. "You'd better call first. Since we're not going out, I think I'll make it an early night."

"Oh . . ." He paused. "All right. I'll —"

"On second thought," she cut in, her mind racing. "Why not just wait and call tomorrow."

Tomorrow. The word reverberated inside Leigh's head in a mocking refrain.

Hadn't she always known there were no tomorrows? She upbraided herself, devastated and hating the feeling of betrayal. She had known what to expect or, more accurately, what not to expect in the first place. So why be surprised, why hurt so damned much when the expected happened?

Leigh knew the answer. Of course, she did. Going against every precept she had held for years, knowing the pain in store, she had foolishly fallen in love with Michael.

The agony of rejection and jealousy she was experiencing was terrible. She didn't eat, she paced.

At one point, she strode to the bedroom, to her closet. Thrusting an arm to the back, she grasped the guardian angel picture, intent on pulling it out, tearing it from the frame and ripping it to shreds.

Then her hand fell away. It was only a picture, after all, and really didn't resemble Michael that much, except in her imagination, she told herself. So why bother?

She went back to pacing.

The phone rang again around eight, freezing Leigh in midstep. Michael? Surely his tryst with Barbara wasn't over already? Positive she couldn't bear seeing him or even hearing his voice over the phone, Leigh shook her head, determined not to answer. With the very next ring she ran for the phone, snatched up the receiver.

"Hello?" She despaired at the breathless, eager sound of her voice.

"Leigh? Hi. I was afraid you might be out."

Her spirits plummeted. "Oh, hi, Brett. No, I had no plans for this evening," she said, thinking not anymore. "What's up? Is there a problem?" she asked, figuring another financial upset for her brother, with ramifications for her, would put the topper on her night.

"No, no problem. Just the opposite." Brett laughed. It had a carefree, exuberant sound. "I thought you'd like to know. I signed three contracts last week, and two more today. My accountant tells me I'm out of the red and actually making a profit — all thanks to you."

"Oh, Brett, that's wonderful. Congratulations," she said, happy for him, relieved for herself, the security of her own business, so long as he could keep Evelyn's sticky little fingers away from the profits.

"Thanks." Then, as if sensing her concern, Brett said, "And, believe it or not, I laid the law down to Evelyn, canceled her credit cards — at least until we're showing enough capital to cover our salaries and personal and business expenses for a year."

"Good for you." Leigh hesitated about prying into his personal life, then shrugged and asked, "How did Evelyn react to that?"

He laughed again. "Surprisingly well." His voice held a lingering note of wonder. "I guess what she needed was a genuine show of strength."

Leigh nodded, but before she could respond, he went on in a musing tone.

"I suppose that's what Dad should have done years ago."

Leigh frowned. "What do you mean?"

"With Mother," he answered. He let out a quick, rueful laugh. "You know, it's almost funny, but after growing up in that house, sleeping in the room next to theirs, hearing Mom whine and nag at him because he wasn't giving her all the things she wanted, the social position she craved, you'd of thought I'd be smart enough to avoid a demanding woman. No. I had to turn around and fall for a woman just like her."

Leigh went still, a sick feeling invading her stomach. "What are you saying?" she snapped out in protest, an inner voice shouting that her mother had not been like Evelyn. "Mother wasn't anything like that."

"Get real, Leigh," he ridiculed. "Of course she was. She always wanted more, more, more. Jesus, was it Dad's fault he had gone as far as he could in the company he worked for? God, how I used to ache for him. Hell, Leigh, he did the best he could, gave her as much as he could. But it was never enough. The sad thing was, he really loved her, and she used sex as a bargaining tool for the things she wanted."

Leigh gasped, shouted, "That's not true!"

"I heard it, Leigh. I couldn't miss hearing it. I was in the next room, remember? You were at a safe distance, down the hall. All you ever heard were her complaints against him." He exhaled, like a man who had just finished a long, hard race. "Water over the dam now. Thanks to you, your willingness to put your own business on the line for me, I've come to my senses, asserted myself at last with Evelyn. Honestly, Leigh, she's a different person lately. And so is Dad. He's finally found contentment with Kathie."

Leigh didn't speak; she couldn't. Her throat was closed, so were her eyes. Tears ran down her cheeks.

"Leigh?" He was concerned. "Are you all right?"

"Yes." Somehow, she managed a marginally normal tone. "I'm fine." She wasn't, but she couldn't let Brett hear her pain, her despair, her self-condemnation.

"I know you said you didn't mind about Dad's relationship with Kathie, but are you sure? You know, I think he's planning to marry her."

"I don't mind," she assured him, feeling tired, empty. "I promise, I'll dance at his wedding."

"Whew, that's a relief." She could hear it in his voice. "Well, I'd better go. Evelyn just called me to come say good night to Andy."

"Okay, good night, Brett, and give Andy a hug from me."

"Will do. Good night."

Shattered by her brother's home truths, Leigh stood unmoving by the phone long after she had cradled the receiver, her feelings lacerated, her self-image in tatters. Her mind replayed statements, old and new.

Men will tell you they love you, just to get sex from you. Her mother's voice, hard and bitter, molding, slanting the thoughts of a young girl.

He really loved her. Brett's voice, shaking the foundations of a now mature woman's beliefs.

Brett was wrong. He had to be wrong.

I heard it, Leigh. I couldn't miss hearing it. I was in the next room, remember?

Oh, God, was it possible she had been wrong all these years, blaming her father, all men, for the blanket condemnation of one dissatisfied woman? Leigh wondered, anguished.

Her answer came, not from words inside her mind, but from a commanding impulse. Without pausing to think, consider, she snatched up the receiver and dialed her father's number.

"Hello?"

Leigh began speaking, babbling actually, at hearing Andrew's voice. Tears washing her face, she poured out her confession to him, begged for his forgiveness. The purging ceased only when her sobs overwhelmed her.

"Oh, Leigh, don't do this to yourself," Andrew said in tones soft with compassion. "I knew. I've always known. Not all of it, of course, but enough to —"

"Why didn't you tell me?" she cried.

"You so obviously adored her," he said, his voice sad. "Loving you, I couldn't tarnish your love for her."

They talked for over an hour, Leigh in tears for much of that time. Before hanging up, Andrew told her he had asked Kathie to marry him and that Kathie had said yes.

"Will you come home for the wedding?" he asked, hesitant and anxious.

"I'll come, Dad," Leigh promised, then reiterated her promise to Brett. "I'll dance at your wedding."

Michael had a bad feeling that he was about to be dumped, if he hadn't, in effect, been dumped already. A new sensation for him, as he had always been the one to end an affair, and he didn't like it.

So much in love with Leigh he couldn't think straight, the last thing he wanted was for their affair to end. He wanted, had been hoping, to expand it into a deeper, more substantive, permanent relationship.

It was late. Leigh had asked him not to stop by if it got late. Yet he sat in his car, uncomfortable and restless, outside her apartment.

Dammit, he should be feeling great. He had found a father — more accurately, his father had found him. Better yet, he liked

Jake. In addition, Barbara had found Shamus, not that he'd been lost. As she had said earlier that evening, he'd been under her nose right along.

And so, by all rights, he should be feeling great, Michael thought. Instead, he was anxious, and all because of the woman he now felt certain was afraid to love.

Somewhere along the way, something had happened to turn Leigh off the concept of romantic love. It was the only answer that made sense to him.

And, though sex with her was more than fantastic, it was no longer enough for him. Michael wanted it all, her heart and soul, as well as her body.

And it was time to lay his cards on the table.

But it was late, almost eleven. He knew he should wait until morning, but . . .

Pushing open the door, he stepped from the car.

Exhausted, mentally drained, Leigh slid the thigh-length nightgown over her head and smoothed the warm satin down over her hips. Sighing, she stared at the music box on the night stand next to her bed. She reached out to grasp it, fling it to the floor, shatter it into a million pieces, but just as

411

her fingers brushed the box, the doorbell rang.

Her eyes flew to the clock. Five of eleven. Now who . . . ? Even as the question formed, she knew the answer.

Michael.

No, Leigh protested in weary silence. She couldn't face him. Their affair was over. But she simply didn't have the stamina to tell him tonight.

She would not answer, would not let him in, Leigh told herself, stalking into the living room to glare at the door. She didn't need him, she assured herself.

Dammit. She didn't need *any* man.

Michael St. Claire could go to hell — and take his precious Barbara with him.

The doorbell sounded again, in short imperative rings, followed by Michael's importunings.

"Open the door, Leigh," he demanded, if softly. "I need to talk to you."

He needs. He needs. Damn his needs, she railed, storming to the door. What about *her* needs? Turning the locks, she pulled open the door to glare at him.

"It's late, Michael," she began, but that was as far as she got.

His expression set, determined, Michael advanced, forcing her to back up. He shut the door with a backward kick, and pulled her into his arms.

"What do you think you're doing?" Leigh said in the coldest voice she could muster.

"If you have to ask," he said, lowering his head to hers, "you're not as bright as I thought you were."

She turned her head away before his lips touched hers, so he kissed her ear instead.

"Let me go, Michael," she ordered, struggling against his hold. "I don't want your kisses." A blatant lie. "I don't want anything from you." A bigger lie; she wanted everything from him. "It's over."

"Why?" He jerked back to stare at her, angry sparks glittering in his crystal eyes.

She managed a careless shrug. It was a mistake.

Michael released her only long enough to grasp her shoulders. Turning her, he backed her to the wall beside the door. Then, ignoring her outcry of protest, he crushed her mouth beneath his.

It was a reenactment of the scene they had played out weeks before. Leigh struggled — for all of three seconds. Desperate for him, if only for one last time, she curled her arms around his neck and clung to him as if her very life depended on the nourishment of his kiss.

While Michael's lips and tongue devoured her mouth, his hands roamed, caressing her shoulders, her breasts, her hips, her thighs. Drinking in her moans, he found the hem of her gown and tugged it up to her waist.

Leigh arched against his pressing hardness. On fire for him, she slid her hand down, inciting him with the stroking of her hand.

His breathing ragged, Michael pushed her hand away with an impatient brush of his. There followed the metallic sound of his belt buckle, the whirr of a zipper, the soft sough of his trousers sliding down his legs. His hands gripped her bottom, lifting her, and then his legs were between hers, his body embedded in hers.

Crying out, Leigh coiled her legs around his waist, sank her teeth into the expensive material of his suit jacket as he plunged into her again and again.

It was madness.

It was glorious.

It was over too soon.

Reality set in as he gently set her on her feet. Shamed by her abandonment of mind and body, Leigh yanked down her gown and moved away, distancing herself from him.

"That was the last time," she said, glaring

at him as he pulled up his pants.

"Like hell," he muttered, stuffing his shirt into the waist band. The zipper went up. The button was fastened. He left the belt dangling. "What in hell is with you, anyway?"

"I won't share, Michael," she said, trembling in reaction to the realization that she probably had done just that. "I want all — or nothing."

"Share?" He frowned. "Share what?"

"You!" she shouted, her control shot.

"Me?" His frown turned to bafflement. "With who?"

"Barbara." There, it was out in the open.

"Barbara?" His astonished expression was almost funny. "You think Barbara and I are . . ." He broke off, his burst of laughter bouncing off the walls. "Damned if I don't believe you're jealous."

Leigh stiffened, furious because it was true. "I'm neither stupid nor a fool, Michael," she scoffed. "All she has to do is call, snap her fingers and you forget me to go running to her. Well, tonight was the last time."

"It might have been," he said, smiling as he moved to close the distance between them.

"Stay where you are," she ordered, afraid she wouldn't have the inner fortitude to deny him anything if he got his hands on her.

"I don't think so." He kept coming.

She turned to run.

He caught her. Kissed her into submission. When he raised his head, tears of defeat were running down her cheeks.

"I love you." Michael kissed her closed eyelids. "I love you." He sipped the tears from her face. "I love you."

"But . . . but . . . Barbara . . ." Leigh cried, wanting to believe him, to believe in love, his love.

He gave a quick, impatient move of his head. "There is not, and never has been, anything of an intimate nature in our relationship."

"But she calls you darling and —"

"Yes," he interrupted, "she loves me, and I call her darling for the same reason." She made to move away. He held her fast. "Listen to me. Barbara found me on the street, took me under her care, when I was a teenager. She has been a mother figure, mentor, benefactor to me. She's the mother I lost. I'm the son she never had."

Now Leigh did feel like a fool, a fool consumed by jealousy. "Oh, Michael, I thought . . . I'm so sorry."

"I'm not," he murmured, brushing his

mouth back and forth over hers. "The air's been cleared between us." Lifting his head, he gazed into her eyes. "Now, please, before I go mad, tell me you love me."

Leigh sniffed and shook her head, still fearful of the word, the commitment it entailed.

"Tell me, dammit!" he shouted, patience gone.

"All right!" she shouted back. "I love you . . . There, are you satisfied now?"

"Not yet, my love. Not completely." A devilish gleam danced in his heavenly eyes. "But I might be, at least temporarily, after I finish showing you how very much I love you."

Over an hour later, content, pleasantly drained by his sensational method of deriving satisfaction, Leigh lay pressed to Michael's side, her fingers combing the whorl of golden curls on his chest.

"You've been recommending me, my work, to prospective clients, haven't you?" she asked, smiling at his sharply indrawn breath when she gently flicked a flat nipple with her fingernail.

"Yes." He grunted in response to the touch of her tongue to the aroused nipple. "As have Barbara and Jake."

Deserting the now hard bud, she raised her head to stare at him in surprise. "Both of them?"

"Ummm . . ." Nodding, he lifted a hand to guide her head back to his chest. "More."

"But why?"

"Because it felt good."

"Not that." She nipped the bud with her teeth, grinning when he shuddered, then groaned with pleasure. "I meant, why would Barbara and Jake steer customers my way?"

"Because they admire your work, and they like you — and me." He caught her hand and drew it down his body, arching into her curling fingers. "Now, please shut up and show me how much you like me."

Content and satisfied, but suddenly not wholly satisfied, Leigh was more than happy to oblige.

The reception hall resounded with laughter and happy chatter. The dance floor was packed.

Standing on the fringe of the throng moving in time with the music, Leigh tugged on Michael's hand.

"I like your father," he said, obviously stalling. "Your brother, too, even though I thought I wouldn't."

She slanted an understanding smile at him, gave another tug on his hand.

Michael stood firm as a rock. "I haven't quite decided about Evelyn, though," he mused aloud. "But I'm already crazy about Andy."

"I'm glad you like my father and Brett." She took a step toward the dance floor. "I feel exactly the same as you do about Evelyn. And I adore Andy," she said, giving another, harder tug on his hand.

Michael sighed and warily eyed the shuffling dancers. "Do you seriously want to dance?"

"Yes." Smiling as he moved onto the floor with her, she circled his neck with her arms and said, "I promised my father I'd dance at his wedding."

ABOUT THE AUTHOR

With over ten million copies of her romances in print, Joan Hohl is an author romance readers can't get enough of. She has received numerous awards for her work, including the Romance Writers of America Golden Medallion. In addition to writing contemporary romances, this prolific author has also written historical romance and time-travel romance. Joan is the author of four contemporary mainstream romances: *Compromises*, *Another Spring*, *Ever After* and *Maybe Tomorrow*. She is currently working on her next contemporary romance, which will be published in 1999. Joan lives in eastern Pennsylvania with her husband and family.

The employees of Thorndike Press hope you have enjoyed this Large Print book. All our Large Print titles are designed for easy reading, and all our books are made to last. Other Thorndike Press Large Print books are available at your library, through selected bookstores, or directly from us.

For information about titles, please call:

(800) 257-5157
To share your comments, please write:

Publisher
Thorndike Press
P.O. Box 159
Thorndike, Maine 04986